AURORA SKY
VAMPIRE HUNTER

NORTHERN
BITES

NIKKI JEFFORD

Cover design by Najla Qamber
Interior format and design by Nada Qamber

www.NikkiJefford.com

Subjects: Teen & Young Adult Paranormal Romance
Teen & Young Adult Loners & Outcasts Fiction

ISBN: 978-1-939997-49-4

For Sébastien, until the end of time.

1

SINNERS AND SAINTS

IF FATE WERE KIND THE only thing I'd have to kill tonight is time.

Our target home, one of two, had yet to draw its curtains, lighting the inside like an aquarium as the last traces of daylight receded into the shadows.

The switch from day to dusk happened in a matter of seconds, at least in Alaska, turning everything black and white.

My tennis shoes crunched over the salted walkway, grinding down pieces so big they felt like small pebbles under my feet. Tennis shoes in winter—not really the best way to keep my toes toasty. Neither was the short pleather jacket, but my parka and winter boots felt too heavy on a mission.

There was no way our targets lived here. A vamp house with skylights…about as likely as the red, white, and pink Valentine's Day flag hanging off the garage.

I wanted to ram a dagger through the limp heart as I passed the stupid flag on the march to the front door. Even if I didn't eschew vandalism, I couldn't have. Not since Agent Melcher revoked my right to bear arms.

Melcher's idea of easing Dante and me back into active duty came down to assigning us each an informant/stand-in assassin. Our duty, our *only* duty, tonight was to do the poisoning (i.e. get bit) then step aside and let our partner go in for the kill.

"No way, I'm all about follow-up," Dante said the moment he heard we were on probation.

"You're lucky we're sending you back in the field," Agent Crist had snapped.

She and Melcher weren't very happy with how Dante's "training" mission with me in Fairbanks resulted in the death of an informant and human, followed by the vampire Renard and his cohorts tracking us down in Anchorage. Of course, Dante missed all that while the Natives in Kotzebue honored his slaying of a rabid vampire with a blanket toss and an all-you-can-eat moose buffet. Dante returned with a bear claw strung from a leather cord around his neck, puffed up like Popeye on spinach until Agents Crist and Melcher lit into him.

Melcher called the incident "too close for comfort."

I still didn't see the harm in keeping a dagger hidden in case things went south. I'd been out of combat training for a week while I recovered from the multiple stabbings Renard's crony inflicted over my body.

Great way to start my second week at a new school.

Strep throat. That's what Melcher's doctor's note said.

More like stabbed throat.

If we ended up with the vamp house, I wouldn't mind stepping aside and letting my *partner* take the beating. To add insult to injury, Melcher assigned Valerie to me and Noel to Dante.

We hadn't spoken since the moment we climbed inside Valerie's red Honda Civic.

Once our addresses checked out we were free to part ways. The sooner the better.

Two nights ago, a pizza delivery boy headed out on his route and never returned. The next morning a jogger found his body at Westchester Lagoon, naked and drained. Melcher felt certain the culprit resided at one of the five homes on the boy's delivery route. When the police questioned them, every resident said they never received their order. The manager at Midnight Pie confirmed that every household on the route had called in to complain that their pizza never arrived.

Dante and Noel were assigned three of the five addresses, Valerie and I the remaining two. The manager at Midnight Pie could only guess which residence the driver headed to first, though he believed the police's theory that the boy had been killed in a carjacking before ever reaching the first home.

The home in front of me did not emit evil. From ten feet away I saw a colorful welcome mat and floral wreath on the door.

Valerie flipped her head from side to side, sending strawberry-brown waves over the shoulders of her pea coat. She looked older without her usual wench's costume.

We walked in sync, neither of us wanting to follow the other's lead. As we bumped shoulders to get to the porch, I spoke my first words. "There's no way this is a vamp house."

"Could be a cover. You'd be surprised at the lengths some vamps will go to hide their activities. I've seen it all." Valerie lifted her nose. "I've been doing this a lot longer than you."

"Congratulations," I said, reaching for the doorbell.

Bing, bong.

A woman in her late thirties came to the door smiling until she noticed the pamphlet in my hand.

"Good evening," I said cheerfully. "We're here to talk to you about Christ our Savior."

"Oh, um. This really isn't a good time. We're about to eat."

"Is there a better time we could come back?" Valerie asked, suddenly all smiles.

"Um…"

My relief at not stumbling upon a vamp house outweighed my embarrassment at interrupting a family's dinner with our phony solicitation.

Valerie and I stared at the woman with twin smiles.

"I don't think so, but thanks for stopping by." The woman quickly closed the door.

"God bless you," Valerie said sweetly. She rolled her eyes the moment the door slammed shut. "Maybe Dante and Noel are having better luck."

"They haven't called," I said, heading back to Valerie's car.

She quickly matched my strides, sprinting for the driver's side as though we were racing for it. At least Valerie respected the speed limit, unlike Dante. Thinking about him made me snort. I had a hard time picturing him sitting back while petite Noel rammed a knife in a vamp's heart. Then again, he'd left me in Fairbanks to do just that without even sticking around. That's what had gotten us into this mess to begin with.

The Honda's headlights slipped across the mailboxes in the next neighborhood. Porch lights dotted the homes up and down the street. All but one house tucked back in the shadows of the yard's prickly spruce trees.

Valerie came to a stop along the curb, three houses from our last address. She stuck her face in front of the review mirror and dabbed gloss on her rouged lips.

I might have kept my mouth shut but then she started rubbing and smacking her lips together.

The thought of those lips all over Fane's made me want to

shove the tube of gloss down her throat. It was bad enough that she blackmailed me into breaking up with him, but Valerie had taken it one step further, reinstating herself as Fane's bitch the moment I stepped aside...or so my source told me. Fane neither confirmed nor denied this the last time we were together. I might have felt guilty over the way it all went down if he hadn't moved on so quickly.

"We're on a mission, not a date," I snapped.

Valerie's lips *smacked* as she gave her reflection one last pucker. She shot me a sly look.

"Maybe I have a date afterward."

Turns out Melcher had been wise to ban me from carrying a weapon. The temptation to do bodily harm to the vixen could strike me at any moment. Like right now.

For a brief second, I hoped we'd get the vamp house. I wouldn't mind watching Valerie get roughed up a bit.

"You're despicable," I said.

Valerie smiled with her now shiny lips. "All's fair in love and war."

"I could report you to Melcher."

Valerie smirked. "You wouldn't risk it. You care about Fane too much."

"More than you, obviously."

"Get over yourself, Aurora. I'd never rat out Fane. We have too much...*history*."

As my fingers stretched down my leg, I had to remind myself yet again that I was unarmed.

"You dated him when you knew from the beginning it was forbidden," I said. "I didn't realize he was a vampire until later."

Valerie faced me. "You moved in on Fane when you knew he

5

was taken." Her words dripped with scorn.

My mouth opened and closed. She sorta had me there. I did kiss Fane on a public bus when they were still together. Not that I could have known for sure. People break up all the time in high school. It's not like I kept tabs on my classmates' romantic status 24-7. Besides, Fane followed me onto the bus, not the other way around.

Valerie took my silence as an acknowledgement of guilt.

"Nothing to say? That's what I thought."

I yanked open the car door. "Let's get this over with so we can go our separate ways."

Valerie slammed her door shut. Good thing we weren't trying to sneak up on anyone. She stormed down the sidewalk. Small wonder she slowed down when I did in front of the house hidden behind a patch of spruce trees.

A set of fresh tire tracks led through the snow to a rusted Oldsmobile beneath the carport.

I headed straight for the plastic trash bin by the side of the car with Valerie hot on my heels.

"What are you doing?"

I didn't answer as I pulled the lid off the bin and placed it quietly on the ground. "Look," I said, nodding into the can.

The vamps hadn't even bothered covering the pizza boxes, a whole stack of them, with other refuse. I lifted the cardboard cover.

Not even a slice missing.

Valerie pushed down the cardboard lid with a huff. "We're not here to go through their trash." She shook her hair over her shoulders. "Let's do this."

Before I could respond, she charged towards the front porch. So Valerie was the jump in head first kind of girl? Why wasn't I surprised?

Valerie knocked on the door.

Five seconds later a young twenty-something man stuck his head out. His greasy hair reminded me of the uneaten pizza sitting in the garbage can.

He didn't say anything, or maybe he didn't have time.

"Do you believe in Jesus?" Valerie demanded.

She leaned forward with her whole body. Valerie didn't have to put on an act—righteousness came naturally to her.

The man looked Valerie and me up and down, his lips forming a sneer. "Boy, did you chicks pick the wrong house."

I stepped forward, waving my pamphlet in front of him. "I think we came to exactly the right house. Are your parents home?"

He scoffed at that. "I don't have parents."

"You live alone?" Valerie demanded.

"Me and my two roommates."

Oh, joy. Three against two. And while Valerie's personality might be toxic, her blood would be no help knocking these creatures out. How the hell was I going to get three vampires to feed on me at the same time? At least I was all juiced up from the stabbing incident.

Calling for backup would've been the smart move, but Valerie had already gotten up in the vampire's face.

"I bet you boys could use some God in your lives."

There's no way Valerie would want to share this bust. The excitement practically bounced off her eyeballs.

"May we come in for a few minutes?" I asked. I couldn't have Valerie thinking I'd wimp out.

The greasy-haired vampire glanced over our shoulders into the dark yard. The bushy spruce needles blocked out most of the neighbors.

"If you insist." He pulled back the door and motioned with his arm to come inside.

Valerie and I stepped forward, placing our first foot on the hardwood floor in unison.

The entry led directly into an open dining room. Two young men, vampires presumably, sat at the table sorting through a mountain of mail. One had piercings in his ears, nose, eyebrow, and chin. He shot me a menacing glare. "What the hell is this?"

The doorman sniggered. "These young ladies from the church want to save us."

"We ain't the ones who need saving."

I lifted my chin. "I think you are."

Pierced guy's chair scraped the wood floor when he pushed back from the table. His companion followed suit.

While it wasn't exactly wise to turn my back on my enemies, I didn't want to trap myself between the china hutch and dining table, either. I went for the living room, spinning around in the center as though prepared to deliver a sermon rather than a battle cry. The pamphlet I'd waved in Greasy Guy's face at the front door crinkled in my hand. If only I could use it to squish them like flies.

Heavy curtains over the living room windows blocked out any passing cars. Good, no witnesses.

Pierced dude and Greasy Guy followed closely behind me.

"Now, where were we?" I asked.

"You were about to beg for your life," the pierced vamp said.

His tongue ring glinted as he spoke. It made a 'screw you, I eat silver for breakfast' kind of statement.

"No," I said, shaking my head. "I was about to save you."

The lips on the pierced vamp drew back so far, I could see his sharpened molars.

8

Jackpot, I thought, right before the vampires closed in on me. "You bitches came to the wrong house."

Oh, we were at the right house all right. The pamphlet fell from my fingers settling by my feet on the hardwood floor. What did vampires have against carpeting? Or heating? I had to hand it to them for practicality. Great way to save on the electric bill and prevent bodies from decomposing too quickly.

Silver Tongue socked me across the face. I had no time to duck. I'd been expecting teeth not a fist. My face snapped sideways. Neck realignment would have to wait until later.

I dropped to the floor before the second blow connected with my jaw. Kneepads would have been nice, I thought, as pain exploded through my leg joints. The words "Jesus Loves You" looked up at me from the pamphlet, receding as Greasy Guy hauled me up by the shoulders.

Not ten minutes from here, Dante was preaching the gospel to some innocent household waiting to see if they took the bait or shooed him away.

Naturally, I'd get the house with the vampires in it.

I squirmed against the vampire holding me.

A bloodcurdling scream ripped through the house followed by crashing glass.

No surprise Valerie screamed like a banshee. The third vampire staggered away from the china cabinet's splintered glass. Valerie must have shoved him right through the wood frame. She cupped her left eye in one hand and gripped her dagger in the other.

I elbow-jabbed Greasy Guy when he turned his attention to the commotion. He grunted but didn't let go. His arms circled my chest to get a better hold. With Silver Tongue approaching I had to do something, so I bit down on my captor's arm as hard as

I could. He screamed and let go.

Take that, you homicidal, bloodsucking savage. Bet he wasn't used to getting bit.

I spit his blood out on the floor. My second taste of vampire blood wasn't any better than the first. Two weeks ago, Renard force-fed me blood from his wrist. Now that I'd tried it again, I could say there was definitely something off about the taste of vampire blood.

Not like human blood.

Silver Tongue smiled. "I see the church still promotes violence."

Before I could answer, he had my arm in a bone-crushing grip. A yelp escaped my lips before I could suppress it. Silver Tongue twisted harder.

Oh God, he was going to break my arm. Just bite me, damn it!

Right before my bones felt ready to snap, Greasy Guy yanked me away from Silver Tongue and smacked me across the face. It stung but at least he didn't punch.

Before I could land a blow of my own, he pushed me backward toward Silver Tongue. The jerk laughed and flung me back to his crony who mimicked his laughter and motion. Back and forth they pushed me as though tossing a ball across the room. It reminded me of a nature program I once saw of two killer whales playing with a seal before they ate it.

The next time I landed against Greasy Guy, I twisted around and dug my nails into his shoulder. He stumbled as he tried to push me away. Before he had a chance to fight me off, I bit straight through his t-shirt to the skin beneath.

He screamed and then grabbed me by the shoulders and shook me. "So, you like to bite, do you?"

Without preamble, he leaned forward and bit my neck.

Silver Tongue took me by the arm. "Better say your prayers," he said into my ear.

He took my earlobe between his teeth and bit down. What started out as a pinch turned into excruciating pain as his teeth pressed through my skin. What if he tried to tear off my entire earlobe? I shrieked so loud I was convinced I would have shattered the glass door on the china cabinet if it weren't already broken.

Greasy Guy fell to the floor convulsing, but Silver Tongue didn't notice. He released my earlobe and covered his own ears while I screamed, then leaned back in to bite my neck. I never saw him convulse.

"Motherfucker!" Valerie screamed right before she plunged her dagger into Silver Tongue's back.

He fell forward, nearly taking me down with him.

Valerie held on tight to her knife. Once Silver Tongue hit the floor face first, she pushed him onto his back with the heel of her boot. He looked dead, but that didn't stop Valerie from kicking him in the side.

The greasy-haired guy twitched on the floor. His eyes widened as Valerie went for him next.

"Son of a bitch!" she yelled, once she finished him off.

She had a shiner around her left eye.

Even though it hurt, the smile was worth it. "Better cancel that date, Val. You don't look so hot."

2

THIS IS NOT A DATE

AFTER CALLING IN THE CLEANERS, Valerie and I jostled for a place in front of the vampires' bathroom mirror.

"Just perfect!" Valerie said, placing a finger on the skin swelling around her eye.

At least she hadn't been bit.

I pulled out what I hoped was a clean towel from the cabinet and wet the corner. I wiped the blood off both sides of my neck. Now that the bites were cleaned up, they looked like red ring marks burned onto my skin. I kept an iridescent midnight blue scarf tucked inside my pocket. I pulled it out now and wrapped it around my neck. It was dark enough to hide bite marks, lightweight enough to stuff inside a purse or pocket.

I looked at Valerie's reflection in the mirror, briefly wondering what happened to her to end up working for the agents. Even if I could bring myself to ask, I doubt she'd answer.

Before heading out, I threw the towel I'd used on top of Silver Tongue's body for the cleaners to dispose of.

By the time we made it on base, Dante and Noel had beaten us back. Valerie and I flashed our passes one last time before heading down the hallway for Agent Melcher and Crist's office. The agents were seated at their desks. Noel sat hunched over in a chair inspecting the ends of her hair. Dante leaned against the wall, one foot propped up. He wore a knit sweater over khakis. It gave him a churchy look apart from the bear claw hanging from his neck.

Dante began applauding the moment Valerie and I entered.

"Bravo, ladies, bravo." He clapped louder.

Crist cleared her throat. "That's enough, Dante."

Valerie rewarded Dante with a full-on voluptuous smile. Her eye had started to swell shut on the drive over, but there wasn't a smudge around her glossed lips.

"Took down all three by myself."

Ah-hem.

"I wasn't exactly sitting there reading the Sunday funnies," I said.

"I can see that," Dante said, pushing away from the wall and coming to my side. He ran his fingers along my hairline, stopping at my temple. "Looks like they tried to take off your ear."

I shot Valerie a look of triumph. That's right, you vampire stealing strumpet. We vampire hunters stick together.

"Back to business," Crist said. "Valerie, Aurora—report."

"I knew the moment I saw the pizza boxes in their trash bin," I said at the same time Valerie launched into her account of taking down the vamps single-handedly.

We glared at each other.

"Good work, team," Melcher said. "The community and law enforcement officials might not be aware of it, but justice has been served."

Crist nodded her agreement.

"Aurora, Valerie, well done," Melcher said in a way that didn't invite a response.

He looked the same as he always did with trim hair cut like a choir boys, wrinkle-free suit, and a smug smile.

"Now I want you all to rest up. Unless we have an emergency on our hands, I'm keeping you off assignment for the rest of the month."

"Off assignment," Dante repeated, pulling away from me.

My skin prickled in the last place his fingers had touched.

"I thought after this you were putting us back on assignment."

Melcher stared across his desk. "It's not up for debate, Dante."

Dante might've been a loose cannon, but he also knew when to roll with the punches. His mouth stretched into a wide grin. "Guess I no longer have an excuse for avoiding my term paper."

Melcher opened a drawer on his desk. "That reminds me. Aurora, Valerie, you need to stay home the rest of the week. Your bruises would draw too much attention."

Melcher leaned across the desk, holding out two slips of paper. I took mine and read over it quickly.

Great, another doctor's note.

Valerie glared at her note. Hopefully hers said "herpes."

"I'll drive you home," Dante said to me, looking sideways at Valerie.

"Thanks."

"Aurora, we'd like to talk to you a moment before you go," Melcher said.

Noel's eyes met mine for the first time since I'd walked in. She'd gotten off her chair and headed to the door. She shot me a thin-lipped smile. "See you at school."

"Next week," I replied, holding up my doctor's note.

"Right," Noel said, grimacing. "Sorry."

"I'll be waiting in the hall," Dante said. He was the last to leave the room.

Melcher gave me the friendly fatherly smile once Dante closed the door. He leaned forward on his arms. "How are you feeling, Aurora?"

I looked him in the eyes. "Great."

"Have you had any more...*cravings*?"

I knew what Melcher was getting at. The last time they patched me up I'd asked point-blank, "Am I turning into a vampire?"

Melcher said blood cravings were one of the nasty side effects of the virus cocktail the government had pumped through my veins while I was on death's door.

"No." The lie came out with such conviction that Melcher dropped it at once.

"Good work, Sky," he said, straightening up. "We are extremely impressed by your commitment to duty."

Even Crist nodded her agreement. The pinch-faced woman wasn't my biggest fan. She wasn't really anyone's fan besides Melcher's.

I wondered if they ever did the nasty. Gross. So did not want to know. My mind had done that a lot since the transfusion—tossed sick and twisted thoughts inside my head like an erotic dinner salad. Besides, it wouldn't surprise me if Melcher was celibate or something, like a monk. Probably even flogged himself at night out of sexual frustration. Again...gross!

I took a step backward.

"Is that all?"

"Take some time off," Melcher said. "You've earned it."

Take some time off? I had a little over three months until graduation and all this time off wasn't exactly impressing my teachers. I once dreamed of going to college at Notre Dame. Now I just wanted to get my high school diploma before some vamp did me in. My list of goals had changed dramatically in the last couple weeks. At the top: graduate from high school.

When I walked out of the agents' office, I saw that Dante

hadn't wandered far. He leaned against the secretary's desk fingering his precious bear claw with one hand while using his other hand to make a stabbing motion. The woman behind the desk didn't so much as crack a smile. She sat ramrod straight, bun at the nape of her neck, dressed in camouflage.

"Hey," I said.

Dante turned. His widening grin was enough to get a smile out of me.

"Ready to roll?" he asked.

"Let's blow this joint."

Dante straightened up. "Nice chatting, Steph."

"Stephanie," the secretary replied gruffly.

I bumped shoulders with Dante as we headed down the sterile hallway.

"I take it you didn't score digits."

Dante laughed. "Negative." He leaned in closer. "Everything A-okay with agents Mulder and Scully?"

I snort-laughed. That's what I loved about Dante. It was hard to take life too seriously with him nearby.

"All good," I replied. "Melcher's impressed with how I'm holding up."

"Well, he should be. You conquered the mountain, battled Goliath, and came out on top." Dante stopped abruptly and placed a hand on his chest. "My protégé. I'm so proud."

I gave him a playful smack. "Get over yourself."

Beatings and bitings aside, it gave me comfort to end the evening by climbing into Dante's Jeep rather than back into the vixen-mobile.

Dante started her up. "Hey, you hungry? Let's get something to eat."

I wasn't hungry, but I didn't want to go home either. Dad was still MIA, and a week ago mom stopped getting dressed altogether. I wasn't exactly chomping at the bit to get home and watch her mope around in her bathrobe and slippers.

I fastened my seatbelt. "Why not?"

"Great, I have a wicked craving for pizza."

"Of course you do," I said, rolling my eyes.

Dante's eyes darted from the road to his speedometer. He braked at the deserted four-way stop. Even Dante knew enough to respect the speed limit on base.

"Lady luck," Dante said cheerfully. "Even with the odds in my favor, you get the vamp house and get paired with Red. I bet she's a ball of fire in action."

"Hey! Don't forget my warning about Valerie."

"Right, no hooking up." Dante shot me a sly look. "Red's not my color anyway."

If he wanted me to ask what color did it for him, I wasn't taking the bait.

Dante chuckled softly when I made no comment and drove more or less responsibly to Moose's Tooth.

"I look like shit," I said, glancing in his review mirror.

"You look good to me," Dante said.

I bee-lined it for the women's restroom while he got us a table. Like my old friends at Denali High, the Mousekeeters, I never left home without concealer.

Valerie wasn't the only one with a shiner. I dabbed a pale shade of liquid concealer around my left eye then touched up with powder. I couldn't do anything about my ear. God, it looked kinky with teeth marks practically piercing the lobe. Is that how Silver Tongue got his piercings?

I started for the door then turned around. At the bottom of my purse, I dug out a tube of red lipstick. If I couldn't cover my bruises completely, maybe I could divert attention to my mouth. I grabbed a square of tissue paper out of the stall and blotted my lips then finger brushed my long black hair over my ears. There. Halfway decent.

Dante had already nabbed us a booth by the time I came out. He whistled as I approached the table. "You clean up good, Sky."

"Thanks," I said, sliding into the bench across from him.

Dante didn't look at me long; his eyes were already devouring the laminated menu.

"I'm hungry," he said.

"You're always hungry." I countered.

Dante didn't look up from the menu. "And you're never hungry."

"Dante—" I started then stopped.

Dante lowered his menu. "What?"

"Never mind."

"What?"

When I didn't answer, he leaned forward with a goofy face. "Sky, what?"

I grabbed my set of silverware and unwrapped the napkin around it.

"Have you ever noticed that food no longer has any taste?" I stared at my silverware as I spoke.

Dante started to laugh then stopped when he saw my face. "You're serious?"

I nodded.

"That's not the only thing. I feel a lot more sensitive to sunlight. Like the other day, it cleared up and…I don't know. It made

18

me feel sick."

"Jesus, Sky. You sound paranoid."

"Maybe." I shrugged.

"Anything else?"

Our eyes locked. I could feel my cheeks heating.

Dante leaned forward when I didn't answer.

Hell would freeze over before I told him how sexual I'd been feeling—my head was in the gutter pretty much 24-7. It felt like a scratch that needed itching.

I focused on the bear claw around Dante's neck rather than his face.

It didn't help that I felt gypped losing my virginity to jock-boy Scott Stevens. At least I didn't have to pass him in the hallway anymore.

Only one person, or vampire rather, knew how to get my blood pumping: Francesco "Fane" Donado.

I hadn't seen him since my abduction when Noel had taken a risk and called him for help. He and Noel walked in right after I finished off Renard's cohort James. If they hadn't patched me up, I would have bled to death. While I recovered, Fane went after the last of my captors. But Anchorage's most popular undead socialite, Marcus, had already taken care of them. The man's upscale parties were strictly no-kill zones…unless, of course, Marcus did the killing.

I'd decided to turn a blind eye to that. For one thing, Marcus had killed vampires, not humans. And he spared me and Fane from having to get our hands bloody. But Fane did have to dispose of the bodies at the dump with the help of Noel's favorite vamps, Henry and Gavin.

Fane hadn't been too happy about that, which surprised me. I assumed a vampire would be used to that sort of thing.

But no, he was a kisser, not a killer.

Not that I'd received so much as a goodbye kiss.

The last night I stayed over we slept separately then talked half the night. Fane knew I'd lied about hooking up with Dante, and he understood why. I was a vampire hunter. He was a vampire. We could never be together.

He accused me of being a vampire created to kill her own kind. I vehemently denied this. How could a person not know they were undead?

"We'll see," Fane had said.

As long as I took the antidote every month, I would remain human. Melcher said they had already started testing a yearly injection and were working on a five-year antidote. I had no doubt the scientists would come up with a stronger failsafe.

I was still lost in Aurora land when our waitress walked up to the table.

"Do you know what you want?"

Dante set his menu down. "I'll have a pitcher of your IPA, the mozzarella breadsticks, and a large chicken ranch pizza. No garlic."

No garlic? Sounded like I wasn't the only one with sensitivities.

The waitress turned to me. "And for you?"

"The raspberry vinaigrette salad, and we'll take the breadsticks without the cheese."

Dante groaned after our waitress left. "Sky, you're killing me. I still *do* have taste buds, you know?"

"Well, there will be plenty of cheese on your pizza. I'm sure you'll live."

"Barely."

Dante cheered up as soon as his beer arrived. "Want some?"

he asked after filling his pint glass.

"I'm eighteen."

"Didn't the agents upgrade your ID?"

I laughed. "I'm sure this isn't what they had in mind."

"Come on, Sky," Dante said, tapping the table with his fingers. "Live a little. Besides, you earned it."

I shook my head, smiling. "I'll pass on the mud water."

Dante gulped the *mud water* down happily. The pint was nearly empty before he set it on the table.

"Look, you have nothing to worry about," he said, leaning over the table. "There's an adjustment period after the transfusion. Our bodies aren't the same. We're…"

"I know," I said with a roll of my eyes. "Superhuman."

Dante laughed. "That's right."

He poured himself another glass of beer. My salad arrived shortly after, but the breadsticks took longer. My plate was nearly clean when the heaping pile of warm, doughy bread arrived.

Since food had lost a lot of its taste, I often focused on texture and temperature. I liked the warmth in my mouth as I chewed.

Dante practically moaned, devouring his first breadstick within seconds. He grabbed another breadstick and held it up, shaking it in front of my face. "How can you not taste this doughy goodness?"

The breadstick flopped around as he waved it.

"Dante?"

A pretty blonde in a sporty ski jacket stood at the edge of our table. Dante's lips were still curved into a gigantic smile.

"Hi, Ashley."

I waited for Dante to explain who Ashley was. He didn't. From the way she glared at me, there had to be history between them.

She stared pointedly at me, but Dante didn't get the hint.

"Are you ready for tomorrow's exam?" she finally asked.

"Ready as I'll ever be."

"How did you do on last week's paper?"

"Pretty decent."

Ashley stood at the end of our table for several beats. When it was clear Dante wasn't going to engage her in mindless chitchat she finally said, "Well, enjoy your dinner."

"See you in class," he said, completely oblivious.

I hoped Ashley was going rather than coming, but she took a seat at a corner table with an older couple—facing me. Great, 'cause I so enjoyed being glared at while I ate.

In the time it took Miss Frowny to get to her table, Dante had already devoured his second breadstick and moved on to his third.

"Ex-girlfriend?" I asked.

"Ashley?" Dante asked, surprised. "She's engaged to an art major."

"Okay," I said slowly. "Then why the evil eye?"

"Evil...oh, I've taken her best friend out on a couple dates."

I raised both brows. "She's not going to be happy when she hears you were spotted with another woman."

Dante chewed a couple more times and then swallowed. "We're not a couple. Besides, if Christine isn't comfortable with me having female friends, then she's with the wrong guy."

I gave Dante a pointed look. "It does look like we're on a date, though."

Dante planted both hands on the tabletop. "You think this is me on a date?"

I lowered my forehead in confusion.

Dante also lowered his head and gave me a hooded look.

Maybe it was supposed to be smoldering. I laughed, thinking he was joking around again, but his lips didn't even twitch. He kept staring.

"Has anyone ever told you that you have the most luscious lips?" Dante reached for my hand.

"What are you doing?" I asked in alarm when he stroked my wrist.

"Your skin is so soft." There was nothing playful about Dante's tone or the way he looked at me. "I'd like to feel your skin naked against mine."

"Hey!" I said, snatching my hand back.

Dante leaned back, smiling. "I bet your heart's beating a little faster."

"Only because you're freaking me out."

I broke off a piece of breadstick and threw it at him.

Dante laughed. He picked up the piece of bread where it bounced onto the table and lifted it to his lips. I thought he'd pop it in his mouth, but at the last second he chucked it back at me.

I threw it back. Dante reached for the plate and threw a whole breadstick at me.

I laughed. I felt much more comfortable with immature Dante rather than flirty, unsettling Dante. Ashley glared at our table. I'd momentarily forgotten about her.

I nodded in Ashley's direction. "Christine is so dropping you."

"Yeah," Dante said with a shrug. "Probably."

3

YOU'RE INVITED

Back inside the Jeep, Dante had George Michael's "Outside" blasting from the speakers. He swayed side-to-side while driving, singing, and tapping on the steering wheel. Dante joined George, singing about how he was done with the sofa, hall, and kitchen table.

I rolled my eyes when he leaned toward me while singing about taking things outside.

I cleared my throat. "Speaking of outside...mind keeping your eyes on the road?"

Dante sang back in return.

God, I swear he had a playlist titled "Songs for Annoying Aurora."

"Wanna come over?"

It took me a moment to register that Dante was asking a real question, not singing lyrics. I looked sideways at him, momentarily speechless.

"I'll let you touch my claw." Dante glanced down.

I burst out laughing. "You are such a dork."

A dangerous dork. The whole 'naked skin against mine' comment still concerned me.

"I should get home before my mom starts to worry."

Doubtful. Every day after school she ran a little later than the previous one. Yesterday she forgot to pick me up entirely. Well, not exactly forgot so much as slept through the afternoon until my phone call woke her up.

While I'd gotten over my car phobia for the most part, I hadn't overcome my driving phobia. Too bad I didn't live in a city with a cool underground metro system.

"Oh, right," Dante said, turning down the music. "How is Mrs. Sky? Still making those delicious cookies?"

More like eating them straight from the manufacturer's box.

"She's okay. She just misses my dad. He's not around much."

Or ever. I had confided in Fane, but I didn't feel like telling Dante my dad had taken off. Dante wasn't capable of taking anything seriously. It went against his nature.

"At least she's got you for company."

"Not for long."

Dante glanced sideways at me. "No?"

"As soon as I graduate, I'm moving into my own place."

"Yep, yep," he said, nodding. "That's the way to go. I know your mom will miss you, but it's not like you're leaving the state."

Not anymore. Before my car wreck, I'd actually made it into Notre Dame, my college of choice. Paradise lost.

The traffic light ahead turned yellow. Dante punched the gas and flew through the intersection.

I bit my tongue. If I screamed it would only encourage him.

"A place of your own is a great idea," he said, easing up on the gas pedal. "In our line of work, we get home at all times of the night. Your mom's going to have gray hair before she's fifty if she's always staying up waiting for you to get home safely."

And maybe dad would return if I wasn't there. He and Mom could work things out, get back to normal. She needed someone and that someone wasn't me. Even with Notre Dame out of the picture, I craved my own life and privacy.

"Get some rest, Sky," Dante said when he pulled up to my house.

"Good luck on your term paper," I said.

As soon as I shut the passenger door, Dante backed out of the driveway and roared down the street.

I crossed the road to our mailbox to collect the mail.

There was a red padded envelope and a grocery bag stuffed inside the mailbox. I opened the bag first and breathed deep. Inside, folded neatly, was my red scarf—the one Renard had claimed as a trophy after kidnapping me.

It had to be from Fane. He'd been the one to dispose of Renard's body at the dump. I pulled it out slowly and let it unravel. In the dark the scarf looked crimson.

What did this mean?

It had to be a message of some sort. Most likely Fane's way of saying we were finished for good.

My fingers tightened into a fist around the scarf. I looked up the hill toward the woods. Without thinking, I headed toward the path leading into the thicket. Ours was the last house on the hill before a dense patch of forest between us and the next neighborhood.

The spruce trees blocked out the streetlights, but I'd walked through these woods enough times to know them by heart.

The upside of anger is it makes you unafraid.

I inhaled the frosty air, practically panting as I rushed through the woods searching the shadows for a silhouette of a man.

The dry snow crunched beneath my tennis shoes.

I stopped midway through the forest and yelled, "Fane!"

After my voice faded in the night, I listened. No answer. I

hadn't expected but rather hoped for one.

Turn around, Aurora. Go home. Standing alone in the woods in the middle of the night wasn't one of my brightest ideas. I still had my phobias, but death wasn't high on the list. Half the time I felt like the walking dead. I wondered if this was how vampires felt, like they'd lost their humanity and could never get it back. The scientists had practically turned me into a vampire. Only a monthly shot of liquid blue prevented that from happening. Still, the side effects were enough to get a taste of what it felt like to be undead.

I trudged back home. I didn't have far to go.

All the lights were off, but the living room walls flashed with the light from the TV. Mom had *The Vampire Diaries* on. Yeah, seriously. Last week she'd finished reading the *Twilight Saga*. She'd downloaded the first book in the *Sookie Stackhouse/True Blood* series but said it was too sexual for her taste. Naturally, I wanted to check the books out.

She seemed to think she was on some kind of research mission.

In her fragile state, I didn't want to burst her bubble that vampires neither sparkled nor glamoured impressionable young ladies into submission. Anyway, it would probably help ease me out of the house if she had the romanticized version of what I had to deal with.

"Hey, Mom."

Her head bobbed around before snatching the remote control. Damon's face froze with his mouth open, and his eyes closed. I nearly snorted.

"Hi, honey." She swiveled her recliner around with her slippered feet. She had gray sweatpants on beneath her blue bathrobe.

She sounded remotely cheerful. She always did when she watched her shows.

Her smile dropped when she saw the red scarf in my hand.

"Your scarf," she said, numbly.

I'd forgotten about it in my hand. To my mother, it represented all the negative changes in our lives, including Dad's departure.

"Oh right," I said, stuffing it back inside the plastic sack. "I found it."

"I like the blue one better," Mom said, nodding at my neck. "It's much prettier."

"Not as warm, though."

"What's that?" she asked, staring at the thick, red envelope in my other hand.

I looked at it for the first time in the light. The package was addressed to me, but there wasn't a return label.

I shrugged. "I don't know. Maybe it's an early Valentine's gift from a secret admirer."

"Someone from West?" Mom asked.

Yeah right, like I was around school enough for anyone to notice me. This time, I really did snort.

"Beats me. Melcher wants me to stay home the rest of the week, so it's not like I'll be able to find out."

Mom nodded absently. Her eyes were already back on the paused screen.

"Well, didn't mean to interrupt your show." I turned to leave. "Dante says hi, by the way."

She smiled. "You should invite him over for dinner again."

"Maybe I would if you put some clothes on," I answered before I could stop myself.

Her eyes narrowed. She'd developed a bit of an attitude over the past couple of weeks.

"I haven't been feeling well, Aurora."

I wasn't in the mood for an argument. "I'll ask Dante what

his schedule's like the next time I see him. He said he misses your cookies," I added.

She smiled again. "You should have let me know you were seeing him today. I would have made a batch."

"Next time. Good night, Mom. Don't stay up too late."

Damon resumed speaking before I made it through the kitchen.

I shut myself inside my room, tossing the sack with my scarf onto the bed. I tore open the padded envelope, pulling out the heaviest object first, something small wrapped in red tissue paper. Inside, I found a silver heart attached to a red ribbon choker. The words "Bite Me" were engraved in the center of the heart. I set it aside and dumped the rest of the contents onto my bedspread. Small sets of wrapped candy tumbled out. There were gummy lips, candy hearts, lollipops, and chocolate hearts wrapped in red foil. It was like Cupid's version of Halloween.

A red envelope had tumbled out with the sweets. I tore it open and smiled when I saw the invitation. If one thing could be said for Marcus, the vamp knew how to throw a party.

I opened the tiny bag of gummy lips and began chewing on a piece as I read over the invitation. LOVE BITES it announced. *No kidding.* The "o" in love was a red heart missing a chunk out of the right corner.

L♥VE
BITES

COCKTAIL PARTY

FRIDAY, FEBRUARY 15ᵗʰ
DUSK

AT THE PALACE
HOSTED BY MARCUS

WEAR RED OR BLACK

I'd only been to the palace once, but Marcus said I was welcome back anytime. Guess he meant it.

I wondered if Fane was going.

If he brought Valerie, I'd rather he didn't.

I put the candy and choker back inside the padded envelope and stuck it, along with the invitation, on my desk then took a shower.

I could still hear the TV downstairs after I finished blow drying my hair. I left my door open a crack. I wasn't big on closed spaces after my initiation with the deranged rabies vampire. I discarded the plastic sack after taking out my scarf. I wrapped it gently around my neck before crawling under my bedcovers. That night I managed to sleep without having any nightmares.

My internal clock woke me up at the usual ungodly hour of five. So much for sleeping in during my time off. I had to get up extra early with my new school being across town. Even though I could have lain in bed half the day—not like Mom would notice—I flipped my covers back and put on a pair of long underwear underneath my sweatpants.

I grabbed my phone off my desk, along with another piece of gummy lips, then walked carefully down the stairs to the entryway.

I did some quick stretches then stepped out into the bitter freeze. Oh yes, I was awake now.

I had started jogging after Renard and his cohorts abducted and attacked me. Mornings were my favorite time to run. It's the only time when I felt like there was only me, existing in a world of my own while the rest of humanity slept.

"Believe" from the *Run Lola Run* soundtrack filled my ears. I ran up the hill to the woods. My feet flew over the forest floor. In no time I reached the neighborhood on the other side and raced past houses with lights beginning to come on as people roused themselves out of bed to prepare for the daily grind.

My mind played over the mission from the evening before and the lack of control I'd felt when the vampires pushed me back and forth. I was tired of getting smacked around.

I ran faster.

Kelly Clarkson's "My Life Would Suck Without You" started up. I hit skip. The next song, "Holding Out For A Hero" by Bonnie Tyler wasn't much better. I really needed to update my playlist.

I jogged in place and scanned my running playlist, selected "You're Going Down" by Sick Puppies, and sprinted the rest of the way home.

I roused my mom out of bed early Monday morning. I wanted time to turn my doctor's note into the office.

I spent all four morning classes at the front of my classrooms, eyes on the teacher or board. No more skipping. No more fighting. No more Fane.

I didn't know anyone in any of my classes except for Noel in fifth-period film elective. I always arrived before her. She was always running late because fifth period followed lunch, and Noel spent lunch with Henry and Gavin. Whatever trepidation she'd felt leaving behind her friends Hope and Whitney at Denali High School was quickly dispelled by spending as many school hours as she could with the suave and sexy vampire duo.

I had an open invitation to eat lunch with them, but I didn't feel like sitting at their crowded table in the cafeteria. I spent lunch in a quiet, empty classroom, chewing my food while getting my homework done.

Today I tapped my foot anxiously, hoping Noel wouldn't walk in just as the warning bell binged. As if on cue, she strode into class. Her shiny black hair looked good with a white turtle-neck instead of her usual head-to-toe black. It was as though Noel had taken on a new persona at West. Her usual Goth garb had been replaced by blue jeans and casual dresses. She smiled more. It was nice to see after how distressed she'd been transferring mid-year. Melcher had made her switch schools. Apparently, he didn't need two informants in one place. At least, as a junior, Noel had time to get to know her classmates before graduation.

"Hi," I said when Noel took her seat beside me.

"Hey." She grinned from ear to ear.

"How was lunch?"

She smiled bigger. "Gavin entertained us by recounting his first, and subsequently last, snowshoeing experience."

Yeah, hard to picture. Gavin looked more like an indoor than an outdoor vampire. "So, what did I miss last week?"

"We watched *Harold and Maude.*"

I shook my head. "Never heard of it." Didn't surprise me. Mrs. Campbell rarely picked movies from the twenty-first century. Film class felt a lot like English with assignments centered on old classics.

"It was a cute show," Noel said. "It's about this boy who is obsessed with death and then he meets this old woman, and they start dating."

I grunted, not the most ladylike sound. Young person dating someone ancient. How appropriate. Too bad I missed it. I'd just have to rent it from the library or the ancient video store near my house. Then again, I might run into Fane and his companion Joss: lover of foreign films and black tea—hater of humankind.

"Did you receive an invitation to Marcus's Valentine's party?" Noel asked.

"Yeah, I ate all the candy."

Noel laughed.

"Are you going?" she asked.

I shrugged. "It's not as though I have a hot date that night… or any night."

"This party is going to be a hundred times better than a date."

"Melcher did tell us to take the rest of the month off, though I'm sure this isn't what he had in mind."

"Melcher knows about Marcus," Noel said, shocking me speechless.

The final bell rang as I shouted, "What?"

Noel looked from Mrs. Campbell to me and shook her head.

Mrs. Campbell was the kind of teacher who started the moment the bell stopped and not a second later. She loved movies, which made her class one of my favorites. Teachers with a passion for their subjects tended to make a lasting impression.

Today I spent the period tapping my foot under my desk and my pen on top. If Melcher knew about Marcus, wasn't he, and every vampire who fraternized with him, in danger? What if the next assignment involved going to one of his parties and poisoning guests? Marcus, Henry, and Gavin were all harmless. The thought of tricking them into biting me and then watching as they convulsed on the floor sickened me. There's no way I could stick a dagger in their hearts.

How could Noel say such a thing so calmly? She was better at this undercover thing than I gave her credit for. I could have sworn she had a thing for Gavin and Henry and even Marcus, despite his same-sex predilection.

Once class ended, Noel and I scooted out of our seats. We walked out side by side. Once we were in the hallway, Noel leaned into me, speaking quickly.

"One of my first assignments as an informant was to work my way into Marcus's crowd. Attending his parties is one of my ongoing duties."

"So, you're spying?" I could feel my mouth gaping open.

"I'm keeping an eye on things."

"What about Marcus, Henry, and Gavin? Are they targets?"

Noel shot me a stern look. "Of course not. They're harmless."

My eyes inadvertently lingered on Noel's neck. Beneath her turtle neck, I knew she had her own *clean* bites. Gavin and Henry were much more gentlemanly, using teeth specifically sharpened to puncture a person's skin and start the flow of blood without chewing through flesh to the vein.

"My job is to make sure no humans are killed or harmed… unwillingly," Noel added under her breath. "And to keep my ears open about any baddies in the area. A serial killer was stopped last year after I overheard some vamps complaining about him at one of Marcus's parties." Noel puffed up her chest.

"Why didn't you tell me before?"

"It's on a need-to-know basis."

I was just relieved to hear I wouldn't be assigned to kick down the doors of the palace. While Marcus was a hospitable host, I had no doubt he'd be every bit as violent as the baddies I'd come up against if I threatened his existence in any way.

He'd already killed two full-grown male vampires just because they'd caused a stir at his party by abducting me.

Marcus had already boasted to me about his music room—the place he took guests who misbehaved. Knowing Marcus there probably weren't any instruments inside the music room. He'd even admitted to me that he still enjoyed killing on occasion. *"When they deserve it."*

Renard and his partner certainly deserved to die a real death, but the ease with which Marcus performed the deed unsettled me.

The warning bell rang up and down the halls.

"Look, don't worry," Noel said. "Melcher didn't have me go to all the trouble of getting in with Marcus only to take him down. His gatherings have been a great source of information."

I nodded slowly.

"Okay," she said a bit louder, straightening up. "See you tomorrow."

"See you," I said, heading for final period.

4

FLIRT

I WASN'T IN ANY RUSH TO get to my locker at the end of the day. It only meant freezing my butt off that much longer while I waited for Mom to show up.

Sure enough, there was no sign of the car when I made my way down the shoveled walkway to the pick-up lane in front of the school.

At least I had my scarf back. Maybe it was silly, but it made me feel better having it around my neck. As I checked my phone for any new texts I may have missed in class, some guy approached flashing a row of perfectly white, perfectly smooth, teeth. He had on a black and orange letterman's jacket. I hadn't even noticed his approach.

"Hi, Aurora."

I squinted at the boy.

"Hi—"

"Mike." He grinned wider. "Are you waiting for someone?"

"My mom." I glanced at the empty pick-up lane. "Late again."

"I can give you a ride home if you need one."

That took me aback. I looked at him closer. Tall, slender, toned, light brown eyes, thick wavy hair—conventionally cute in every way.

I glanced behind Mike's shoulder at the small group of guys, his friends presumably, watching us. They were equally fit and clean-cut. Probably part of the popular crowd, not that I knew or cared. I hadn't spent enough time at West to figure out who belonged to the "it" crowd. And I had no intention of finding out.

"Yo, Mikey!" one of Mike's friends called out, sounding arrogant and impatient.

"Just a minute, man." Mike turned back to me. "I don't mind giving you a lift."

"Thanks, but I'm sure she's on her way."

She better be on her way.

Mike flashed me a grin full of confidence. "No problem. See you in class tomorrow."

We had a class together? Lovely, I suppose now I'd have to say 'hi' when I saw him in whatever the hell class we shared.

Call me jaded, but I'd already been through this charade with Scott Stevens back at Denali High School. The silly smiles and shy hellos. The part where he admitted to having a crush on me. The sloppy, horrible kisses. The even more horrible sex. Pass!

I hit the play button on my playlist before I even got the buds in my ears. "Fake It" by Seether blasted through the small speakers. My foot tapped impatiently.

Just when I was about to call my mom, she drove by and took the turn into the school's parking lot. I walked up to the curb, reaching out for the door handle on the passenger's side before she'd come to a complete stop.

"I'm so sorry, honey," she said as soon as I'd tossed my backpack in the back seat and buckled up.

For once her lateness served my purpose. I'd been struck by a flash of brilliance in fourth period. Grandma had a townhouse only minutes from West and it was unoccupied half the year. Maybe Mom would consider letting me live there given she wouldn't have to drive back and forth across town anymore.

I leaned back in my seat, eyes on the freshly plowed road.

"It's okay," I began. "It doesn't seem fair making you drive across town four times a day."

I left a very long pause in the air. There's always that anticipation right before you're about to ask for something you want and don't know if the person will surprise you or shoot you down on the spot.

"I've been thinking. Gran's apartment is only a few blocks away from West, and it's not like she uses it in the winter. If I lived there, I could walk to school." It was so perfect. How could she say no? We'd have to ask Grandma, of course, and you never knew with her. She'd want to know why I'd transferred in the middle of senior year, why I still wasn't driving, and a thousand other questions, but it would be worth it to get a shot at her apartment. I'd only get about three months out of it before Gran came up for the summer. Just enough time to finish senior year and start looking for on-campus living at the University of Alaska Anchorage.

Mom actually straightened in her seat. Even her voice was on edge. "Out of the question. You're in high school."

"Not for much longer."

"Well, you are now, so we can talk about this again after you graduate."

I could still see Mom's rigid stance out of the corner of my eye. A frosty silence settled inside the car as she pulled away from West. I didn't realized I'd clamped my teeth together so hard until my jaw began to ache.

I heard a small sob and looked over.

"Am I so terrible to live with?" Mom asked in a breaking voice.

Oh, crap. I turned in my seat.

"No, Mom. I just feel really bad making you drive back and forth five days a week."

"I don't mind," she said through sniffles.

There went my dreams of independent living...for now. Hopefully she would be in a less fragile state when I brought it up after graduation. Better yet, maybe Dad would return before then so she wouldn't be alone.

Mom wiped her eyes on her coat sleeve and sniffed. She wore it unzipped over an old sweatshirt and sweatpants. She'd shucked her slippers in favor of a pair of ankle-high winter boots with a fuzzy lining.

She sniffed a couple more times then took her usual detour up Benson Boulevard's one-way street, swinging back around to Northern Lights. Today she chose the Taco Bell drive-through. In addition to not dressing, she no longer cooked, either.

"Do you want your usual?" she asked as she turned into the parking lot.

Her voice had taken on a much more cheerful tone.

"Sure," I said.

A rice and bean burrito was my usual. It reheated nicer than a taco. Wherever we ended up, Mom always ordered something to warm up later for dinner and a snack for when we got home. The fast food was probably her real motivation for getting off the couch to pick me up every afternoon.

As soon as we got home, I dumped my backpack in my room and changed into my running gear. Mom was eating a taco from the paper wrapping when I came bounding down the stairs. I wasn't always able to get myself up in time to jog before school. On those days I made it up as soon as I got home.

I did my warm-ups in the living room then headed up the hill, music playing gently into my eardrums. I kept the volume down during afternoon runs. There was more traffic, and I liked to keep tabs on it. I'd already been through a gruesome car accident.

It would be just my luck to get hit on foot.

I started out with a light jog through the woods then picked up the pace in the adjacent neighborhood. I slowed at the intersection then raced across when it the road was clear. The sidewalk passed in front of a strip mall with one of the last surviving video stores, a take-out pizza place, and laundromat.

A quick glance at the parking lot revealed no sign of Fane's car.

I don't know why I tortured myself this way on afternoon runs. And I don't know why I thought his car might appear today. It was probably the scarf. I gave it a gentle tug for reassurance.

Maybe I would have better luck spotting his car if I ran at night. Or better yet, maybe I should let go and move on with my life.

There were other bears in the woods. I snorted to myself. Like pretty boy Mike. Please let the guy back off and leave me alone. That's the trouble with it. Guys liked girls who were a challenge. Maybe tomorrow I should dress up all cutesy and giggle at every sentence that came out of his mouth. That would scare him off. Yeah, right. I could never pull it off with a straight face, but it was a funny thought all the same.

I turned the volume up on my music once I reached the stretch of woods leading home.

It turned out Mike and I shared history class together. He plopped into the seat beside me Tuesday morning. He ran his hand over the surface of his desk. I heard a click followed by scraping. I glanced over. In addition to the jacket, he had a big honking class ring on his finger. The orange oval jewel was set in a gold band. Flashy.

"What's up, Aurora?"

I did my best not to visibly grimace. "Not much. How are

you?" I pasted a smile on my face. I was fine with my role as one of West High's nobodies, but I'd sooner graduate without becoming known as The Loner Bitch.

"You're really serious about graduating," Mike remarked.

"What do you mean?"

He nodded towards the board, six feet in front of us. "Sitting in the front row, taking notes all hour."

"Oh," I said.

I looked down at my spiral notebook, already opened to a new page, dated at the top, my pen laced between my fingers.

He chuckled. "We should enjoy our last semester while we can, don't you think? Once we get to college it's all up hill. Textbooks the size of encyclopedias. Lectures designed to cause serious migraines. Late night cram sessions. Never ending homework. You get the idea."

I looked at him with more interest. At least he planned on pursuing a higher education. That kind of conversation made me more comfortable.

"Where are you going to college?" I asked.

Mike's desk moved when he leaned in closer.

"Boise State University. Yep, gonna be a Bronco." He dipped down in his seat as he said this, lifting the front legs of his desk several inches off the ground before hitting the floor again. "What about you?"

This used to be my favorite question. I hated telling people I was staying in-state, like I wasn't adventurous or smart enough to leave Alaska.

"I'm going to the University of Alaska Anchorage," I said without enthusiasm.

I always had to fight back the urge to add that I had been accepted into Notre Dame, but it was no use. I'd only have to come up with lies about why I wasn't going. In the end, it didn't impress anyone, anyway. Bottom line: I was an in-state loser.

"You should look into woo-wee," Mike said.

"Woo-wee?"

"W-U-E, Western Undergraduate Exchange. You can go to participating out-of-state colleges for in-state tuition." Mike grinned. "That's what I'm doing. There're a lot of universities in the WUE program. Colleges in Washington, Idaho, Colorado, California, Arizona, Oregon…even Hawaii."

If only my problems were financial. If the government hadn't forced me into a life of servitude, even the WUE colleges wouldn't be far enough away from home. Take me East any day.

"Maybe I'll look into it," I said.

"You totally should. I don't know about you, but I want to get the hell out of dodge come graduation."

Mike succeeded in making me laugh. I was reminded momentarily of the story Dante shared with me about taking off for Amsterdam after his initiation. He's lucky the agents gave him a second chance. There'd be no European tour for me. No east coast college experience. Not even a western one in the WUE program. My laughter dried up.

Mr. Young walked in and was bombarded by several students. They were still talking to him after the bell rang.

"Hey, why don't come to the school dance with me Friday?"

Ugh, the dreaded proposition. I had to hand it to Mike; he didn't waste time. Maybe that was a senior year thing. *Carpe diem* and all that jazz.

I laughed—a genuine amused laugh. "Isn't this Friday the Sadie Hawkins dance?"

I never got why they always scheduled it around Valentine's

Day. Big time lame.

"Yeah," Mike said, smiling bigger.

"I hate to break it to you, but boys aren't supposed to do the asking."

Mike shrugged. "I don't mind breaking the rules…for you."

A wave of heat shot through me. I couldn't tell if I was flattered, embarrassed, or both. I wanted nothing more than to hightail it out of the room.

I took a steadying breath before answering. "Thank you. That's really nice, but I'm going to a party Friday night."

"So, do both," Mike said without missing a beat.

"That wouldn't really work."

"The school dances are pretty lame, anyway," he said. "So, what's this party?"

"Nothing special," I said quickly. "Mostly hanging out, drinking. It's an older crowd."

Mike grinned. "I like older crowds." No doubt he liked drinking, too.

Thankfully Mr. Young shooed the last student away from his desk and began roll call before I had to think of how to respond to Mike's obvious fishing.

I shot out of my desk the moment the bell rang at the end of class.

"See you later," I said to Mike, avoiding eye contact and rushing out of the room. Luckily he didn't follow me out.

Still, I felt unsettled enough to spend lunch with Noel, Henry, and Gavin rather than risk Mike walking by an empty room I happened to be studying in.

"Wow, is that Aurora Sky?" Gavin asked when I approached their table in the cafeteria. He squinted up at me. "I almost forgot you go here."

Henry elbowed him before flashing me a brilliant smile. "Have a seat. It's good to see you."

They looked preppy in their Calvin Klein jeans and sweatshirts. They dressed nice, unlike Fane who had his whole Neo/Matrix look going on. But unlike a moth, I was drawn to the dark.

"Thanks," I said, pulling a chair out beside Noel. "Where's the rest of your posse?"

"They decided to go out for lunch," Noel said. She looked clearly pleased to have the hunky vamps to herself.

I couldn't blame her. I was glad it was just the four of us.

"You and Fane going to Marcus's party?" Henry asked.

I tried not to flinch. Fane had done me the kindness of letting Henry, Gavin, and Marcus believe we were together so they'd keep their teeth out of me.

"I'm going," I answered evenly, studying the tabletop.

Henry and Gavin exchanged a look.

"What are you wearing?" Noel asked. "Red or black?"

She piled small pieces of orange cheese and sliced turkey onto round crackers from her pre-packaged lunch. Henry and Gavin didn't have lunches. My sack lunch was made up of the standard peanut butter and jelly sandwich, and a Ziploc filled with chips. Noel and I weren't exactly paragons of health.

I had fully intended to wear black to Marcus's party in protest of the dreaded holiday, but that was before I took the public bus to the mall and fell in love with a short red dress. The top had a scoop neck that practically came off the shoulders. The color accented my pale skin and long dark hair in a way black never could.

I needed to look stunning in case Fane showed up with Valerie, although I don't know how we'd explain that one since the only thing warding off potential biters was the fact that Marcus and company thought Fane and I were together. I didn't know how long he'd agree to put on the charade. Returning my scarf could be his way of signaling the end of that.

"Red," I said to Noel. "What about you? I presume you're wearing black."

Henry laughed. He had a great smile. "I'd be willing to put money on it."

"Black's my color," Noel said before popping another cracker sandwich into her mouth.

"And you look great in it," Gavin said.

Noel blushed, which was almost comical. Her color was certainly red now.

Noel turned her attention quickly back to me. "Do you need a ride for the party?"

"That would be great. Do you mind picking me up in front of school? I told my mom I was going to the dance Friday night."

"No problem," Noel said.

Henry and Gavin pushed their seats back and stood. "See you, ladies, later."

"Have fun in history," Noel said. She, Henry, and Gavin began laughing.

"I hope I didn't scare them away," I said after they'd gone.

Noel shook her head. "Nah, they have a presentation to give about the Civil War. Gavin has the visual aids in his car...artifacts from his 'grandfather.'"

I sighed. "School must be such a breeze for those guys."

Noel shrugged.

"What's up with you and Gavin, anyway?" I asked. "Is he ever going to ask you out or are you friends with biting benefits?"

I bit into my sandwich and chewed.

Noel's face colored. "Gavin and I are friends. Besides, I haven't been assigned a vampire."

I stopped chewing. "Assigned a vampire?"

Noel frowned. "Never mind."

"Noel, what are you talking about?"

Noel shrugged. "It doesn't matter. Anyway, now that we're alone I have something to tell you about Fane."

Oh, she was devious changing the subject like that. I planted both arms on the table and leaned in.

"I wasn't sure if I should tell you this, but Whitney doesn't think he's with Valerie anymore."

Whitney was one of Noel's old friends from Denali High and had been one of mine briefly between my car accident and transfer to West. A short friendship. But she had called me to report seeing Fane and Valerie lip-locked right after Valerie blackmailed me into breaking up with Fane.

I didn't know which one of them I had been angrier at. Valerie for threatening me or Fane for moving on the moment I ended our relationship.

"Well, Whitney should get her facts straight," I said. "She told me they were back together."

"'Cause they were," Noel said. "For a day."

Why would Valerie go to the trouble of pulling Fane and me apart only to hook up with him for one day?

Maybe Fane had realized his error and dumped her a second time. Lovely thought. One that would take some of the edge off St. Vomit's Day. At this point, even the possibility that Valerie and Fane were history was enough for me.

5

SUCK BUDDY

I MADE IT THROUGH THE WEEK without having to deal with Mike. On Friday morning there were no more seats beside me when Mike arrived in history class. I could sense him hustling to follow me out at the end of the period. Just as I felt him closing in, a girl called out, "Mike, wait up!"

His footsteps slowed, mine hastened, and I was in the clear. Hopefully, Pretty Voice, whoever she was, asked Mike to the dance.

Special thanks went out to Mom for not keeping me lingering in front of school. That afternoon I saw her waiting in the pick-up lane when I walked out. Ever since I'd mentioned moving out, she'd been either on time or early.

Five hours later the sky had drained of color and we were back at school. I felt bad making Mom drive out here three times in one day, but she wasn't exactly Noel's biggest fan. She'd ask less questions if she thought I was going to a school dance. Even though she knew about vampires, she needed her illusions, one of which consisted of a daughter who did normal things like attend school dances.

That didn't stop her from worrying. "But who do you know here?" she asked, chewing on her lower lip.

"I've met a few people," I said.

"Well, you look beautiful, honey."

"Thank you."

I wore my hair down and stained my lips in a blood red shade that could hold their own against Valerie's. I wasn't usually big on eye makeup, but tonight I'd outlined my eyes and put on mascara. I pushed the mirrored visor back up once I'd double-checked that I had no smudges around my eyes or lips.

"What time should I pick you up?" Mom asked.

"I'll get a ride home. One of the guys I'm meeting mentioned going out for dessert afterward if that's okay with you."

Mom's eyes narrowed. "Is this boy nice?"

"Very nice and very boring. All he talks about is college."

"There's nothing wrong with thinking about the future," Mom said quickly.

At least my comment worked in taking the sting out of her voice.

A group of girls in short dresses walked past the car.

"Will you look at that," she said. "Those girls are going to end up catching colds without a coat on. In this weather..." She shook her head.

I'd tried to walk out of the house without a jacket earlier, but Mom insisted I take her full-length coat. It looked too fancy on me, but then again there was no such thing as too fancy or too elegant at the palace.

I leaned over and kissed Mom on the cheek. "Thanks for driving me over...again."

"Don't worry about that. I'm happy to."

"Don't wait up," I said after I exited the car.

"Don't stay out too late," she countered.

I gave her a little wave then turned and headed for the school's double doors. Knowing her, she'd watch me until I safely entered the building. A guy in a tux held the door open for his date and then ushered me in ahead of him.

"Thanks," I said.

The students who had worn coats were hanging them up on the long metal coat racks that had been wheeled into the hallway outside the gym.

I swung around to the farthest set of double doors and peered out the glass into the parking lot. No sign of Mom's car. No sign of Noel, either. I wasn't particularly keen on hanging around the school in case Mike showed up.

I made my way across the parking lot. Cars poured in one after the other as though they were part of a Friday night funeral procession. With any luck, Noel would pull in before I reached the street.

She didn't.

I paced the sidewalk along Hillcrest Drive until I heard a honk.

Noel pulled up alongside the curb, and I got inside her car.

"Sorry!" she said before I even closed the door behind me. "I didn't notice the time."

"Don't worry about it."

I pulled the "Bite Me" heart pendant out of my coat pocket and clasped it around my neck. I hadn't wanted to wear it in front of Mom. She would have wanted to know where it came from, who gave it to me, why, and so on and so forth.

Noel looked over and smiled at me. "I've got mine on, too."

Marcus didn't live too far from West in downtown Anchorage. His condo sat about as close to the inlet as you could get.

I shucked off Mom's coat and tossed it in the backseat of the car.

"You look nice," Noel said, doing the same with her jacket.

"You look good yourself." And she did in her little black dress. I held offered my arm. "May I escort you inside?"

Noel grabbed hold. "You may."

We knocked on the carved wood door with its custom

stained-glass windows. A young man in a tuxedo ushered us inside.

"No coats, ladies?"

"We left them in the car," I said.

The young man nodded once. "Please make yourselves comfortable and have a magnificent evening."

Noel and I looked at one another. I had to bite my tongue to keep from laughing.

"Thank you," Noel said.

"Joyeux Noel and Aurora Sky!"

It was impossible to miss Marcus in a living room full of black tuxes. He wore a pair of black trousers and a red silk shirt, half unbuttoned. Guests parted as he made his way through the living room to join us.

"Welcome, my black-haired beauties."

Marcus kissed Noel's cheeks and then mine. He eyed our pendants and said, "Very good."

Marcus had the same heart pinned to his shirt.

"Thank you for inviting me," I said.

"But of course." Marcus had a voice as silky as his shirt. I didn't feel particularly comfortable around him, but you couldn't find a more hospitable host.

"You know where the drinks are," he said, sweeping an arm toward the kitchen.

"Thank you," Noel and I said in unison.

Marcus stepped in the way before I could follow Noel. He leaned forward, lips curving. "Try not to behave."

I shivered involuntarily and Marcus chuckled before rejoining the guests inside his living room.

A young man dressed like the guy at the front door walked out of the kitchen with a tray of drinks as I walked in. At least

Noel and I had the space to ourselves. I looked around the counters. Last time there had been a champagne fountain.

My eyes landed on a silver tray lined with shot glasses and filled with thick, red liquid.

My eyes widened. "Is that…"

"Blood," Noel said.

I opened my mouth to speak, but she cut me off. "Don't worry, it comes from the blood bank. There's wine in the fridge or champagne if you prefer."

"I think Aurora would prefer the blood."

Goosebumps rose over my flesh at the sound of Fane's voice. I turned slowly. I couldn't stop myself from staring once I saw him. Fane wasn't cute in the conventional sense. A lot of girls would probably cross the road to avoid passing him on the street, but they didn't know the way he kissed. The way his lips teased me until I was breathless. If he kissed that good, I couldn't begin to imagine him in bed. Actually, I could. And therein lay the problem.

"Hello, Fane," I said cordially.

Noel looked between us then asked, "Have you seen Gavin?"

"He's in the living room," Fane said, not taking his eyes off me.

"Cool," Noel said. "See you soon?"

And then she left me. Alone. With Fane.

His grin widened as Noel passed him on her way out of the kitchen.

"Alone at last," he said, inching closer. "Don't look so scared, Aurora. I'm the one who should be afraid." Before I knew it, he was at my side. "Hunter," he whispered inside my ear.

I took a step away from him. "I'm just here to have a good time, like everyone else."

"I'll drink to that." Fane grabbed two shot glasses off the

tray and handed one to me.

Without thinking, I grabbed the shot then scowled. "I don't drink blood."

Fane gave me a dubious look then tossed back his blood shot and set it on the counter with a clack. "Yes, you do," he said, running a tongue across his lip.

I set the shot beside his empty one and glared. Now that he was closer, I could smell cigarette smoke on him. He'd quit once for me. Back when we were together. Back when I thought he was human.

"Thanks for returning my scarf."

"You're not wearing it," Fane said. He pushed my hair over my shoulders then sucked in a breath when he saw the bite marks on my neck.

Henry chose that moment to enter the kitchen.

"Jeez, Fane! Get carried away?"

Fane's back was to Henry, so the other vampire didn't see Fane scowl. His expression changed almost instantly to one of smug satisfaction.

"You know me, I like the rough stuff."

I felt my cheeks heat when Henry glanced back at me, unsure how to respond. I knew how he felt. I was utterly without words. Unlike Fane. The fiend.

"Speaking of which…Aurora, may I speak to you upstairs?" Fane asked.

"Upstairs?" I repeated. The room expanded as my eyes did.

"Yeah," he said. "I need to *talk* to you in private."

I nodded, once more speechless. My heart beat erratically as I followed Fane out of the kitchen.

"Hey," Henry called.

When we turned around Henry held out two shots of

blood to Fane.

"Why don't you take a couple of these, Fane? Go easy on her."

Fane's upper lip curled when he smiled. "Thanks, bro," he said. He downed the first shot in one gulp then lifted the second one in the air. "One for the road."

With Fane's free hand he slipped his fingers over my arm and steered me through the living room to the spiral staircase.

"What are you doing?" I whispered frantically.

Fane looked around the room. "Have to keep up appearances, don't we?" he responded testily.

Fane knew that if we didn't keep up the act of being together then eventually one of the vampires at these parties would want to bite me, and if they bit me, the gig was up. At least Fane didn't want me dead. How romantic.

I nodded mutely and followed him up the custom iron and wood spiral staircase leading to Marcus's many private guestrooms upstairs. Fane walked down the hall into the October room—a spacious quarter painted in various shades of orange. He pulled the silver bat dangling from the doorknob inside the room and moved it to the outer knob—Marcus's clever "do not disturb" signal.

He didn't bother turning on the overhead light. Candles blazed from all corners of the room. It smelled like orange peel and clove.

Once he'd shut the door, Fane held up the shot of blood. "Still going to pretend you don't want this?"

"I don't want it."

Fane shrugged, but rather than down it he set it beside an orange pillar candle on the dresser. The blood flickered in the light.

"We're alone now," I said impatiently to mask my jangled nerves. "What did you want to talk to me about?"

"Who said anything about talking?" Fane walked over to the bed.

My breath caught in my throat as he ran a hand along the quilt while skirting the length of the bed to the headboard.

I swear every move he made was a deliberate attempt to unnerve me.

I expected Fane to sit on the bed, but he rested his back against the wall and folded his arms. "You have a lie to maintain, and I have a reputation to uphold."

"Some reputation," I said under my breath.

He smiled. I tried not to stare at his lips too long.

They puckered right before he began speaking. "How's the new school?"

"Same shit, different faces."

Fane leaned forward when he laughed. I felt my body relax as his did as though our minds were somehow hardwired together. "Are you staying out of trouble?"

"I'm West High's model student. Early to class. Front row. Attentive."

Fane nodded. "I'm sure that makes your mother happy."

I shrugged and sat on the edge of the bed. The doorknob settled in my direct line of vision. I'd forgotten how easy it was to talk to him even after the whole vampire/hunter revelation and breakup. Easy didn't exactly equal comfortable. I hadn't yet formulated the words to ask if he and Valerie were together. It's not the kind of thing that flowed naturally into a conversation.

"Have you made any new friends?" Fane asked carefully.

I couldn't tell if that was Fane's roundabout way of asking if I had a boyfriend.

"I don't need friends. I need to graduate." I turned and met his gaze. "As long as we're in private maybe you can confirm something for me."

Might as well go for it.

Fane raised a brow. "And what's that?"

"Are you with Valerie?"

I didn't care how it sounded. I had to know.

"The only reason Valerie threw herself back at me was so she could ditch me a day later." Fane chuckled. "I forgot what a hellcat she is."

He said the last part a little too fondly for my liking. And I suppose Fane considered me a kitty in comparison. I don't know why Dante and Fane perceived Valerie as the feisty one. I thought the news would relieve me, but now that I knew, it seemed irrelevant. If Valerie hadn't dropped him, Fane would still be with her. That's what mattered.

Fane honed in on my frown and grinned. "Don't worry, she may have gotten the last word, but I got the last bite."

"That's enough," I said, balling my hands into fists. "We've put in our time. Now if you'll excuse me." I stormed toward the door.

"Aren't you forgetting something?"

Against my better judgment, I stopped and followed the direction of Fane's eyes to the shot of blood on the dresser.

One sip. What harm would it do? I could taste blood, unlike food. Not that blood tasted particularly fantastic. It's the way it made me feel: my whole body humming to life, radiating warmth, all my senses fully engaged.

Fane took advantage of my hesitation. He fetched the shot and lifted it between me and the door.

"I'm leaving now," I said.

I couldn't blame Fane for not taking me seriously when I did nothing to push past him.

His voice dropped. "I know all about the cravings. I know

about the unbearable thirst that can only be quenched with blood." He stepped closer. "I know you think about it all the time, like a lover you can't get enough of."

I closed my eyes and shuddered. "Stop," I rasped.

Fane chuckled softly.

I cracked my eyes open enough to see him throw back the shot, but he didn't swallow. He leaned forward. Even knowing both the blood and kiss were off-limits, I leaned in. His lips curved up as they closed in on mine.

A knock at the door jolted me back to my senses. My body jerked. Fane swallowed the blood and cursed.

"Aurora?" a voice called from the other side.

My heart momentarily stopped. It couldn't be, but even from the few conversations we'd had, I recognized Mike's voice.

6

PARTY CRASHER

Fane OPENED THE DOOR HALFWAY, folding his arms across his chest as he leaned against the frame. "Can we help you?"

I tried to regain my composure.

Mike stood in the hallway trying to look over Fane's shoulder. He smiled when he saw me. "Hey."

"Apparently you *have* made friends," Fane said sardonically.

I didn't respond. I had a bigger problem on my hands. "Mike, what are you doing here?"

Before he could answer, Fane jumped in. "Mike, is it?" I couldn't see Fane's expression with his back now facing me, but there wasn't anything friendly in his tone. "You see this here ornament on the doorknob?"

Mike glanced down. "Yeah."

"When the bat's in flight, we're getting down tonight—if you know what I mean."

I pushed past Fane. "That's not what it means," I said. "Come on, Mike. We can talk downstairs. Fane, I'll see you later."

Fane stretched in the doorframe. "Got some spare Trojans burning a hole inside your pocket?"

I whipped around and scowled at Fane so hard my jaw ached. The only thing burning was my face from rage and humiliation…a lethal combination. I flipped him off right before I grabbed Mike's arm and steered him down the hall. It took a bit of pulling—he kept staring into open rooms, at statues, and other curiosities decorating the palace.

"Sorry, Aurora, I didn't mean to interrupt anything."

"There was nothing to interrupt. I was just leaving when you knocked."

Mike grinned. "Oh? That's good. Who was that guy?"

"Mike," I said, stopping at the railing beside the spiral staircase. "What are you doing here? How did you even find this place?"

Mike grinned. "I have a little confession to make. I followed you here."

"What?"

"I hadn't planned to," he said quickly. "I drove to school to meet my buddies at the dance and then I saw you outside. Before I had a chance to park and ask what you were doing, I saw you get into a car with some chick."

"So you followed me?"

"I remembered you saying you had a party to go to, and it didn't look like you had a date. I thought if I showed up we might get a chance to hang out."

Oh, Mike. This was so not the place to hang out. I had to get him out of here immediately.

Mike stared down at the guests mingling in the living room. "This is quite the shindig. Glad I dressed up for the dance."

"Speaking of the dance, you should get back before your friends worry about you."

"Nah, I texted them before I came inside."

If I'd had any color left in my pale skin, it would have drained. "Did you text them the address?" I demanded.

"No, I just told them I decided to go to a party instead."

My shoulders relaxed. "Good, now let's get you out of here." I looked back in annoyance when Mike didn't follow me to the top of the stairs.

"What's the rush?"

I tightened my fingers around the iron railing. My patience had just about run out.

"The rush is that this party is by invitation only, and you weren't invited. Now come with me before the host notices you've snuck in."

I scanned the living room for Marcus as I spoke. He couldn't be hard to locate in his red shirt. As luck would have it, he wasn't around. Hopefully he'd snuck off in one of the upstairs rooms with their dangling bats.

Mike looked ready to protest until I took his hand and pulled him toward the stairs. He smiled and gave my hand a squeeze.

I led Mike down the spiral staircase. The moment we reached the living room I let go of his hand. Before I could steer Mike out of the living room, he said, "Hey, I know you."

I tried not to grimace as Henry turned slowly. He looked from Mike to me then back at Mike, saying nothing.

"You go to West," Mike added.

Oh God, Henry did not look happy, and I couldn't blame him. I would have clamped my hand over Mike's mouth if it wouldn't draw more attention.

"Come on, Mike. The door's this way." I gave his arm another pull.

"Aurora's throwing me out," Mike said with a laugh. "See you around."

I felt a surge of relief when I finally managed to get Mike past the kitchen. The front door was in sight.

"Did you bring a coat?" I asked.

Before Mike could answer, we were stopped by a mass of

muscle, staring sensually at Mike. Marcus. Perfect timing.

"And who is this delicious treat?"

"No one. He's leaving."

Mike reached his hand out. "Hey, man. I'm Mike."

Marcus's eyes shined under the track lighting above his head. "Handsome and well mannered—I insist you stay. My name is Marcus."

"Is this your place?" Mike asked. "I didn't mean to crash your party."

"Crash? Don't be silly," Marcus said, still holding on to Mike's hand. "You can crash here anytime. Aurora knows I never turn down objects of beauty."

Mike's smile faded. He moved closer to me.

I squared my shoulders. "Too bad Mike has another engagement he's late for."

"I'm sure he can cancel," Marcus said, winking at Mike.

Before Mike could answer, I said, "Unfortunately not. He's kept his friends waiting long enough already and like you said, he's too well-mannered to keep them waiting any longer. Mike?" I said sharply. "I'll walk you to your car."

"Maybe another time," Mike said, following close behind me.

"Anytime." Marcus's brows jumped, and he turned back toward the living room.

Mike walked out the front door as though in a trance until the cold air hit him.

"Wait, what about my jacket?"

"Forget the jacket. I'll bring it to school on Monday."

"Are you mad at me?" Mike asked.

Now that we were outside, I felt free to talk as loud as I liked.

"Yes, I'm mad at you! You can't just follow me to a party and show up uninvited."

"I know. I'm sorry. I wasn't stalking you or anything. I'd just rather hang out at a party than a school dance. And it would have been cool to hang out. Marcus didn't seem to mind."

I stopped on the sidewalk and leaned into Mike. "You have to promise me you will never come back here." I really needed to find a way to hammer that point home. It's not as though I could warn Mike about vampires. "It's Marcus, you see. He once had a thing for me, and he still gets jealous of other guys. I know he acts friendly, but you can't trust him to have the best intentions."

"Marcus?" Mike asked dubiously.

I nodded, hoping he'd buy it.

Mike watched me carefully. "But you're not into him?"

My expression was proof enough—my entire face wrinkled. "I've never been into him that way."

Mike stopped beside a blue Honda Civic and kicked at a clump of frozen snow on the sidewalk. He kept at it, making no move to the driver's side.

The cold made my gums feel numb. I cleared my throat. "Drive safe, Mike."

Mike stopped kicking at the snow. "So, you're going back inside?"

"Only to get your coat and find my ride. I'm ready to go."

"I'll drive you home," he said.

"I promised my friend we'd hang out afterwards," I said.

"Okay, well, I guess I'll see you Monday."

Unless I found another high school to transfer to. Yeah, right.

"Drive safe."

"See you later, Aurora," Mike said.

I lifted my hand in the air and turned my back to him before he could say anything more, hurrying back to the warmth of the palace.

Henry was waiting for me in the kitchen with a tight frown

forming wrinkles on his chin. I eyed the blood shots on the counter beside him. I could really use one. Blood made me feel strong, in control.

"What was Michael Peterson doing here?" Henry demanded.

My brain had a whiteout moment before registering that Henry was referring to Mike.

"I didn't invite him," I said defensively.

"That wasn't my question."

I reached for a bottle of red wine on the counter. If I couldn't drink blood in public, then I was going for the next best thing. Red wine had its own warming quality, especially in winter.

"Allow me," Henry said, ever the gentleman even though displeasure filled every crevice of his face.

"He followed me here," I said as Henry poured.

"You seem to have a knack for drawing unwelcome attention," Henry said, eyes never leaving the flow of wine. He lifted the bottle when the glass was half full and handed it to me.

I didn't feel like drinking anymore. It's not as though I could argue with him—as much as I wanted to. It had been nice of him and Gavin to help dispose of my captors two weeks ago. Now here I was leading a clueless classmate straight into the bat cave. If I didn't watch myself I'd be banned from the palace.

"What does he know about us?" Henry asked, watching me with a stony expression.

"Nothing."

"But he knows where to find us."

"This isn't his scene," I said quickly. "He came looking for me."

"What's to stop him from looking again?"

"I told him not to." Sheesh, what was with the third degree?

Henry narrowed his eyes. "Where's Fane?"

"Upstairs."

"He left you unchaperoned?"

A gagging noise gurgled in the back of my throat before I could speak. "This is the twenty-first century, Henry. I don't require a chaperone."

Henry looked me up and down. "That's debatable."

"Well, he wanted me to fetch him another drink. How does that sound?" Henry probably had no problem seeing me as a serving wench. Who knew how old, or more importantly, *old-fashioned*, he was. I nearly knocked over my wine glass reaching for a shot of blood. Having a vampire watch my every move was unnerving. Wine in one hand, shot in the other, I marched out of the kitchen without a second glance.

Marcus shot me a wicked grin as I made my way through the living room to the spiral staircase. Upstairs, the door to the October room remained open, but there wasn't any sign of Fane. I didn't know what I'd been expecting, and I didn't know where he'd gone. I hadn't seen him in the living room, and he couldn't have left without running into me. Not through the front door, anyway.

I glanced at the window. Doubtful.

I tried to convince myself that the only reason I felt disappointed was he'd gotten away with only the finger for that Trojan remark. What did Fane think? Because I'd messed up once I'd do it again?

I took a quick glance around and then downed the shot of blood. One gulp. I felt shaken, and I needed something to calm me.

Calm wasn't exactly the right word. The blood excited me. I felt like I'd taken a hit of adrenaline. I wanted to dance. Why didn't Marcus have dancing at his parties? Everyone stood around yapping and sipping cocktails. What a bunch of old fogies. Literally.

I took a large sip of wine to wash down any trace of blood

on my teeth.

I felt like walking home, but I wasn't dressed for it and I wasn't about to disappear on Noel again.

Where was Noel, anyway? Probably shut off in a room with Gavin. I hadn't seen him in the living room when I passed through.

Guess there wasn't much else to do besides sip my wine in a corner downstairs and not talk to strangers. As I retreated down the hall, I found a tray with empty glasses and stashed the shot glass there before descending into the living room. Noel sat in a corner by the window staring out at the dark inlet. Her frown reflected in the glass.

"Noel?" I said, taking a seat on a cushy chair beside her. Marcus and his partner, Richard Stanton of Stanton's Fine Art Gallery, kept the rooms filled with so many antiques and art objects that there wasn't much legroom. My knees bumped into Noel's legs.

"Oh, hi." She sighed.

"What's the matter?"

"I don't know what's going on. Gavin is being so cold to me tonight."

I raised a brow. "He's a vampire."

"Ha, ha," Noel replied. "What about Fane? Is it true he broke up with Valerie?"

"He says they were only together a day." I slumped forward. "He was rather cold, too."

Noel sighed. "Why can't we like normal guys?"

"Because we're not normal girls." I followed Noel's gaze to the window. From that vantage there were no city lights, no buildings, no land. Just ocean.

During the day, Cook Inlet looked about as gray as the overcast sky. At night it was as black as oil. Anchorage didn't have beaches. We had mudflats. The fine glacial silt turned to quicksand any time an unwary victim ventured too far and became stuck in the mud. Last summer, the Anchorage Fire Department had to rescue two teenagers who got stuck before the tide swallowed them whole.

"Ready to get out of here?" I asked Noel.

"Sure."

All I wanted to do was collapse into bed, but as Noel's Volvo chugged up the hill, I saw my entire house lit up from within as though it were radioactive.

"That's odd," I said when we pulled up.

"Is everything okay?" Noel asked.

"I don't know. Guess I'll find out."

The moment I walked in I heard the kind of sobbing that could only mean one thing. Someone had died. And that someone could only be my dad.

"Mom?"

My heart constricted, and I fought for breath. My vision swam. I tried to think back to my last memory of Dad—his last words. What I remembered was Mom begging him not to leave. Great last memory to take with me for the rest of my life.

I found Mom in the kitchen, plates broken at her feet. She'd stopped sobbing as soon as I called out her name, but her face was a red blotchy horror.

"Aurora, I wasn't expecting you home this early," she said in a voice that was freakishly normal.

She'd lost it all right.

"It's Dad, isn't it?"

Mom's eyes confirmed that it was.

"Oh, God." Without warning, I collapsed against the counter and made a choking sound. "I was such a snot the last time I saw him. And now…" I started sobbing uncontrollably.

Dad hadn't been especially nice after my accident, but in his defense, he'd been out of the country and had no idea how close I'd come to dying or of the deal Mom had made with the agents.

It came back to me then, his last words. *I'm not sure I like this new attitude of yours.* I sobbed harder. If only he'd known what really happened. I couldn't imagine him sitting idly by, allowing a secret government agency to dictate the rest of my life. He would have fought for me.

"My poor girl," Mom said, taking me into her arms. She stroked my back as I cried into her bathrobe.

I leaned back and looked her in the eyes. "How did it happen?"

Her hand stilled on my back and her lips pinched the way they did whenever she didn't want to talk about something. "I don't want to worry you with it," she said.

"That bad?" I asked, barely above a whisper.

I took her hand in mine and squeezed gently. "Mom, I have to know."

Please don't let it be a vampire or a car accident. The truth couldn't be as gruesome as what my brain was throwing at me.

Mom sighed. She pulled her hand out of mine and went to the far side of the dining room, coming to a rest in front of a stack of papers. She took a deep breath. Her eyes didn't seem capable of meeting mine.

"He's been having an affair for two years," she started.

"Affair?!" My jaw went slack.

She met my eyes now and squinted as though trying to read the expression on my face. "I didn't want to shock you with this. We don't have to talk about it."

"Mom, I thought Dad was dead!"

"Dead?" she repeated. "No, your father wants a divorce." She visibly shuddered as though divorce was worse than death. "He had the papers delivered earlier this evening." She looked down.

I stormed to the table, raking my eyes over the stack.

"That dick!"

I could say that now that I knew he was alive and dicking around with another woman. His long absences suddenly made sense.

"I'll clean up the kitchen," I said, wanting to distract myself with something.

"Don't worry about that," she said.

I got out the dustpan and broom anyway and began sweeping up the broken bits of plate.

"What does this mean?" I asked, crouched on the floor. "Do we have to move out of the house?"

"We're not going anywhere," Mom said in a voice that brokered no argument.

She was understandably angry. I should have left it at that, but I didn't.

"Maybe this would be a good time to sell the house. I plan on moving into an apartment after I graduate. This is an awfully big house for one person. You could spend time with Grandma." Like many retired Alaskans, Gran divided her time between Alaska and Florida. I swept the last of the pieces of broken plate into the dustpan and stood up.

Mom had been deathly silent as I spoke. When I ventured a glance her way, she looked ready to snarl. "I am not running off to hide in Florida. If Bill thinks he can run me out of the state and out of my home, he has another thing coming!"

"Okay, Mom. Calm down. What do you want to do?"

She took the kind of breath that lifted her shoulders halfway to her ears and released. "I want Bill to come home. We could work this out if only he'd try."

"You…want him…back?" I couldn't believe my ears.

"Spare me your judgment, Aurora."

Now I really didn't believe my ears. Mom never said stuff like that to me.

"I'm not judging," I said defensively. "But he cheated on you—for two years!"

"And we've been together for twenty. You don't just walk away from something like that. He's going through a phase is all. How much do you want to bet that woman put him up to this? Of course she did. Bill has a wife, a daughter, a home. He wouldn't just walk away from that."

I doubt Mom was in the right frame of mind to be reminded that he already had walked away from all that. He wasn't coming back. She might not be able to see that, but I did.

7

MYSTERY MAN

I DIDN'T TAKE MY USUAL SEAT up front in history on Monday. I chose a desk with seats occupied on either side. I wasn't in the mood for Mike's antics. Not today. Not tomorrow. Not ever.

I really needed to put on my big girl panties and lay down the law. If I could fight vampires, I could let a boy down gently.

First I had to return his jacket.

I gave silent thanks when the final bell rang with no sign of Mike.

Homework was the furthest thing from my mind when lunch rolled around. Maybe I could convince Noel to leave the love nest and go out for a bite. I needed to tell someone about my dad.

I took my wallet out of my backpack before stuffing the bag inside my locker. Hopefully Noel would let me steal her away.

I made tracks for the cafeteria. If we left within the next five minutes we might still have time to order our food at one of the nearby fast food chains and eat it.

A giggling freshman collided into me while joking around with a friend. I nearly pushed him aside.

"Sorry," he said quickly.

I took a breath. *Be nice, Aurora.* "That's okay."

Four girls sat around Henry and Gavin today—none of whom were Noel. Henry watched me wearily. Probably still bent out of shape after being IDed at the palace by Mike.

"Where's Noel?" I asked.

Henry lifted his chin. "Library."

"Thanks." I turned abruptly and walked out.

I found Noel slouched over a tabletop in a back corner of the library. My lips lifted as I approached her. When she sat up I noticed her hair. She'd cut it short! Although Noel and I looked nothing alike, we'd had almost identical long black hair. Noel's had been streaked with pretty blue highlights that disappeared once she transferred to West. Now it was all black and barely reached her shoulder blades. Like Valerie, Noel had a way of wearing red lipstick as though it were a natural eye color. She looked good without the hoodie and with her hair styled in an attractive bob.

"I love your hair," I said immediately.

Noel didn't so much as crack a smile. "Thanks."

"What are you doing in the library? Get hit by a case of nostalgia?" Noel and her friends Whitney and Hope used to hang out in the school library at Denali High all the time. "What's the matter?" I asked when she didn't respond.

"Valerie," Noel said, anger rising in her voice.

I slipped into the seat beside her. "No argument there. What's the vixen done now?"

Noel glared at the tabletop. "She hooked up with Gavin."

"When? How?" I sputtered. "They don't even go to the same school." And just when Noel had gone and gotten a makeover. What rotten timing. Or maybe this was Noel's way of showing Gavin what he was missing.

"After I dropped you off Friday night I went back to the party and there they were making out on the couch." Noel's lip curled back. "One of Marcus's guests told them to take it upstairs…and they did."

Noel's head dove forward into her arms.

"I'm so sorry, Noel." I patted her back gently. Maybe not the best time to bring up my philandering father.

"Want to grab a sandwich with me?"

"I'm not hungry, but I'll come with you. I just want to get out of here." She pushed away from the table.

As we headed down the hall, the intercom crackled.

"Aurora Sky and Noel Harper, please report to the front office immediately."

Noel and I looked at each other. I imagine I looked every bit as alarmed as she did. My hands instantly balled into fists. Noel and I headed to the office without a word. I didn't know about Noel, but I could do without any more surprises.

Noel stepped up to the front desk. "I'm Noel Harper and this is Aurora Sky."

The secretary handed us each a slip of paper. "You've been excused from your afternoon classes," she said.

Noel and I huddled together with our matching notes.

Report for duty immediately.
-Melcher

"So much for taking the rest of the month off," I muttered.

"Duty calls," Noel said, sounding pretty sarcastic herself. "Do you need anything out of your locker?"

"Yeah, can I grab my books? I have a history test to study for tonight."

"Meet you out front," Noel said.

My phone rang on the way to my locker. It was Dante.

"Have you been called in?" he asked.

"Yep."

"Need a ride?"

"I'm coming in with Noel."

"I'll save you a seat at headquarters," he said, abruptly ending the call.

"It's not a race," I muttered under my breath.

I certainly wasn't in any hurry to get on base.

It took me a moment to remember my new locker combo. Once I had the door unlatched, I sifted through my pack, leaving behind the textbooks I knew I wouldn't touch that night. I eyed Mike's coat in the back of my locker—one more thing that needed taking care of.

I dialed my mom as I walked down the hall and told her the agents had called me in, and I'd catch a ride home with Dante. For once she didn't ask if everything was okay. Probably too hung up on her own problems.

Noel had her car idling in the pick-up lane when I walked out. She had the black hoodie back on with the hood pulled over her head. I'd grabbed my red scarf that morning and wrapped it around my neck. Old habits die hard.

"Valerie is the absolute last person I feel like seeing right now," Noel grumbled after I got in.

"Sorry."

"Melcher better not try to pair her up with me."

"Nor me. Once was enough." I scrunched up my face. "How did you and Dante get along, by the way?"

"Fine, even though he would have rather been with you or Valerie."

Now she was really pouting.

I kept my eyes on the road because Noel looked spaced out. At least we were driving on snow, not ice.

Noel and I didn't speak the rest of the way. My thoughts drifted back to the divorce. I wished I could tell Fane about my dad. Could we ever be friends again?

I handed my ID badge to Noel at the gated checkpoint leading on base. The military man at the window took both badges with his standard frown then handed them back.

"About time," Dante said when Noel and I walked into Melcher and Crist's office.

I rolled my eyes before taking a seat. "I'm surprised the agents left you alone in their office."

Dante leaned against the wall and grinned. "I tried to get into the file cabinets, but they're locked."

Noel fell into a chair and pulled her hood further down her face.

Dante's eyes flicked from Noel to me. "How's school?"

"School."

"Really? Tell me more."

I started to chuckle when Valerie strode in, tall brown boots pulled over skinny jeans, a fire engine red cowl-necked sweater on top. She sighed dramatically.

"Don't tell me I've been called in to babysit Aurora again."

"Good thing you came," Dante said smoothly. "A call girl's gone missing, and Melcher needs you to work through her clients until you find the culprit."

I laughed and then choked trying to hold it back.

Valerie chose to direct her anger at me. "Something funny?" she demanded, leaning toward me.

Dante tsked. "Careful, Red. I've seen Aurora in action."

"So have I. By action, I assume you mean getting her ass whipped."

Dante grinned. "You have my attention now."

I pushed myself out of my chair, prepared to yell at them both when Melcher walked into the room.

"Oh good, you're all here."

I hardly noticed the man who walked in behind Melcher. He pushed the door closed forcefully, hanging at the back as though guarding our only exit. Melcher stood behind his desk.

"Team, I have bad news."

Since when did Melcher ever call us in to share good news? Something was definitely up, though. For the first time, he wasn't smiling. He looked us each in the face. "Agent Crist was found dead over the weekend."

"What?"

I'm not sure who said it—maybe all four of us. Noel's head shot up. Dante lowered his foot to the ground. Valerie's jaw dropped.

Melcher nodded grimly before taking a seat. "One of our own...gone."

Crist and I were never close, but I never wished her ill—and certainly not dead.

Melcher cleared his throat. "Agent Crist served her country well, and while the community might not know it, her sacrifice will never be forgotten. Not in our unit. She put duty before her personal life. Honor before pride. Loyalty above self-interest."

I slouched in my seat. At least Melcher's rambling served the purpose of numbing my initial shock, though I was waiting like everyone else to find out exactly what had happened.

"Agent Crist worked tirelessly by my side for over three years. She understood our mission better than anyone I've ever worked with."

The guy behind me yawned.

As much as I wanted to turn in my seat and get a better look at him, it didn't feel appropriate with Melcher talking about the former Agent Crist.

"Did a vamp get her?" Dante demanded the minute Melcher

concluded his tribute to Crist.

"I'm afraid so." Melcher's speech had loosened his lips, relaxing his frown into something more Melcher-like.

"Do you think he, or whoever, was aware of her involvement in this organization?" I asked.

That's what had gotten me into trouble with Renard and his cronies. What if Crist had talked? Shared names? I gripped the armrests of my seat.

"From what the autopsy showed it appears this was a rush job. We believe Crist was simply in the wrong place at the wrong time."

What were the odds of that happening? I actually felt sorry for the poor woman no matter how prickly she'd been. No one deserved death by vampire, especially not someone who'd dedicated her life to stopping the creatures from harming human citizens.

Dante smacked his fist against his hand. "Any leads?"

Melcher glanced over our shoulders to the man in the back. Mr. Mysterious made his way to the front, taking a seat on the edge of Crist's desk.

"That is what Jared is here to help us with," Melcher said in answer to Dante's question.

"Agent?" Dante asked, raising a brow.

"Just Jared," the man said.

I thought Melcher was smug. This guy exuded conceit. He looked around the room as though he owned the space and everyone in it. His chest looked rock solid under a thin ribbed t-shirt with long sleeves. He didn't wear a suit like Melcher, and he couldn't be much older than thirty, though he held himself up like some kind of Fortune 500 CEO.

Melcher cleared his throat. "Jared is our top recruiter. He's taking time out to help us find Agent Crist's killer."

"Where do we start?" Dante asked, looking between Melcher and "Just Jared."

"We found another body dumped beside Agent Crist," Melcher said. "We believe the second body will lead us to the culprit."

"Who was the second victim?" Dante asked.

Melcher formed a steeple with his fingers and looked directly at me. "It was a boy named Michael Peterson. He went to West High School."

For one glorious second, I didn't recognize the name. Then I stopped breathing. It wasn't until Melcher's gaze turned to Noel that I was able to get oxygen to my brain.

Mike!

How was that even possible? Melcher must be mistaken. There was absolutely no link between Mike and Crist—no reason for their lives, and deaths, to collide. Mike couldn't be dead. I had his coat. I still needed to return it.

"Aurora, did you know this boy?" Melcher asked, studying me carefully.

I could see a question forming on Dante's lips. Both men stared at me. Out of the corner of my eye, I saw Jared stifle a yawn. I knew in our line of work we had to desensitize ourselves to a certain degree, but he didn't have to act so bored by the death of an agent and a high school boy.

"We both did," Noel spoke up. "He followed us to Marcus's party Friday night. The moment Aurora noticed him at the party she escorted him out to his car. That's the last we saw of him."

I felt torn between awe and appreciation at Noel's succinct account of Mike's appearance Friday night, and a pain of betrayal that she'd reported my after-hours activities. Well, what could I expect from an informant?

"Marcus," Jared said, grinning. He snapped up the name like a grizzly grabbing a salmon mid-jump.

Melcher shook his head. "He doesn't like to get his clothes wrinkled, let alone his hands bloody."

Jared smirked. "He's not the only one."

"It's not Marcus," Melcher reiterated, sitting up in his chair. "He wants to draw as little attention to himself as possible."

How did Melcher know so much about Marcus? My head started spinning. At least the attention wasn't on me.

Melcher's eyes zoomed in my direction. "You were at Marcus's?"

Whoops, spoke too soon.

Before I could formulate a response, Noel spoke up. "We've been seen together at West, so the guys inquired about her and extended an invitation."

Melcher thought this over then nodded. "And what was the other boy doing there?"

"He saw Aurora getting into my car Friday night and followed us. I think he had a crush on her."

Now my mouth really dropped. I didn't mind Noel speaking for me at first, but I was starting to now.

Dante whistled. "Heart. Breaker," he said, beating a fist against his chest.

I glared so hard I swear I strained my eyeballs.

"I didn't even know the boy! We had like one conversation. Maybe two."

"Two too many." I heard Valerie say under her breath.

Maybe she'd like a shiner to match the one she got the week before.

"Who all was at this party?" Melcher asked.

His question was directed at Noel, so I sat back. If she

wanted to do the talking then, fine, she could be the one to out everyone in Marcus's inner circle. As soon as they let us out of here, I was warning Fane. I didn't think Noel would have been the vindictive type when it came to Gavin hooking up with Valerie, but then you never really knew a person until a boy ended up dead.

Melcher had a notepad out. He picked up a pen and looked at Noel.

"Obviously, Marcus was there," Noel began.

She began reciting names. I couldn't imagine how she'd become familiar with so many. Someone knew how to do her job.

As the list continued, my fists tightened, my fingernails leaving crescent indents in the palms of my hands.

Noel stopped speaking. I didn't look at her for fear of attracting attention, but now that she'd finished, I noticed she'd left out Gavin, Henry, and Fane from the guest list. I loosened my fists. I shouldn't have doubted her.

Valerie didn't pipe up, either. Maybe she really did want to protect her suck buddies.

"And that's everyone?" Melcher asked.

"Everyone I can think of," Noel replied without hesitation. "If I think of anyone else, I'll let you know."

"Very well," Melcher said. "I need you all to wait in the hall while Jared and I talk. We'll call you back to deliver your instructions so don't wander far."

8

PARTNERS

THE FOUR OF US FILED out in silence.

Valerie began texting the moment we walked out. She leaned against a corner at the far end of the hall.

"I had no choice," Noel whispered.

"I know," I said.

There wasn't time to say anything more. Dante slipped in between us. "Poor Agent Crist, who would have dreamed?"

I nodded solemnly. "It's horrific. And Mike." I had to stop talking. My throat constricted.

I felt like such a wretch—always bellyaching about not leaving the state for college. At least I got to go to college. Mike wasn't going anywhere anymore. No bucking bronco at Boise State. I tried to swallow the lump in my throat.

Dante put an arm around me and Noel. I thought he'd say some words of condolence or support. I should have known better. "What's with this party I wasn't invited to?"

I pressed my shoulder against my ear. Dante's breath tickled against my neck.

"You wouldn't last five minutes with Marcus," Noel said.

Dante chuckled. "So, he's a biter, is he?"

I rolled my eyes. "Only when it comes to hot younger men."

Dante leaned into me. "You just admitted you think I'm hot."

"Did I?" I raised a brow.

Dante nodded slowly, staring me straight in the eyes. "Can't take it back now."

"I can't believe you two, flirting when Agent Crist's killer is on the loose."

I gave a little jump when Valerie appeared behind us. "We're not flirting!" And don't tell me she hadn't been off texting with Gavin.

"Speak for yourself, Sky," Dante said and winked.

Valerie made a sound of disgust. She folded her arms beneath her bosom, pushing up both breasts, and tapped her foot. "Do they plan on keeping us here all afternoon?"

I took a breath. "Val, it's been like three minutes."

Valerie stopped tapping and glared at me. "Don't call me Val. Only my close friends have permission to call me Val."

"Whatever," I said, throwing up my hands before I walked away.

Noel quickly followed me.

"That time of the month?" Dante asked Valerie before joining us.

Dante put an arm around me. I didn't want him to, but I couldn't exactly shrug him off when he'd dissed Valerie on my behalf.

"That one's wound tight," Dante remarked, massaging my shoulders.

Noel watched Dante's hands at work on my back. When she met my eye, I gave her what I hoped was a "we're just friends" look.

Noel's lips twisted. "I'll be right back."

Maybe she misread me and thought I wanted some privacy.

I pulled out of Dante's arms as Noel disappeared around the corner. I faced Dante with my arms folded over my chest. He shot me a lopsided grin.

"Feel better?"

"A little." Not even close.

Dante leaned into me. "Listen," he said, glancing to the side and then back. "As soon as I arrived, I had a chat with Melcher."

"Oh?" Now what?

"I requested he pair us up again. We work well together."

I nearly laughed. My arms actually dropped. "Dante, we don't work together at all. You left me alone with two vamps in Fairbanks…during my *first* mission. You weren't even in town when Renard and his henchmen abducted me."

Dante listened to all this with the kind of expression that indicates a guy isn't listening at all but rather rewriting everything you say inside his head to fit his version of the facts. "What about when we went back to interrogate the boy? We got him into the cabin together. You tied him up. You even handed me the knife when it came time to interrogate the subject."

I shuddered. This wasn't exactly something I wanted to remember. Great teamwork—torturing and killing a human.

Dante took me by both shoulders and dipped down to look me in the eyes. "What's the matter, Sky?"

I shook my head. "I still can't believe they're dead—Agent Crist and Mike."

"Did you like this boy?"

My lower lip threatened to tremble. "No. That's just the thing. I thought he was annoying. I was relieved he wasn't at school today, and that makes me feel a thousand times worse."

"Hey." Dante squeezed my shoulders gently. "There's nothing wrong with being honest."

A phone rang behind us. The secretary informed us that we could go back inside Melcher's office. I looked over my shoulder and saw Noel reappear from around the corner.

Valerie walked in front of Noel and took her former seat.

Noel stumbled on the way, quickly righted herself, and went for the next available chair. Dante took his usual stance against the wall. He looked from me to the spot beside him. I joined him. Better than sitting beside Valerie.

"All right everyone, let's get down to business," Melcher said.

He and Jared were in the same positions we'd left them in: Melcher at his desk, Jared on top of Crist's.

"Two of the guests at this party have left town. We'll start with them."

Jared slipped off the edge of Crist's desk in one fluid motion and stood. "Listen up, rookies. We're splitting into two teams."

It was almost worth being called a rookie to see the scowl on Valerie's lips.

Almost.

"Ginger and Raven, you're with me."

Should have known I'd get paired with the vixen and Commando.

"We have names, you know," Valerie retorted.

"Not on mission, you don't," Jared said. "You two," he said louder, looking between Dante and Noel. "Moose and Mouse. You're a team."

I snorted. "You're kidding."

"No, I'm not."

I swear I saw Jared grin at me. In a flash, it disappeared.

"We have a person of interest in Sitka and one in Fairbanks." Jared set a quarter with a *click* on Crist's desk. He slid it across the surface and then scooped it up off the edge. He looked directly at Dante. "Heads you go north. Tails, south."

Dante grinned. This was the sort of game he liked to play.

Jared used his thumb to flick the quarter in the air. We all leaned forward.

Heads, heads, heads, I chanted in my own head. I'd sooner go to Siberia than back to Fairbanks.

Jared caught the quarter mid-air and slapped it on his arm. "Heads," he announced.

I smiled and let out a breath. It was pretty funny seeing as there wasn't anything to be relieved about. I still had to leave town on mission with "Ginger" and Jared.

I met Jared's eye. "What do we call you on mission?"

"Just Jared."

Naturally.

"Why do you get to keep your name?" Valerie asked, her lips forming a pout.

"Because I'm in charge on mission."

"It's settled," Melcher said. "I'll book three seats on Alaska Airlines leaving tomorrow."

"Tomorrow?" My jaw dropped. "What about school?"

"Sorry, Aurora. This takes precedence."

I might have left it at that, Lord knows I didn't want an audience, but my stomach had twisted into angry knots and something inside me snapped. "You're kidding! I can't go to an out-of-state college, and now I can't even finish high school?"

I hated Melcher's nonchalant attitude. I hated the lack of concern in his smug expression.

"You'll get your degree, Aurora. If you get too far behind this semester, I can always arrange correspondence. Just hang in there another few months. Here." He handed me a slip of paper.

"What's this?" I asked after taking the paper from him.

"A doctor's note. Have your mother deliver it to your school."

Something awful and ugly twisted in my gut. I didn't bother

checking my latest malady before crumpling the note into a wad. I squeezed the crumpled paper one last time then let it fall to the ground.

"What's the point?" I turned on my heel and stormed out of the room.

The secretary frowned at me as I walked by. Usually, I smiled at her no matter how unfriendly she acted. Not now.

I hurried down the hallway past closed doors and bland walls. My vision swam with unshed tears.

"Aurora, wait up!" I heard Dante call behind me.

I turned around, startled to see him looking very serious. He squeezed the claw at his chest and pulled it over his head. Dante held the cord out to me. "Take it for luck."

"You're giving me your claw?"

Dante grinned. "I'm loaning it to you. Just watch yourself, Sky. I have a funny feeling about all this."

Great, Dante had a funny feeling. He usually lived for this stuff.

Dante fished his car keys out of his pocket. "Here, wait in the Jeep if you want. Melcher and the new general want to brief Noel and me. Shouldn't take long."

I thanked Dante and headed out into the cold. I retrieved my backpack from Noel's car and tossed it inside Dante's Jeep. I turned the key in the ignition and turned the heaters up full blast. While I waited for Dante, I turned the bear claw over in my hand. Poor beast. Hopefully this one had lived to a ripe old age and died of natural causes before having his claw stripped from his carcass. Well, I needed all the luck I could get. I slipped the cord around my head.

There was nothing to see outside the windshield except for parked cars and Melcher's base of operation. It looked about as welcoming as an army barrack. I never thought I'd be summoned back so soon. I curled my fingers into fists, angry with myself for entertaining any ideas of self-pity.

Crist and Mike were dead.

I hated knowing the victims. Worst of all, I hated feeling somehow responsible.

I'd walked Mike to his car. He'd gotten inside. What went wrong?

A vamp must have been waiting in the backseat of his car. Or followed him. Maybe he'd returned to the party. No, I would have seen him from my spot in the living room. I could have sworn his car was gone when Noel and I left.

What about Fane?

He'd seen Mike and me together, and it hadn't made him happy. Where had he slipped off to?

I didn't even want to think about it. It was ridiculous. Fane wasn't a killer.

What about Henry?

He hadn't liked Mike seeing him at the party and there was the location of the bodies to consider. The Anchorage dump was literally becoming a dumping ground for dead bodies. Fane, Gavin, and Henry had used it before to ditch Renard and his associate after Marcus ripped them apart.

It seemed unlikely he would be so obvious, but then again, he probably didn't plan on the bodies being discovered. Not to mention he had no clue I was part of a secret government organization specializing in vampire activity.

I was deep in thought when Dante climbed inside the Jeep. "Feels like a sauna in here," he said. He switched the heat off completely.

"Feels nice."

"Good thing you're headed south."

Sure, into the wet cold. Anchorage was so dry that if you dressed right, you'd be fine. Southeast Alaska with its damp winters chilled a person right down to their bones.

Dante pulled out of the parking lot. It was still light out. Before he could turn on the radio I asked about his briefing.

"They're sending us to Fairbanks to check out some dude who comes into Anchorage every couple of months. Noel thinks the whole thing's going to be a bust—says he likes beer better than blood." Dante leaned back in his seat. "Oh well, I'm always up for a road trip."

Dante began tapping the steering wheel. He always did that around these parts. I knew he couldn't wait to get off base and start speeding.

"Melcher has us all on a wild goose chase. I bet the killer is right here in Anchorage," I said. Maybe right under our noses.

"Oh yeah?" Dante said, sounding interested. "Got a suspect in mind?"

"I've got a funny feeling is all." Dante wasn't the only one.

"And you didn't want to share this with Melcher?"

I scrunched up my nose. "Melcher's a freak."

"And we're his little Franken freaks."

I laughed.

Dante smiled sideways at me.

"Did you hear anything about the vamp I've been assigned?" I asked.

"Just a name and origin: Andre Morrel, formerly of French citizenship. The sergeant doesn't seem keen on small talk."

"Yeah, he's a real bundle of joy."

Jared scared me a little, but that meant he'd scare any vampires we ran into as well. Maybe this time I wouldn't get beaten and bruised.

Then again, a quick in and out to Fairbanks with Dante was beginning to sound better. At least I knew the journey would include comedy relief. I wouldn't wish Valerie on Noel, though, especially after she'd sunk her claws into Gavin. Maybe I could get to the bottom of that development as long as I was forced to work alongside the vixen. Maybe Valerie and Gavin had teamed up to take out Agent Crist and Mike. Nah, it was too much to hope for. While Valerie had shown no love for Crist, Mike's death made no sense. None of it made any sense. I still couldn't wrap my brain around the connection. The effort had begun to exhaust my brain.

"Have you ever been to Sitka or Juneau?" I asked Dante, switching topics.

"Sadly, no. Melcher's always sending me north. He knows I have a way with the natives." Dante winked. "I envy you, Sky. You get to take on the capital."

"Not really. I'm only passing through on the way to Sitka."

"Even better. Back in the day, Sitka was the capital of Russian America. They called it the "Paris of the Pacific.""

I snorted. "Paris? Give me a break."

Dante squeezed my thigh. "Come on, Sky, show a little enthusiasm. This is a chance to see the world, go back in time before The Alaska Purchase. You have the chance to stand outside St. Michael's Cathedral and the old Russian blockhouses. Even better, you get to see Mount Edgecumbe. It looks just like Fuji."

Paris and now Japan. Big stretch.

I only half listened. My concentration had flown out the window when Dante put his hand on my thigh. He had it back on the steering wheel where it belonged a moment later.

"I'm jealous," Dante said.

"Don't be, I'm stuck with Hothead and Strawberry Suck Cake."

A devious smile spread over Dante's lips.

"What?" I demanded.

"Maybe a trip out of town is just what the two of you need to bond."

I gave a rude laugh. "Let me assure you right here, right now, that I will *never* bond with Valerie Ward."

Dante's brows shot up. "Never say never."

"Never."

9

MISSION SOUTHEAST

THE NEXT MORNING, I PACKED my raincoat and dagger, secure in its sheath. Melcher hadn't verbally lifted my ban on weapons, but he hadn't prohibited it on this mission, either. I wasn't about to go in unarmed.

Mom didn't seem particularly concerned that I had to leave town. She had one thing on her mind at the moment: the divorce. Not that she'd accepted it. She told Dad she wouldn't sign the papers until he agreed to meet with a marriage counselor.

I kept what I wanted to say to myself. *"He moved on. Shouldn't you?"*

Then again, what did my mom have to move on to? She didn't have a career or many friends. Soon enough, she wouldn't be responsible for me any longer. It was bad enough staying in state for college. I sure as hell wasn't staying home. The apartment search was marked on my mental calendar for the day after graduation. If I graduated.

Dante had brought a fresh doctor's note with him from the meeting.

"Take it," he'd insisted. "The only person you're hurting is yourself by not turning in the note."

He could be annoying but sometimes Dante made perfect sense. I zipped up my duffel bag then slung it over one shoulder and stopped in front of my mother's bedroom door. I knocked. "Mom? Mom, it's time to go. Mom?"

No answer.

"Mom, do you want me to call a cab?"

"I'll be right out," came her gravelly voice.

I headed downstairs, ate a piece of bread without toasting it, and downed a glass of orange juice. I glanced at the oven clock. I really needed to get to the airport.

The stairs creaked with her slow descent. She appeared in the foyer in her slippers and open bathrobe. I took it she wasn't getting dressed before seeing me off.

Mom shuffled to the fridge and pulled out a can of Diet Coke. She got a glass out and plunked a handful of ice cubes from the freezer inside before pouring the soda into the glass.

"Uh, Mom? We need to go."

She nodded and took a sip. She set the glass down and tied her robe closed. "I'm ready."

Mom followed me to the garage, not even bothering to put on shoes. At least the airport wasn't far.

"Is Dante going with you?"

"No, he has to go to Fairbanks. I'm going with another girl and our team leader." I wasn't sure what to call Jared.

Mom hummed. "Another girl? That's nice. Is she your age? Are you friends?"

"Yes. Yes. And no."

"It might be nice to have a friend who shares the same line of work."

"I have Dante." And Noel, but Mom didn't know that, and it wasn't for me to share.

"I meant a female friend," Mom said.

"Guys make good friends." Better friends...except when they were trying to hit on me.

"Maybe this trip will give you girls a chance to get to know one another better. What's her name?"

"You know I can't give out that information, Mom."

"Oh, right, I forgot."

"Don't worry. You can call her Ginger. That's her codename on this mission. I'm Raven." Raven was a heck of a lot better than Mouse. I couldn't imagine Noel was too thrilled about that, or that she and Dante would stick with those names. Dante liked to use the name Peter, as in Peter Pan, the boy who never aged. I doubted he'd make Noel his Wendy. He reserved that name for me.

Mom pulled into the departure's lane in front of Alaska Airlines and put the car in park. I glanced at her slippers. What I wanted to do was lean over, kiss her on the cheek, and get out of the car, but Mom pulled on the handlebar and stepped outside. I hustled around to the trunk and took my duffel from her hands.

"Thanks for dropping me off, Mom."

She nodded, looking me over. "You be safe."

"I will." I gave her a quick hug.

"Call me after you land."

I hoisted my duffel over one shoulder and walked to the curb.

"Let me know as soon you return, and I'll come pick you up."

I lifted my hand. She took a step toward me. Now that I was leaving, she couldn't seem to say goodbye. I would feel more relaxed once she got back inside the car.

"Aurora, I love you."

"I love you, Mom. I'll be home in a couple days." I had no idea when I'd be home. That was part of the job we had to accept. I went where the agents told me for however long it took. I couldn't imagine this mission taking long. It seemed to me like we were shooting in the dark. I guess it made sense to start with the most obvious candidates and make our way down the list from there—though being from out of town didn't strike me as particularly sketchy.

The night before I'd tried to psyche my mind into believing I was headed out on a mini holiday…with two of the last people on the planet I wanted to be stuck with.

"I'll call you when I land," I said again, then turned toward the sliding doors leading into the terminal.

I caught one last glimpse of my mom standing in the drop-off lane in her slippers and robe.

Warm air greeted me as I stepped into the terminal. Valerie came out of nowhere, practically bumping into me as she pulled a small suitcase on wheels behind her.

"What's with your Mom? She looks like she escaped from a mental ward."

"My mom's not a morning person," I said defensively.

Valerie parked her suitcase at the back of the check-in line and put her hands on her hips. "Where's Jared? He has our tickets."

"We might as well wait in line till he gets here."

She tapped her foot as the line inched forward. She wore a fashionable trench coat that stopped above her knees.

My raincoat was the outdoorsy kind. I'd stuffed it inside my duffel bag along with Dante's bear claw in case TSA tried to confiscate it. For the plane trip, I had on my standard jeans and pleather jacket. I'd left the red scarf at home. The last time I wore it on mission I was abducted and nearly killed. Didn't want to jinx myself.

The closer we got to the check-in counter, the faster the line moved. At least I wasn't the only one flustered. Once we were next up, Valerie glanced over her shoulder and huffed. "Don't tell me he got the time wrong."

"Next!" a ticket agent called.

Valerie and I stood in place. Just as I was about to admit defeat and head to the back of the line, Jared gave us both a shove from behind toward the check-in counter.

"Hey!" Valerie said.

"Hey, yourself, Red."

She snorted in disgust. "Really? Is that the best you can come up with?"

"Works for me," Jared replied, pushing between us to get to the counter.

"Dipshit," Valerie said under her breath.

"Three to Juneau, final destination Sitka," the clerk said. "I have you all seated together in aisle twenty-three. Will you be checking in any luggage?"

"Three bags," Jared said.

It's not like we could carry all our knives and hazardous materials on board.

"What seats are we in?" Valerie asked as the three of us waited in line at security.

"I'm taking the aisle," Jared said. "You two can flip for the window seat."

Valerie shook her hair over her shoulders. "I'm not flipping for anything. I call window."

Great, stuck between Ginger and Mr. McCreepy.

"Fine," I said. "I'll take window on the way back. It's only fair," I said when Valerie began to protest.

Jared and I went through security first while Valerie unzipped her boots and removed all her jewelry.

Since we were in the back of the plane, our aisle was one of the first to be called for boarding. Jared held onto all our tickets. It felt patronizing, which I suspected is what he was going for. I had no choice but to follow him and Valerie down the Jetway to our plane.

There were people in the front rows, standing in the aisle, stuffing everything they could into the overhead bin. Rather than wait for them to finish and take a seat, Jared bumped passengers from behind and kept moving. He stopped at the row after ours.

Valerie ducked under the overhead compartments and plopped into her window seat. I took the dreaded middle seat. Once Jared had us blocked in, I buckled my seatbelt, and rested my head against my seat, earbuds in place, music playing. The volume wasn't loud enough to block out the screaming child who ended up in the seat in front of me. I turned up the volume and closed my eyes.

I had to leave my musical cocoon during takeoff. The seat in front of me shook when the boy screamed, "I don't want the puzzle. I want to color!"

"You'll have to wait until after takeoff," the mother said.

"I don't want to wait."

"You have to."

"I don't want to!"

"Here, have your jellybeans."

"No!"

Jared kicked the seat in front of him. I didn't think the mother noticed because I could see her through the space between chairs leaning forward, rummaging through her big carry-on tote bag.

I couldn't see Valerie behind the book she held in front of

her face. *Blood in the Snow* the title said in big, bold red letters. Below it, the subtitle announced: *The True Story of a Stay-at-Home Dad, his High-Powered Wife, and the Jealousy that Drove him to Murder.* I would've thought she was more a *Glamour* magazine type reader. Then again, I wasn't exactly surprised that Valerie got her kicks reading about cold-blooded killers.

Sometimes, I felt as though my love of reading had been taken away by my new commitments. It was hard enough keeping on top of school assignments and secret missions. The written word took more focus and effort than it used to. These days, music helped me to relax and escape reality in small doses.

As soon as we reached cruising altitude, I lowered the seat tray in front of me. Dante had grabbed a copy of the University of Alaska Anchorage's summer schedule for me to look at. The fall schedule didn't come out until mid-semester. I pulled the catalogue out of my messenger bag along with a highlighter, flipping through the registration dates, deadlines, and introductory pages until I reached the course listings with their dates and times.

Jared had his iPad out, playing Angry Birds beside me, legs stretched into the aisle.

My tray jiggled when the boy in front of me squirmed in his seat.

Valerie lowered her book and nodded at my open catalogue. "What's that?"

"The summer schedule at UAA."

"Are you taking summer classes?"

"I don't know. I just wanted to get an idea of what they offer."

"Can I see that?"

"When I'm done." I found it hard to concentrate with Valerie watching me. "Are you going to UAA or something?" I asked.

"I start this fall."

"Really?"

"Where else would I go?"

That surprised me. I guess I never thought about it before, but informants were probably under the same set of strict rules as assassins—forced to live, work, and study in-state. Still, I wasn't a hundred percent sure. "Are you in Alaska because you have to be?"

Valerie huffed. "No, I'm here for the beautiful sandy beaches and great tanning weather."

Sarcastic much? Valerie sounded even more disenchanted about being stuck in Alaska than I was.

"Here," I said, passing Valerie the catalogue. Maybe I could see which classes she was interested in and avoid them. I watched her thumb through the pages. "What degree are you going for?"

Valerie sighed in utter annoyance. "It doesn't make a damn difference what degree I get. Our careers have already been chosen for us."

Jared looked up from his iPad. "Whiner."

She very slowly lifted her middle finger at him, her expression totally badass. She would have made a great actress, even though I'm sure she would've ended up being a diva from hell.

What happened to Valerie Ward to get her stuck in this program in the first place?

The only stories I knew were my own and Dante's. Dante had nearly died in a snowboarding accident. Noel didn't want to talk about what happened to her. I bet Valerie wouldn't either, but I couldn't stop myself from asking. "What happened to you?"

"None of your damn business!" she snapped as soon as my words were out. I swear she knew what I was going to ask before

I asked it.

The woman in the seat in front of Jared lifted her head above her seat to glare at us. "Do you mind?"

Jared set his iPad on his thighs and leaned forward. "You keep your brat quiet, and I'll see what I can do about mine."

The woman's frown reached her chin, but she seemed incapable of speech with Jared staring at her like some kind of maniac begging to be provoked.

Her head disappeared. "Keep it down, Sammy," I heard her say.

Valerie turned her attention to the catalogue. As we began our descent into Juneau, I leaned over her to get a look out the window. Valerie sighed but didn't say anything.

Patches of blue sky broke through the gloom. Mountains rose endlessly all around us, half covered in snow. From above, Auke Bay looked like a river flowing between the rugged coastal mountain range. The entire landscape was tinted blue.

Valerie and I watched out the window the whole way down. We hit the landing strip roughly, bounced back up, and hit it again. The boy in front of me shrieked, but I barely noticed. Happily, he and his mother got off in Juneau.

Passengers continuing on to Sitka were asked to remain on board.

Valerie unbuckled and hovered halfway out of her seat. "Excuse me," she said.

She wanted out, which meant I had to nudge Jared who'd slipped his iPad into the seat pocket in front of him and closed his eyes.

I cleared my throat. He didn't respond.

"Jared? Valerie needs out."

Jared's eyes opened. He looked at Valerie. "Where are you going?"

"To the bathroom. Where do you think?"

He stretched in his seat before slowly standing and stepping into the aisle. He blocked the way to the front of the plane, eyes sliding lazily over me as I stepped out, and homing in on Valerie when she reached the aisle.

She made a snort of disgust. "Do you think I'm going to make a run for it? In Juneau?" She started laughing.

It was pretty funny. Juneau might be Alaska's capital, but it wasn't accessible by road.

Jared didn't so much as crack a smile.

Valerie headed toward the back of the plane, laughing as she went.

"I'm going to use the restroom too, as long as I'm up." I hated explaining myself to Jared, but he looked at people in a way that made you feel like you had to narrate your intentions.

The flight from Juneau to Sitka was under forty minutes but it felt good to stretch my legs. I beat Valerie back to our seats.

Jared stood, leaning against the headrest of the chair across from our row.

"It's a shame we don't have a chance to look around. I've never been to the capital," I said, trying to make conversation. He stood impassive. "Someday I'd like to see Mendenhall Glacier."

"You seen one glacier, you've seen 'em all," Jared said in monotone.

Sure, print that one on the brochure.

Passengers began boarding. A young woman had to squeeze past Jared when he didn't move aside. I really hoped that once we found Agent Crist and Mike's murderer, Jared would go back to recruiting and disappear from our lives.

The plane was almost ready for departure by the time Valerie reemerged. She had a look on her face like a cat that just ate the canary. I moved into the aisle, and as Valerie slipped in, I caught a whiff of perfume and cigarette smoke.

If Jared noticed, he didn't say a word.

We weren't at cruising altitude for long, but I listened to music the entire time we were, ignoring Valerie and her smug little smile.

Our plane landed on Japonski Island. Once we deboarded, and picked up our luggage, Valerie lit up a cigarette while I called my mom to let her know I'd safely landed. Jared pulled up in a compact rental car. Valerie threw her cigarette on the ground before tossing her suitcase in the trunk beside my duffel. She took the seat in back, so I took the one up front. If I could survive three hours mashed up beside Jared on a plane, I could get through a short car drive riding shotgun. By this time, it was almost noon.

Jared drove across the O'Connell Bridge connecting the airport on Japonski Island with Baranof Island and Sitka. The road was wet but free of snow and ice. Sitka's climate with its overcast sky and constant drizzle resembled the Pacific Northwest more than the Alaskan interior.

Within minutes, Jared pulled up to the Westmark Hotel. Valerie and I grabbed our bags out of the trunk and followed him into the front lobby, straight up to the check-in counter.

"Welcome to the Westmark," the woman at the counter said cheerfully.

"Reservation for Jared."

The woman had it up on her computer in no time. I couldn't imagine tourism booming in February.

"I see you right here, Mr.—Jared. Two rooms. One with a king-sized bed, the second with two doubles."

Valerie abandoned her suitcase and took a giant step to the counter. "What do you mean two rooms? There are three of us."

"You and Raven are sharing," Jared replied evenly.

"No way. It's the middle of winter. I'm sure there are lots of rooms available."

"Sorry," Jared said in a voice that conveyed the opposite. "Budget cuts."

"Here are your keycards," the clerk said, moving on with the check-in procedure. "We offer lunch and dinner in the Kadataan Lounge, or you can walk to the harbor and find more options downtown. We are also within walking distance of the National Historical Totem Park."

Good, because I doubted Jared planned on lending us the car even if we were stranded on an island.

"Now what?" Valerie asked when Jared stopped in the hallway between our two rooms.

"Now we wait until night. We'll meet in my room at eleven."

"That's eleven hours from now," Valerie said.

I'm glad she mentioned it. It's what I was thinking.

"What are we supposed to do until then?" I asked.

"Watch TV. Take a nap. I don't care." He slipped his keycard into the slot. It clicked once, and he pulled the door open before looking over his shoulder one last time. "Remember, my room, eleven o'clock."

"Just great," Valerie said once Jared left us alone in the hall. "Notice he took the room with the harbor view."

At least she wasn't bitching about sharing a room…at the moment. Valerie swiped the keycard into the door across the hall. Our room didn't have an ocean view, but it was nice, aside from the beds barely resting two feet apart.

She rolled her suitcase to the far bed by the window and set her baggage on top of the chair.

Her phone vibrated and she plopped onto the edge of her bed to look at the screen. She gave a girly laugh before texting back to the person who had messaged.

I dropped my duffel and messenger bag on the floor beside my bed then began digging out the things I wanted to take with me when I went exploring. I needed my wallet, of course, and phone. Sitka might be as far south as I'd get for a while, at least until Melcher cleared me for out-of-state vacation leave. I planned to document the trip even if I was technically on business. I switched my pleather jacket for a raincoat.

Valerie stared at her phone then started giggling. She typed quickly then tossed her phone on the bed beside her.

"So, you're with Gavin now?" I asked.

Valerie glared at me as though she'd caught me reading over her shoulder.

"How is that your business?"

"I'm just curious," I said, sticking my things inside my backpack. "Why do you have a thing for vampires?"

"It's my job. Hello? Informant. And there's the sex," Valerie said. She laughed when she saw my face. "Does that shock you? It shouldn't—you've been with Fane after all."

I hadn't exactly mastered the art of the poker face. Valerie noticed at once. She stood and took a step toward me, coming in for the close-up. A wicked grin lit up her face. "Oh my God, you and Fane never hooked up, did you?"

I glared at Valerie. "And that's none of your business."

She snorted. "Don't tell me you're saving yourself for marriage."

"I'm not saving myself for anything," I retorted. I grabbed my backpack.

Valerie followed me to the door. She had a look on her face

like she wouldn't let me out of the room without an answer. Well, she could suck it. That's what the vixen did best. "Then why in God's name didn't you do the deed?"

"We weren't together long enough," I said coldly. "You made sure of that."

10

SITKA

IT WAS STILL DRIZZLING WHEN I stepped outside. The Toyota hadn't moved. I guess Jared decided to take his own advice and watch TV or rest. I doubted he would use the time to report to Melcher. Somehow Jared didn't strike me as a check-in with home base kind of guy.

I pulled my hood over my head and walked through downtown until I reached the harbor. Mid-sized boats were tied up along the docks.

The rugged coastal mountains served as a backdrop in every direction. They all looked so close, unlike downtown Anchorage where the Chugach Range touched the skyline in the distance.

I pulled my hood back and fished my phone out of my coat pocket, hitting "call" next to Fane's name before I had a chance to talk myself out of it. I couldn't help feeling less alone when I heard his voice.

"Aurora Sky," Fane said, drawing my name out when he answered. "Are you on lunch break or skipping?"

"Neither. I'm on assignment."

"Ah. Fairbanks?"

"I can't say."

"Who have they sent you to kill this time?"

"Hopefully no one. We've been sent to check out a person

of interest."

"Then you admit vampires are people."

"Of course they're people," I said.

"Are you with Dante?"

What was with the third degree? I ought to be the one asking the questions.

"No."

If only Fane knew the truth—that I was stuck with his former suck buddy. I could see his eyes falling out of their sockets if he heard that one.

"Oh, that's right," Fane said. "You've moved on to numb nut number two. I saw you leave the party together. Did jock boy get lucky?"

"Excuse me?" I said in an icy voice. I felt equal parts relieved and enraged. If Fane thought I'd hooked up with Mike, it meant he didn't sneak away and off the poor guy.

Then there was the enraged part. He must think me terribly pathetic to drop my panties a second time for some high school *numb nut* as he liked to call twenty-first-century jocks.

"I mean, that is the only way you'd let a guy stick it to you, right? If he's one hundred percent human he's on the 'okay to bang' list."

My chest tightened in indignation. "Screw. You. Fane." I was so mad I felt like chucking my phone into the harbor. Instead, I jabbed my thumb on the end call button so hard I probably left behind a permanent fingerprint.

"Jackass. Jerk. Shit brain. Pig!" I said at the phone, even though he was no longer on the line. Might as well cuss like a sailor while standing in the harbor. I tried to hold onto the anger as long as I could, but I eventually ran out of breath.

Vampire or not, men sucked.

I walked to the end of the dock. Small ripples lapped the beams below my feet. Beyond the harbor, the bay unfurled toward the horizon like an oil canvas. Clouds clung to the sides of Mount Edgecumbe, but it was beautiful nonetheless. I should have taken a picture, but I was feeling too bleak at the moment.

I lifted my face to the mist, relishing the cold moisture on my cheeks. Nature had so many emotions. Right now, I swear she understood mine.

If I'd never known the real Fane, the sweet man behind the rough exterior, I wouldn't hurt the way I did now. If he were just a jerk, so be it. But we'd had something. Something I'd never felt for anyone. When Fane and I were together, he didn't just get my mind off things, he made me feel better. He'd told me he wanted to be with me for as long as possible…right before I broke it off.

It would have had to come to that, anyway. He knew why now, well, mostly. Fane didn't know about Valerie's hand in the matter. Even if I could get over my aversion to dating a vampire, it wasn't safe for us to be together and would only lead to heartbreak. Why delay the inevitable?

Those thoughts didn't stop me from mourning what I'd lost. Sometimes, late at night, I liked to play back scenes from our short time together like a favorite hits list. The time he'd beat our opponents at badminton in gym class. The afternoon I ran into Fane in front of the video store and he walked me home in the snow. Our first make-out session on the bus. Fane's goofy attempt at *car rehabilitation*, and the way he never hesitated to call and check in on me. Washing dishes together the time he came over for dinner. Skipping class to walk to Portage Glacier. Making out in his car overlooking Cook Inlet.

That Fane felt like a figment of my imagination.

At least he cared enough about me to want me alive. He'd been convincing enough when Noel went to him for help after my abduction. But the moment I was better he couldn't get me out of his sight quickly enough. And now he'd taken to tormenting me.

What did I expect? That I could dump him and then pick back up as friends?

No, nothing would be the same again, and it was my own damn fault for calling him in the first place.

I was glad Fane had spoken to me so harshly. I needed it. I needed to wake up and smell the blood.

With a final glance across the bay, I turned and retraced my steps across the dock.

On my way to the totem park, I popped into the local food co-op and bought a bag of granola.

The totem pole at the park entrance was as tall as the surrounding trees. The next stood in front of the visitor's center. I moved on, grabbing handfuls of granola and munching on it as I walked from pole to pole further into the forested park.

I stopped in front of a wolf pole, shrugged off my backpack and exchanged the half-eaten bag of granola for my phone. Sitting on top of the wolf with his pointed ears was a village watchman wearing a hat that reminded me of an orange construction cone. I looked around. It would be nice if someone could snap a photo of me by one of the totems, but the forest was quiet. Just me and a couple of ravens watching from the trees. I took a picture and moved down the wooded path to the next totem. They were cool and creepy with their sharp beaks, teeth, unsettling grins, and big black eyes.

I moved deeper into the forest and paused, face-to-face with a wood bear carved at the bottom of a totem. He had what looked like a very long shrimp in his mouth. I turned on my phone's camera, so focused on taking the picture, I never heard the footsteps behind me.

"Ridiculous, isn't it?"

I nearly shrieked. Whatever expression I had on my face made Jared grin.

"I think it's beautiful," I retorted, putting the annoyance I felt into words.

Jared stood directly beside me. I fought the urge to take a step away from him. "A Michelangelo is beautiful. A Rembrandt is beautiful," Jared said, eyeing the totem disdainfully as he spoke.

Sounded like he and Fane's roommate, Joss, had something in common. Total art snobs. "That's like comparing ice to sand," I said.

Jared gave me a weird look. "Are you ready for tonight?" he asked, turning his back on the totem.

I stuffed my phone into my pocket. I wasn't about to ask Jared to snap a picture of me after he expressed such obvious distaste for Native art. "Ready as I'll ever be."

"It could get messy."

I lifted my head and shot him my "I'm numb to the world and its horrors" look. I'd seen it in the mirror, and it had a certain familiar feeling, or rather unfeeling, whenever it came over my face. "It always gets messy," I said, enunciating each word, letting them freeze in the air as I spoke.

Jared's lips twisted into a smile. "I'm trying to decide if you're tough or just acting tough. I think you're acting."

"Think what you want," I said, maintaining the same cold expression. "I made it through initiation and my first and second missions without any formal training."

"Do you recognize me?" Jared asked abruptly.

I didn't have to think about that one. I'd never seen Jared before he appeared in Melcher's office. He had a vibe about him that I'd remember even if I'd been foggy about his looks.

Instead of answering, I replied with a petulant, "Should I?"

Jared kept watching me without blinking. It was more unnerving than usual. "I was there the day of your accident."

"That must have been a pretty sight."

Jared cracked a small smile. "I'm accustomed to it."

I guess he would be if he was the first one on-site anytime a potential recruit got into an accident, but that didn't explain how he happened upon the scene of my accident. My mom had told me the agents appeared at the site before the ambulance had a chance to haul me off to a regular hospital.

"How could you have possibly known about my accident so quickly?" I asked. I stared at Jared's face, looking for clues in his demeanor, but he had the "I'm dead to the world" expression down better than I.

"I have my own team. We monitor candidates between the ages of fifteen and thirty-five around the clock, all over the world."

By candidates, I knew that Jared meant people with AB-negative blood, the rarest blood type in the world, making up less than one percent of the population. Thanks to Noel, I also knew that they'd tried recruiting people with AB-positive blood, the second rarest blood type, but their virus-laced transfusions didn't take. That's how candidates like Noel and Valerie ended up as informants rather than assassins.

Jared stretched his arms over his head. "Melcher has us set up with a fancy software program. It's designed to alert us whenever a candidate's name comes up on a police scanner, newsfeed, or hospital database. I have people monitoring that database. I also have people on surveillance, myself included. I was tailing you the day of your accident."

I stood there for a minute, speechless, as still as one of the totems lost in the trees. My brain told me I ought to be angry and lash out accordingly. What Melcher and Jared were doing was a complete invasion of privacy. They probably knew my entire medical history—everything from braces at age fifteen to chicken pox at nine years old. They probably had files on all of us ABers. As if that weren't creepy enough, they had people stalking us. Even Jared had joined the fray.

The forest went out of focus. I spoke to Jared without looking at him. "How long had you been following me?"

"From the moment you left school."

"So, you saw the accident?" I asked numbly.

"From a certain angle."

"Is that the first time you've ever followed me?"

"No."

That didn't surprise me. "How often did you follow me?"

"We shadow candidates anytime an opportunity might present itself—icy road conditions, extreme sporting events, motorcycling, intoxication, overdose, gang involvement, depression, recent breakup with a violent ex—you get the picture. There wasn't much to go on in your case. You went to school, went home, didn't drink, didn't do drugs, didn't date. Didn't do much of anything."

My jaw tightened. How thoughtless of me to be such a responsible, law-abiding bore. Good thing I lived in a state with extreme weather conditions. It wasn't much to go on, but it was something.

My mind filled with sarcasm, but I kept it to myself. I was saving my anger for Melcher. Still, I couldn't help saying, "How lucky for you that I happened to get hit when you were tailing me."

That had to be like winning the lottery in recruiter terms. The trillion-dollar lottery. I mean, what were the chances?

I met Jared's cold gaze. I could picture him standing in the rubble, looking down at my unconscious body without a trace of emotion.

"It was lucky," Jared said. "Your life is much better than it was before."

My jaw dropped. "How can you say that?"

"I don't understand some of you recruits," Jared said. "You act like you were abducted from some sort of meaningful, fulfilling life. Where would you have been if you hadn't joined our ranks?"

"College! In another few months, I would have been attending school at Notre Dame."

"And then?"

"What do you mean and then?"

"What's after college?"

"A career."

Jared gave me a pitying look. "That's the best you could come up with? Go to work, go home, eat, sleep, repeat?"

God, he was maddening. So I'd been a complete bore in my past and now he'd managed to make my future sound equally pitiful in the space of a sentence.

"At least it would have been my choice," I snapped before turning on my heel. I started down the path, backtracking through the forest. Before I could go another step, Jared had my arm in a bone-crushing grip.

"I didn't say you could go."

Fear seized me in place. Jared looked capable of anything at that moment, including breaking my arm.

His grasp tightened even though I hadn't so much as

breathed. My heartbeat quickened. There wasn't a thing I could do about that, and I swear he could hear it.

I heard a warbling and clicking noise in the trees that turned into a ranting *ah, ah, ah, ah, ah* before two ravens took flight. I wished I could join them.

"There goes my namesake," I remarked. My voice reflected nothing of the panic I felt inside. Something told me the best way to deal with Jared was to stay calm, not try to fight him.

Thankfully that instinct proved right. Jared's grip on my arm loosened as he followed the raven's flight with his eyes.

"Pesky birds," he remarked, letting me go. "Eleven o'clock. My room. Don't be late." He pulled down the edges of his open jacket with a firm jerk then took off down the path.

I didn't move until his receding figure disappeared into the woods. I just needed to get through tonight and get back home. After this, there was no way I'd work with Jared again. I'd make Melcher promise. I'd sooner stick a stake in my eye than go on a mission with the psycho stalker.

I could handle Dante and his appetites for food and other less savory activities. I could even handle the backstabbing vixen, but there was something off about Jared. If he'd been anyone else, I might have asked for details regarding the aftermath of my accident. Did he call it in? What condition had I been in? No, too morbid. Had the other driver died instantly? All Melcher had told me was that the guy in the other vehicle hadn't made it.

I tried to picture the guy's face. It had been so crystal clear in those last moments. He had looked maybe twenty or young thirties. The most I remembered about him now was the blue bandana he'd worn tied around his forehead, Karate Kid style.

Too bad he hadn't had AB negative blood because the agents

would have saved him, too, if there'd been an ounce of life left in the poor guy. Even the agents weren't that lucky.

I pulled out my phone. The time said it was half past three. I meandered my way back through the park, ready to get out of the forest but not ready to return to the room. I listened to music as I explored downtown, getting a picture of St. Michael's Cathedral. That one was for Dante. It wasn't the Notre Dame cathedral, but he'd enjoy it.

"Paris," I huffed under my breath, remembering Dante's brief history lesson.

When the damp air began giving me the shakes, I ducked into a café, ordered a large black tea, and settled at a corner table. Once I'd warmed up and killed some time, I hit the streets. I passed a Mexican restaurant, did a one-eighty, and walked inside. The granola and tea weren't exactly sitting well, and I wouldn't want my stomach to grumble if we had to do any sneaking around on assignment.

I ate my vegetable fajitas slowly, allowing them time to cool. Not like I was in any rush to get back to the room.

I wished Noel were with me. I wished she were sitting in front of me now. She was good company and easy to talk to. I would have loved to discuss the case with her and tell her what happened with Jared in the totem park, to say nothing of his stalking methods.

Had Jared been nearby when Noel died? Or Dante? Or Valerie, for that matter?

For the zillionth time, I wondered how Noel had gone down, but she seemed even more reluctant than Valerie to discuss it—at least she had the one time I tried broaching the subject.

I checked the time on my phone. Almost eight, which meant

Dante and Noel must have made it to Fairbanks hours ago—with Dante at the wheel, naturally. I wondered what Noel thought of the speed demon. She seemed capable of handling anything. I just hoped she got over Gavin quickly. Anyone who would go out with Valerie had issues—Fane included. Why couldn't Noel crush on Henry? He always struck me as the nicest of the pair. But that's not how the heart operated.

The heart was one twisted organ. At least I had an excuse. I'd literally lost my heart, and this new one hadn't done me an ounce of good.

11

XENA: WARRIOR PRINCESS

I SPENT ENOUGH TIME AT THE restaurant to finish all my food. Mom would have been pleased. I wasn't exactly a regular at the Clean Plate Club. I left a tip on the table and dragged my feet back to the Westmark.

Luckily, I had just missed the vixen changing clothes. She'd traded in her jeans and sweater for a pair of workout pants and tank top. When I walked in she was perched on the edge of her bed lacing up her sneakers.

An empty tray with dirty dishes and half-eaten food sat on the room's desktop. There was a glass of red wine on the nightstand beside the bottle.

"Enjoying room service?" I asked.

"The choices were limited, so I made do."

"Looks like you ordered one of everything," I remarked. "Did you put it on the room?" I already knew the answer—of course she put the meal on the room.

Valerie stuck her nose up. "Melcher will take care of it. Budget cuts, my ass. Make sure to save your receipts. Everything we eat during mission gets reimbursed."

"Including alcohol?" I asked, raising a brow.

"Especially alcohol."

Somehow, I doubted Melcher would agree to that, but I

didn't feel like starting a new argument with Valerie. It looked like she was on her way to the fitness center. I couldn't have timed my return better.

"Where have you been?" she asked.

"Walking around town. I went to the harbor and the totem park. Did Jared come by while I was gone?"

"No, thank God," she said. "He's a real piece of work. Total dick. Have some wine." Valerie inclined her head toward the nightstand.

I grabbed an empty glass beside the ice bucket and poured myself a small portion. The first swallow warmed my throat all the way down.

Valerie stood up. Her phone buzzed beside the wine bottle. I moved aside as she grabbed it. "Nice timing," she said. "I was just on my way to work out," she spoke as she typed out her text.

A moment later she erupted into giggles.

"Want to know what Gavin said?"

"No."

"He said he wished I was getting my workout with him."

I took a bigger gulp of wine than I meant to.

"Look at you," Valerie said. I didn't appreciate her smug smile. She set her phone on her nightstand and looked me over.

"What?"

"You're turning totally red."

"Because I just drank wine."

"Two sips."

I took two more swigs as she spoke.

Valerie circled me. "Have you even kissed a guy before?"

If only I'd walked in five minutes later we wouldn't be having this conversation.

I got that feeling inside. The same one that came over me

when we stormed into the vamp house together. Like I had to prove something to her. "I've done everything," I said.

"Oh, *everything*," she said, grinning wider. "Was it with anyone I know?"

I shrugged.

"You're bluffing."

I could tell she said it to weasel a name out of me, but I played into her hands all the same. "Fine. I hooked up with Scott Stevens."

Valerie's nose wrinkled. "Ick."

"Excuse me?" Yeah, he was a jock with the personality of a tree stump, but *ick*? From someone who did the seesaw with vampires?

"Don't try to tell me you enjoyed it."

"Fine, I won't." I swirled the last bit of wine inside my glass then tipped it back, downing every last bit.

"No wonder you're so repressed. Sleeping with Scottie Stevens is probably worse than being a virgin."

Sadly, I had trouble arguing with that.

"What about Dante?" Valerie asked.

What about your workout? I wanted to ask back. Shouldn't she go work off all that room service?

Valerie looked me up and down. "He wants you bad."

"Well, it's not going to happen."

"Why not?" She sounded more curious than crude. "I get that his personality leaves something to be desired but at least he's got one. There's nothing worse than a man without character. And his body's hot. You can't tell me you haven't noticed those rock-solid pecs."

Oh, I'd noticed all right. I'd noticed the moment Dante showed up on my doorstep to introduce himself as my mentor. I was with Fane at the time, but I wasn't blind.

"Yeah, he's built," I said slowly.

"What is it? Are you still hung up on Fane?" Valerie challenged.

I should slap her for saying his name, but she'd read too much into that one. The bottle of wine called to me from the corner of my eye, but I wanted a clear mind for the mission ahead. "Dante and I work together," I said, rather than responding to Valerie's taunt. "We have a responsibility to this unit, and I doubt dating on the job would be a wise decision." Plus I wasn't attracted to Dante that way. Maybe a little more than previously, but it would take a lot more to convince me he was boyfriend material.

"Oh my God," Valerie said with disgust. "How old are you? I swear you just sounded thirty."

I glared at Valerie. At least I hoped I was glaring.

My phone buzzed inside my pack. Relieved by the distraction, I turned my back to Valerie and dug it out.

Speak of the devil. I'd received a text from Dante.

Dante: Any action?

Aurora: Not yet. You?

Dante: Nothing. Where are you?

Aurora: Hotel room.

Dante: What are you doing?

Aurora: Just chilling.

"Just chilling?" Valerie repeated over my shoulder. "That's all you've got?"

I held my phone against my chest. "Do you mind?"

"Come on. Let's see what he said."

"I don't know why you need to see it." Nonetheless, I pulled the phone away from my body and held the screen so we could both see.

Dante: Cool.

Aurora: Not really. I have to share a room with Valerie.

"Good one," Valerie said. And she sounded like she meant it. "Nothing on this planet gets a guy's blood pumping like the thought of two women sharing a bedroom." She leaned in closer to read Dante's next text with me.

Dante: Just remember, if you're going to fight, use pillows…

Valerie snorted. "See? Typical."

Before I could respond to Dante's text, he sent a follow up message.

Dante: And you can only wear underwear. Hey, I don't make the rules. ;)

Whatever, I typed.

"Give me that." Valerie grabbed the phone out of my hands before I could send the message. She deleted "whatever."

"Dante's messing with you, and you're playing right into his hands. This is exactly what he's expecting, Aurora. It's time he got a dose of his own medicine." Valerie began typing. I tried to see, but her hair blocked my view when she leaned forward. Only when Valerie lifted her head did I see what she'd written and sent.

Aurora: Actually, she stepped out, so it's just you and me.

I breathed a sigh of relief. That wasn't too bad.
Dante messaged back instantly.

Dante: Meaning?

I wanted to ask Valerie the same question.
Valerie smirked as she typed a response.

Aurora: Meaning I'll strip if you strip.

"Valerie!" I cried.

She held up a hand. "Let's see what Mr. Hot Shot replies to that."

I had to admit I was curious. We watched the screen. It remained blank.

Valerie snickered. "Two can play this game, Don Juan."

"I am so telling him you who wrote those messages."

"I don't care." Valerie finger combed her hair over one shoulder with her free hand. She had the most gorgeous head of thick, wavy red locks. The color made her look like some fabled siren who beckoned men out to sea before drowning them. If I was honest, I'd have to admit I envied her confidence. She had a way of intimidating even the school's most popular girls. When we were in gym class together at Denali High, she walked around the locker room in her lace bra as though it were as comfortable as a cotton tee.

No doubt smoke would blow out Dante's ears if I could shoot him a mental image of Valerie from our gym days.

As I watched Valerie twirl a piece of hair around her finger, I decided I didn't want to tell Dante she was behind the texts. It would only make her seem more daring.

Valerie had already broken Fane and me apart and stolen Gavin from Noel. I wasn't letting her have Dante, too. He was my friend, my mentor, my wingman. If he wanted to flirt with someone, it would be me, not Valerie.

Valerie began typing on my phone.

"Did he respond?"

"No, I'm adding my number to your contacts."

"Hey!" I said. If she were snooping through my contacts, she might see that Fane was still in there. "Why would I need your number?"

"In case we get split up tonight." Valerie rolled her eyes, finished typing, and stretched across her bed. Suddenly she propped herself up on her arms. "He took the bait!"

I hurried to join Valerie's side, leaning into the phone with her.

Dante: My pants are off. Yours?

Aurora: Not yet.

Dante: What are you waiting for?

Aurora: Give me a sec.

Dante: Counting down.

Valerie laughed. It sounded a little too sultry for my liking. "This is better than TV."

I reached my hand out. "I want my phone back."

Valerie pulled back. "Hold up. Can't leave the poor guy standing there with his pants around his ankles."

I tried to grab my phone, but Valerie held it above her head. She rolled to the edge of the bed and stood up, glancing at the screen. She burst into laughter.

"What?" I asked, annoyed, but also not wanting to miss anything.

Valerie held the screen in front of my face showing me the message from Dante.

Dante: Need help?

While I screeched in dismay, Valerie dashed into the far corner of our room. "Naughty boy," she tsked, her eyes glowing in the light of the screen. "Hm. How to respond?" Valerie looked at me a long while. Her lips slowly formed a devious smile. Her head bent down as she typed.

"What are you saying?" What was wrong with me? I wanted

her to stop but another side of me silently urged her to keep going.

Valerie lifted the screen in front of her face and read. "No help necessary. Would you like me to take off my thong or leave it on?"

I felt my eyes bug out of my head. "Okay, that's enough." I stormed over to Valerie and ripped my phone out of her fingers. She didn't have a very good hold on it, seeing as she was laughing her pretty red head off.

"And now Miss Prude spoils the fun. Poor Dante. I think I might actually feel sorry for him."

Valerie grabbed her phone off the nightstand. "I'm going to the fitness center," she said, scooping her sweater off the back of the chair. "Tell Dante I said hi and to text me if he's feeling lonely." Valerie laughed and ducked out before I could tell her to shove it.

I listened to her receding footsteps in the hallway then sat on the edge of my bed for several moments in silence. My palms sweated. Why was I so nervous about reading Dante's response? Dante, for crying out loud. Goofy, annoying, reckless Dante.

I glanced at the bear claw pendant on my nightstand. That had been really sweet the way he lent it to me. Dante loved that stupid claw.

I wasn't attracted to Dante. Well, maybe a little at the moment, but probably only because I felt *repressed*, as Valerie liked to remind me.

I sat at the top of my bed, back against the headboard, legs crossed. Time to face the music. I took a deep breath and stared at my phone.

Dante: Aurora Sky wears a thong? If I wasn't shocked before, I am now.

I laughed. That wasn't too bad. Not bad at all. In fact, it was a good place to sign off. I tried to come up with what to say next and had decided on "Now you know one of my secrets. I think that's enough for tonight," when my fingers tapped out something else entirely.

Aurora: What about you? Boxers?

Dante: Commando. ;)

I laughed. Dante was messing around, too. That was probably about as true as me wearing a thong. Sorry, boys. Butt floss wasn't my thing.

Aurora: Better put your pants back on before you freeze your buns off.

I laughed. *Good one, Aurora.*

Dante: Don't you worry about my buns of steel. I'm snug in bed...pitching a tent.

It took me a moment to figure out what he meant. When I did, my whole face burned.

Aurora: Perv!

Dante: You started it.

But how to end it? And how to face Dante when I went back home?

Aurora: Just killing time.

Dante: Wish we were killing time together.

My first response would have been "In your dreams," but that's not what Valerie The Seductress would say.

Aurora: So it goes. I'll let you go amuse yourself.

Dante: Wait! You can't leave me hanging.

I smiled as I typed.

Aurora: Sweet dreams, Dante.

Dante: Tease.

If anyone was a tease, it was Dante and Fane. Taunting me, teasing—tormenting. Boys with their wicked words and suggestions. They knew how to get under a girl's skin, and make her body respond without so much as a touch.

I hadn't been in the mood before, but now I wouldn't mind kicking some vampire butt.

I turned on the TV and drank more wine. Valerie returned an hour later. "So, you cut him loose, didn't you?"

I didn't bother looking away from the TV or answering. Valerie walked in front of the screen to her side of the room then crossed again and closed herself in the bathroom. A minute later the shower came on, followed by the hair dryer a good fifteen minutes later.

She strutted out of the bathroom in a matching bra and panty set—black lace. Her hair flared over her smooth shoulders. Locker room flashback.

I guess she didn't care that our curtains were open. She rummaged through her suitcase and pulled out a dagger. Not like I wanted to watch her strut around in her panties, but it was pretty damn distracting when I was trying to watch television, especially when she began posing in the window's reflection with her dagger in hand. She probably saw herself as some kind of Xena, Warrior Princess.

I grabbed the TV remote and turned the volume up, even though Valerie wasn't speaking. Out of the corner of my eye, I saw her make a show of laying out her clothes before actually putting them on. Once assembled, she slid her dagger inside her right boot.

I turned off the TV, tossed the remote on the bedspread, and got to my feet.

I had a new belt sheath I attached around my waist before slipping my dagger in and pulling my shirt over it. I liked it a lot better than having to pull up my pant leg to get to my weapon.

Valerie reached into her bag and pulled out a revolver. Once again, she stilled in front of the window with the weapon in her hand.

I tensed. Guns made me nervous. Probably because I'd never fired one before. I liked that Melcher stressed combat training and knives.

"What's that for?" I asked, trying to sound calm.

Valerie turned, facing me. "It's called backup."

I watched in silence as she took a small box out of her suitcase. She shook bullets loose onto the bedspread. They clinked together. She loaded the bullets one at a time into the cylinder's chambers. When she was done, she snapped the revolving cylinder back in place and slipped the gun inside her coat pocket.

Before heading out, I put the bear claw over my head, hoping very much it was as lucky as Dante claimed.

12

CRIST'S CROSS

AT EXACTLY ELEVEN, WE KNOCKED on Jared's door. It opened and Jared filled the frame in a pair of jeans and a dark cotton tee that formed against his solid muscles. He gave us each a menacing stare. "Well, don't just stand there, come in."

Jared had the curtains closed and the lights dimmed. I settled into one of the armchairs and Valerie did the same. I suspected she didn't want to sit on Jared's bed any more than I did.

Jared cracked his knuckles, sending each of us a sneering glance. "While you two were taking it easy, I gained access to the house."

"You mean you broke in?" Valerie asked.

"I did more than that." He reached into his pocket then dangled a gold cross from its chain in front of us. "I found this inside a wood box in the bedroom."

Valerie squinted. "What's that?"

"It's Crist's cross."

Try saying that five times real fast.

"How do you know?" Valerie asked.

"Shouldn't it be silver?" I added.

I knew the whole silver warding off vampires thing was a myth, but Crist always struck me as a traditionalist.

Jared huffed in disgust. "Rookies," he said, rolling his eyes. "Crist wore this cross all the time."

It looked pretty generic to me, and I didn't remember ever seeing any jewelry on Crist, but maybe she slipped it under her shirt. Melcher and Jared knew her better than I ever did.

"What about Mike?" I asked.

Jared squinted at me. "Mike?"

Really? I waited for the name to settle in, but Jared kept with his blank gaze. "The boy who was killed! Did you find his class ring?" I demanded.

"It's probably inside the wood box. I wasn't looking for a ring."

Wow, great detective work.

"What's the plan?" Valerie asked, sitting up in her chair.

Jared began pacing. "We sneak in when they're sleeping, secure the house, split up, and take them all out simultaneously. They won't see it coming."

This didn't sound good. "What do you mean *them*?" I asked.

"Andre, Henriette, and the two teenagers," Jared answered without blinking.

"They have kids?!"

"A lot of vamp teams pose as families. It's not uncommon," he said.

"But…"

Valerie huffed and added her two cents. "They can't have kids, you idiot. They're vampires. Do you need me to explain the ABCs of vampire sex and reproduction? They're dead. Sterile. It's not possible. End of story."

I looked from Valerie to Jared. Trying to reason with either of them was like trying to wrestle a pair of wolverines. Those things were nastier than grizzlies. At least with a grizzly you could play dead or make a lot of noise and in most cases scare it off.

Valerie crossed then uncrossed her legs and leaned forward

in her chair. "Look, if these vamps are all hanging out together, they can't be up to any good."

"So that's it then? Guilt by association?"

"Pretty much," Jared said in his arrogant, brutish way I'd come to loathe a thousand times more than Melcher's cool condescension.

"Are they asleep now?" Valerie asked.

Eager beaver. Either that or she wanted to get it over with.

"Maybe. We'll check it out after I go over the game plan." He slid the gold cross on top of the desk. It made a scraping sound. "I'll see to Andre and Henriette. You two will take care of the boy and girl."

"I'll take the boy," Valerie said. Of course she would.

"What are their names?" I asked.

"What does it matter?" Valerie retorted.

Jared surprised me by answering, "Etienne and Giselle."

Now that our targets were no longer nameless vampires, Valerie frowned. "And how exactly do you want us to *take care* of them?"

Jared looked between us with a slight smile then headed to the far corner of his room. He bent down. I couldn't see what he was doing with his bed blocking my view. Jared returned with two small brown bottles and two rags. "Chloroform," he said, setting the bottles and one of the rags on the desk. He moved around Valerie's chair. "You wet the cloth and then hold it over their mouth and nose." As Jared said this, he swooped in, affixing the rag over Valerie's mouth.

The cloth muffled her scream.

Valerie's eyes widened. She began clawing at Jared's arms, but he held firm.

I was on my feet in an instant. "What are you doing?"

128

A glint appeared in Jared's eyes. His smile looked more like a snarl. Although I'd stood up, I suddenly felt unsteady.

As I regained my footing, Jared released Valerie, straightened up, and took a step back. "That's how it's done."

"I think we get the gist," I said angrily. "No need for a demonstration." God, for a second I thought he really intended on knocking her out. It might be Valerie, but I didn't want to be left alone with el creepo.

I looked at Valerie. It surprised me that she hadn't reacted yet. She had something of a shell-shocked look on her face. The expression changed in a flash to one I recognized—Valerie in a fit of rage. She got up from her chair and turned to Jared. Without warning, she threw a fist at him, but Jared was ready for her. He took her arm as it extended and twisted her around so that her back was against his chest. Valerie cried out. His grip on her arm looked painful. I knew how it felt.

"Nice try, Red, but no amount of advanced training will prepare you to take me on."

"Hey! We're all on the same team," I said. The way Jared exerted his authority was really starting to creep me out.

"Then start respecting your leader," he said right before releasing Valerie and giving her a shove backwards.

She regained her footing, rubbed her arm, and glared daggers at Jared, but she didn't go after him again. She didn't call him a dick either, but I knew she was thinking it.

"Both of you take a rag and a bottle. While I deal with Andre, see that Etienne and Giselle remain unconscious."

"And then?" I hated to ask, but it would come up at some point.

"I'll take care of them."

Why didn't that relieve me? If Jared took care of them, it

meant I wouldn't have to. He'd even provided chloroform and rags, which meant I didn't have to blemish my precious neck.

But something about the whole thing made me sick. It wasn't very sportsmanly to knock the kids out without giving them a fighting chance. There, I said it. It didn't feel right.

"Ready?" Jared asked.

I looked at Valerie. She had her eyes on Jared, and I swear she was thinking of pulling the gun on him. I hadn't known Jared long, but I was willing to bet he'd break her arm if she went after him a second time.

I grabbed the bottles off the desk quickly and thrust one in Valerie's hand. "Here, let's get this over with."

She stared at the bottle. "I need a rag."

I handed Valerie the one I'd gotten off the desk then bent down and picked up the demonstration rag that had fallen on the floor.

"Coming?" Jared asked from the doorway.

We followed silently behind him. At the car, Jared swung around when Valerie reached for the door handle behind the driver's side. "You, next to me."

Maybe he was afraid she would try and chloroform him from behind while he drove.

Valerie walked around the car without comment and plopped into the passenger's seat. I took the seat behind her.

Jared seemed to be in no hurry as he drove down the dark, deserted roads. I looked out my window, but at times like these my eyes didn't connect to my brain. I squeezed my fingers around the claw, careful not to let the tip prick my skin. Too bad I couldn't brain-text Dante. I'd tell him Jared was nuts.

Gravity pulled me back in my seat as we curved our way up a hill. Small rocks crunched under the tires and pinged against the bottom of the car when the road turned to gravel.

Jared slowed then turned onto a paved driveway, pulling right up to a house, and parking the car.

"Won't they hear us coming?" I asked.

Jared leaned back in his seat and swung his head around, a smirk on his lips. "This place is vacant. I checked it out earlier."

Jeez, did he stake out the entire neighborhood? Jared had been a busy boy when he wasn't tracking me down in the park or gagging Valerie with a rag. Someone took his job seriously. Way too seriously.

The driver's door creaked open. "We walk the rest of the way."

Valerie and I opened our doors simultaneously and stepped out. Her eyes met mine briefly and she glowered. For once, I knew it wasn't intended for me. She patted her right coat pocket. The one with the gun.

I didn't know what she meant by it, but I shook my head. I didn't want anyone getting shot tonight.

We followed closely behind Jared who led us back to the gravel road. It snaked up into the trees, and the higher we climbed, the bigger the houses were. Lights dotted downtown. The surrounding islands had turned to dark silhouettes against the Sitka Sound.

The gravel rolled and crunched under our feet.

In the distance, the road came to an end at a three-story mansion that looked like a palace made out of smooth slabs of stone. The driveway led directly up to a row of four garage doors. On the far left there was a set of stairs leading to a balcony at each level. They were surrounded by tempered wind-blocking glass.

"Look at the size of this place," I said.

Jared grunted. "Yes, Andre has done quite well for himself."

I wrinkled my nose. "Do you know him or something?"

"I don't just keep tabs on future recruits."

Meaning he also kept tabs on future targets. Now I really had the creepy crawlies.

I nodded my head toward a window on the middle floor. "There's a light on."

"Don't worry about it," Jared said. He led us under the porch beside the garage doors. "Etienne and Giselle live upstairs. There are three ways in. The garage, the door around back, and up to the porch. You can access their bedrooms from the upstairs porch."

"How are we supposed to get in?" I asked. The agents poisoned my blood and then sent me into the field without practical skills like lock picking.

Jared sneered at me. What a jerk. If Valerie and I were such an annoyance, why bother bringing us? He looked like he did fine as a one-man show. "We're on a small island. No one locks their doors. How do you think I got in earlier?"

I shrugged. "How would I know?" I'd never considered myself a city girl being from Alaska, but Anchorage was the last place you'd leave your doors unlocked. We were constantly ranking in the top five of the nation's most dangerous metropolitan areas.

Anchorage's crime rate was one of those fun facts Dante liked to share with me. He seemed to find it encouraging for our line of work.

Valerie began moving toward the stairs. Jared stepped in front of her. "Knock the kids out quietly then wait with them until I get there. Make sure they don't wake up." He headed up the stairs ahead of us and didn't make a sound as he crept up.

Valerie and I waited until Jared eased back a sliding door and slipped inside the house. I looked at Valerie, and she looked up at the third floor. I waited for her to go first, not wanting to make noise jostling for first place.

Every step we made produced sound against the composite wood porch, but we kept going as quietly as we could. As I passed the sliding door Jared had taken, I took a quick peek inside. There was a massive kitchen on the other side. All the appliances looked brand new. The whole place had an open, modern feel to it, unlike Marcus's palace.

Valerie reached the top deck four steps ahead of me. I was surprised she waited for me to catch up. When I did, Valerie crouched down. I did the same.

The awning had kept the porch dry along the house. I leaned against the outer wall of the house and pressed my forehead to the glass. The door led into a rec room. I looked at Valerie and she nodded.

I gripped the edge of the sliding door with my nails. My fingers slipped off the door on the first try. I used my finger pads instead to ease the door gently open. Once I had an inch of space between the door and frame, pushing an opening large enough to slip through was easy.

With my hands and legs, I lifted myself over the sliding door track and scooted into the room. It had thick carpeting. Finally. The chill from outside followed me in. Valerie came in behind me.

She gently closed the door. We listened. The upstairs was silent.

We got to our feet quietly and walked to the hallway.

"I'll take the right, you take the left," Valerie whispered. "Whoever you get, go for it. If your target wakes up before we get a chance to knock them out, entice them into biting you."

Roger that, team leader two.

At the moment I didn't care if Valerie wanted to get bossy. I was on edge, and I had a feeling she was too. She seemed calmer giving orders. Whatever it took to stop her rushing in, guns blazing, was fine by me.

For a moment I thought she was going to wish me luck, but that would be stretching her goodwill too far.

Valerie looked to the right, indicating she was going for it. I nodded and crouched as I took ginger steps down the hallway.

I didn't look behind me to see if Valerie had made it to the bedroom on the right. My focus had switched to my personal mission.

Luckily, the bedroom door had been left cracked open. I crouched to the floor and pushed the door open further without pause. Better to do it in one motion than with tiny creaks. I crawled into the room and then stopped to listen. If I weren't so on edge, I'd feel pretty ridiculous right about then on my hands and knees sneaking into someone's bedroom.

At first, I heard nothing, but then the sound of light breathing drifted over from the bed eight feet away.

I looked around the tidy room. There wasn't much to see. The room had the usual furnishings and there were framed scenic photographs on the walls. This had to be the boy's room. It had a musky masculine odor.

I scooted my way to the bed, right up to the side where a dark blue or black bedspread hung over the edge. I rested my back carefully against the bed and listened to Etienne breathe. *Inhale. Exhale.* It put me momentarily in a trance.

I dug the bottle and rag out of my coat pockets, squeezing one in each hand. Then I leaned to the side and quietly got to all fours. Slowly, I rose to my feet.

Etienne slept on his side, back facing me. I sucked in a breath. He looked so angelic with his eyes closed, chest softly rising and falling. He had beautiful thick brown hair. I wondered what color his eyes were. I'd be in trouble if I had occasion to find out.

I took a deep breath and held it—just in case—before unscrewing the cap on the travel-sized bottle of chloroform Jared had provided. I emptied the contents onto the rag.

If I stopped to think things through, I'd hesitate. And once I hesitated, I might lose my nerve. So, I replaced the cap and pocketed the bottle then dove forward.

Etienne woke briefly. I felt his body jolt when I clamped the rag over his nose and mouth. His body went slack as suddenly as it had jerked. I felt a moment of exhilaration followed by a sickening sense of guilt.

I pulled the rag away. The boy looked the way he had before I knocked him out. I stared at the rag in my hand before setting it on Etienne's bedspread.

Time to wait.

I walked around the room carefully, studying each framed photograph close up. I recognized the one of Saint Michael's Cathedral in downtown Sitka. The other photos were of castles and cathedrals that looked vaguely familiar. The room was spotless. There wasn't so much as a t-shirt tossed on the ground or on top of the furniture. The only object on the dresser was a set of keys on an electronic key fob with the Mini Cooper logo on it.

I passed by Etienne's open door several times, glancing into the dark hallway. On the eighth pass, I stepped out and listened.

An unsettling silence gripped the house.

I looked to the right, curious if Valerie had chloroformed the girl. She'd probably beat me to it. I wondered what she was doing now. I heard no sounds. Either way, Valerie would probably shoo me off and tell me to stand guard over my unconscious vampire.

A set of carpeted stairs descended to the left.

What was taking Jared so long? What if Andre or Henriette—or both— overpowered him? Jared might be a nasty brute but that didn't change the fact that he was up against two vampires.

If anything happened to compromise Jared, Valerie and I were sitting ducks.

I listened at the top of the stairs. Hearing nothing, I took the first step down as though it would help me hear better.

Crashing glass and fighting were so familiar to me that the silence felt unnatural.

I stopped halfway down the stairs and reached around my back for my dagger. Gripping the handle in my right hand, I continued down quietly.

The stairs ended at a hardwood floor. This was as far as I should go. I needed to turn around and wait with Etienne as Jared had instructed. But I couldn't bring myself to turn around. My fear had detached itself from my consciousness like a scab falling off an old wound.

I placed one foot and then another onto the hardwood floor. I looked right then left. A soft glow traced the outer edges of the wall on the left. I headed toward the light, each step placed carefully.

I stopped once I reached the curve at the end of the hall, listening again. This time I picked up faint chattering.

I crouched down and carefully looked around the corner. The hallway widened, and the light became brighter. I thought about turning back. I didn't.

I walked heel first over the floor, slowly lowering each foot, heel to toe, before picking up again. I moved to a long oriental rug in the middle of the hallway. Much as I wanted to inch along the wall, the rug would offer a more muffled approach. The hall led into the kitchen I'd seen from outside. The fridge hummed softly. I sheathed my dagger, crouched to the floor, and made my way to the long counter in the middle of the room.

The kitchen connected to a large dining room, and the dining room opened into a vast living room. Right off the dining room, the faint glow brightened.

I crouched behind the kitchen counter. The voices continued, so at least no one seemed aware of my presence. Once my heart rate steadied, I strained to hear what was being said. It took me a moment to realize I couldn't make out the words because they weren't in English.

The voices were from a man and a woman. They spoke rapidly. The woman did most of the talking, and she sounded agitated.

I got on my hands and knees and crawled from behind the kitchen counter to the dining room. I ducked under the table. The woman was still talking when I stopped to calm my breathing. Once I felt I could control it, I looked at the living room furniture, trying to decide if I dared go any closer. I might be able to crouch behind the sofa. The voices were coming from the far corner of the gigantic living room. I'd like to get a look at their faces and see what was going on. Obviously, Jared hadn't made his move yet.

On second thought, I should crawl my way back to the kitchen and get my butt back upstairs. If Jared was hiding and I bumped into him, I was dead meat.

I had just started turning on my knees when a familiar laugh stopped me cold.

The woman spoke again with urgency in her voice. "*S'il vous plaît ne blessez pas les enfants.*" I recognized the French now. Before they had been speaking too fast, but the woman's last sentence had been simple enough to understand.

Please don't hurt the children.

The next voice was Jared's, and it was just as chilling in

French as it was in English. "*Ma pauvre Henriette. Vous avez l'air effrayée et cela pour de bonnes raisons.*"

I crawled to the nearest sofa while they were talking and peered around. It didn't do much good. All I saw were the legs of a coffee table, a large area rug, and a couple of recliners.

The woman began speaking again, but I couldn't make anything out. She spoke too quickly. Then her voice cried out, crystal clear. "We have money. We can pay you."

Jared laughed. "Money doesn't interest me," he said, switching to English.

"You loved me once."

"I never loved you, Henriette."

The house fell silent. I wanted them to continue talking. Conversation was the only thing preventing violence. Suddenly steps began running toward me. I laid flat on the floor. As if that would do any good. But before the person could reach me I heard a cry of alarm, followed by a struggle. Something fell to the floor.

Ignoring the voice inside my head telling me to stay the hell down, I lifted my head just over the sofa's back and caught a glimpse of Jared struggling to get a hold on the woman squirming in his hands.

"Andre!" she screamed.

Jared's mouth opened so wide I thought he would bite her. His lips pulled back in an animalistic snarl.

Henriette's shoulders sagged after shouting Andre's name. Jared wrapped his arms around her neck.

My breath caught.

I didn't close my eyes in time.

In one swift motion, Jared twisted Henriette's neck as though it were no more than a plastic cap on a bottle of Dr. Pepper, but instead of the *phish* sound, it was followed by a *snap*.

13

THE SHINING

THE MEXICAN FOOD FROM EARLIER rose up my throat. I clamped a hand over my mouth and hit the ground behind the sofa.

I was too sick to worry about the sound I made. Besides, Jared couldn't hear me over the thump of Henriette's body landing on the floor. Once she'd fallen, I heard footsteps hurrying to the living room from across the room.

"What is going on?" a man cried. Andre, presumably. "Xavier," he said next, pronouncing the name as though seeing a ghost. I expected them to pick back up in French, but they didn't.

"Hello, *brother*."

"How can this be, Xavier? I thought you'd been hanged."

Jared began laughing then stopped abruptly. "While you sat back and did nothing to help me."

"What could I have possibly done? Stormed *La Force*? Don't look at me like I'm to blame. You got yourself in that mess, Xavier. How many times did I warn you to be more cautious?"

"You know what I think?" Jared said. "I think you all couldn't wait to be rid of me."

"How did you find us?"

"I have connections now."

In the silence that followed, I realized I hadn't breathed in a long time. I held it until the talking resumed.

"What have you done to Henriette?"

"I delivered the same fate she left to me."

"You should not have done that, Xavier. Henriette wasn't responsible for your actions. None of us were. You have no one to blame for your capture but yourself."

"Ah, but you see, I didn't remain in captivity, and where were all of you when I got out?" When Andre didn't answer, Jared said, "Have you enjoyed screwing my wife over the last two centuries?"

"She thought you were dead. We all did."

Oh no, I thought. *Jared's a vampire.*

Their conversation faded from my mind.

What was a vampire doing working for a vampire hunting unit of the government? Melcher hated vampires. Did he know? He had to know! How could he not know? Which brought me back to my first question. Why was a vampire working with the government?

Laughter interrupted my thoughts. It was male, but not Jared's.

"Arrogant as always. Do you really believe you can take me on, Xavier? I should remind you I've been around much longer than anyone in this family."

"Which means you should die before me," Jared said.

My body finally sprang into action. I scuttled on hands and knees back to the dining table as the first fist smacked skin. The living room erupted into a chorus of angry shouts and loud thumps.

I'd never crawled so fast in my life. I was like a crab making tracks across the scorching sand. Once I'd passed under the table, I didn't care about stealth. I jumped to my feet and ran for the stairs, taking them two at a time.

Valerie stood at the top. "What the hell is going on down

there?" she demanded.

"Jared!" I gasped, barely able to get enough air in my lungs to speak. "He's a vampire."

"What?"

"He's a vampire! This is a personal vendetta. He already killed the woman. Now he's fighting with the man."

"Shit!" Valerie said. "What do we do?"

I looked down the hall. "Did you knock out the girl?"

"Of course I did!"

"Okay, okay." I shook my hands in front of me trying to think. "We have to get the kids out of here."

Valerie dropped her arms. "Are you crazy?"

"If we don't, Jared will kill them."

"Not my problem."

"Valerie…"

"How the hell are we supposed to get two full-grown teenagers out of this house…from the top story, no less?"

Valerie was right. There was no way we could do it in time. It would take two of us per body. We had to at least try.

"We hide the boy and get the girl." Valerie's mouth opened to protest. I didn't let her. "We carry the girl down the way we came. You take her legs. I'll take her arms. Then we come back for the boy. Once they're both out front I'll enter the garage through the side door, find Etienne's car, and get the doors open. Once I open the garage door, we need to get them inside the vehicle fast. After tha,t we blast out of here."

"And go where? We're on a fucking island!"

"Can we please concentrate on getting out of this house alive and then worry about that?"

I felt ready to snap. There wasn't any time to argue.

"What if Jared gets up here before we have time to get them out?" Valerie demanded.

"We'll just have to hope Andre keeps him preoccupied long enough." Or better yet, wins the fight. I wasn't willing to wait and find out.

Valerie followed me into Etienne's room without another word. While I flipped his bed cover aside, she opened the closet door. "Too obvious," she said.

I crouched on my knees to get a look under the bed, but it was barely half a foot off the ground.

"There's a bathroom over here," Valerie said.

"We'll put him in the tub, just in case."

Valerie grabbed Etienne by the shoulders. I took his feet and led the way to the bathroom. We laid him in the tub and pulled the shower curtain closed.

I pocketed Etienne's car keys as we passed his dresser on the way out. Valerie led the way to Giselle's room at the far end of the hall.

We entered a room with pink walls. Unlike Etienne's room, every available surface had been put to use. The dresser had an army of fairies holding wands, sitting on flowers, and dangling in flight from stands. Stuffed animals filled an entire shelf above the fairies.

Valerie rolled her eyes before nodding at the four-poster bed with a pink comforter.

I'd been expecting someone younger, but the girl lying unconscious looked the same age as us. Her blonde hair fanned out across the pillow. Two swords were mounted and crossed above the headboard. They looked odd against the pink wall.

Valerie went to the head of the bed. I tried not to get annoyed at her defiance of my plan—I'd told her to get the girl's legs. Even in a situation like this, Valerie felt the need to be stubborn. There wasn't any time to worry about it. It didn't matter anyway.

I grabbed her legs, and we pulled her off the bed. The girl had on a pair of pink cotton shorts and a white tank top. We'd almost reached the door when a gunshot ripped through the house.

Valerie dropped Giselle. I wasn't able to do much good holding on to her legs. The girl's head hit the floor. At least she landed on the carpet.

Valerie and I looked at each other.

The shot was followed by yelling. No one was dead. Yet.

"We have to get out of here," Valerie said. Before I could open my mouth, she added, "Now."

I looked down. "We have to help them first."

"Are you insane? If we waste any more time none of us are making it out of here. Do you think Jared's just going to let us go back home now that we know his little secret?"

"He doesn't know we know."

Valerie made no move to take the girl's arms. Instead, she took a step toward me. "You saw the way he manhandled me earlier. I don't think he ever had any intention of bringing us back alive. He'll probably tell Melcher we died in combat. He's going to kill us and drink from us. Well, me anyway. He won't be able to drink from you, but he sure as hell isn't going to leave a witness standing around. You know I'm right. He's been watching us like a wolf watches mice from the moment we left town. Melcher will have no reason to doubt his story."

"We can't just leave them."

Valerie took a step toward the door.

"Fine, it's your funeral. I'm out of here."

Before she could take another step, a second shot rang out. This one wasn't followed by angry shouts. It wasn't followed by anything but silence. I dropped Giselle's legs. From the look on Valerie's face, I'd say her heart momentarily stopped, too.

There was no way to know who the last vamp standing was. Either way, we were in deep shit. If Andre had offed Jared, he'd have no problem taking care of the human sidekicks. He might even drink from us. If we were lucky he'd go for me first…before he shot us both, hacked up the pieces, and tossed them in the bay.

Seriously, how could Valerie read creepy stuff like that for entertainment?

I looked at Valerie's coat pocket. The one with the gun. She shook her head. I didn't know whether that meant she didn't have the gun, didn't know how to use it, or didn't want to use it.

There was no time to get the girl out, but I couldn't leave her helpless on the floor in case Jared was the victor of the fight below. I squatted, grabbed her ankles, and dragged her toward the bathroom.

Valerie didn't assist, but thankfully she didn't flee either.

I pulled Giselle into the bathroom, leaving her on the floor. I didn't have the strength to get her inside the bathtub. I looked at the inner doorknob. Sure enough, there was a push-down lock on the brass knob for securing the room from the inside. I pressed it down.

As I moved back into the bedroom, I began pulling the bathroom door closed behind me.

"Someone's coming up the stairs," Valerie said, her words ending in a low hiss.

I stopped and listened for footsteps. I heard Jared's voice instead. "Oh girls, where are you?"

I looked at Valerie. She put two fingers to her lips. Quiet? No shit! What did she think I was going to do? Call out, "In here?"

Jared would see us in the hallway if we tried to make a run for the sliding door.

Slowly, we backed up toward the bathroom. Our quiet steps were followed by louder ones as Jared stomped his way up the stairs. He entered the first room. "And where has Etienne gone to?" His voice had an unsettling way of carrying through the walls.

There was a metal scraping sound as Jared yanked back the shower curtain in the bathroom down the hall.

"Nice try, girls," he said.

The following gun blast shook the walls. My eardrums rang in protest. I thought I saw Giselle twitch on the floor, but it must have been my eyes playing tricks on me. Valerie and I were in the bathroom with her in a flash. Valerie slammed the door shut behind us and leaned her body up against it.

"It's locked," I said.

Jared rammed against the other side. Valerie shrieked, jumped away from the door, and grabbed me. I screamed. She let go. The ramming noise stopped. "Come on girls, I know you have Giselle in there. Open up and I'll finish the job."

For one sick moment, I considered tossing the girl out. Maybe Valerie was wrong. Maybe if we went along with the plan Jared would spare us. I looked around the bathroom. No windows. No way out.

"What's with the gun?" Valerie called back. I had to give her points for asking in a steady voice.

"Andre pulled it on me. Damn fool. Half the homes on the hill probably heard, which is why we need to stop wasting time." The last three words were spoken with more menace than the beginning of Jared's sentence. "Open the door."

I looked at Valerie. She looked at the door. "No."

"Open the door now, Red. You do not want to get on my bad side."

I didn't doubt that for a second after witnessing how ruthlessly he'd snapped his ex-wife's neck, but Valerie hadn't heard the conversation below.

"Do you think I'm stupid? I know what will happen if I open this door."

Jared didn't respond. I couldn't make out any movement or breathing on the other side of the door. I tried to listen, but all the keeping quiet had frayed my last nerve. My breath came out ragged. I tried to still it, but I couldn't.

"You had your chance," Jared said calmly.

I heard a brusque movement in the room then silence.

"I think he left," Valerie whispered.

"Probably to get an ax," I whispered back.

"Then we should make a run for it now."

My body tensed. "No way! What if he's waiting in the hall?"

Valerie chewed on her lower lip. I looked at the girl lying at our feet. Sorry, G, I tried. At least her death would be painless and terror free.

"Hey," Valerie whispered. She reached into one of her coat pockets and pulled out the brown bottle. "I still have half a bottle." She pulled a pink washcloth off a stack of folded towels on a metal rack above the toilet. Valerie handed the cloth and bottle to me.

I took them in my hands. "What am I supposed to do with these?"

Valerie pulled her revolver out of her pocket. "I'll hold him at gunpoint while you chloroform him."

If I weren't freaked out of my mind, I would have laughed at her insanity. "No way!"

"Shh!" Valerie hissed louder than I'd spoken. She held up her left hand and we listened as Jared returned.

Something banged against the door. Valerie and I screamed. Jared whacked the door again.

Oh God, it was *The Shining*. Unfortunately, I actually had been present the day Mrs. Campbell played the Jack Nicolson horror film in class. The movie might be dated, but it had still freaked me out, especially the part where Jack's wife locked herself in the bathroom, screaming as Jack hacked it down with an ax.

I could just hear him breaking a hole through the door and announcing, "Heeere's Jared," all creepy and crazy-eyed.

He hit the door again.

And again.

Valerie pulled back the hammer on her revolver, and aimed it at the door. She nodded at me once.

My heart froze in my chest. I'd battled baddies and fought for my life, but this I couldn't do. I shook my head.

Valerie shot me a stern glare. It was sort of comforting to see her give one of her normal bitchy looks.

Jared beat at the door without pause. Each blow made a sickening crack. The wood splintered at eye level, but he hadn't broken through.

Valerie gave me another look, full of unspoken orders. She gazed pointedly at the spot beside the door.

One way or another we were going to have to fight for our lives. I moved beside the door, jumping slightly when Jared smashed against it. I looked at Valerie. She looked at my hands. I unscrewed the bottle of chloroform and dumped the remaining contents onto the pink washcloth.

"All right!" Valerie yelled. "We'll come out, but first you have to promise you'll calm down."

Jared whacked the door in answer.

A look came over Valerie's face, anger replacing fear. She placed her left foot in front of the right and held the gun steady.

I wished whatever calmness had come over her would rub off on me a little. Sheer terror coursed through my bones. At that point, I didn't even care about looking like a scaredy-cat in front of Valerie.

Jared continued hacking at the door.

The wood splintered around the hole he made when he broke through. We caught a glimpse of his weapon. At least it was an aluminum bat, not an ax or sword. That also meant he didn't have the gun in his hand.

Jared whacked at the hole several more times then reached through. I screamed when his arm shot inside the bathroom and grabbed the doorknob. The lock clicked open when he turned the handle. He yanked his arm back and threw open the door.

I froze.

Valerie didn't.

She fired her pistol without a second thought.

Jared's murderous look turned to one that seemed perplexed. He took a step back and dropped the bat. He looked down. Valerie had gotten him just below his shoulder blade. Blood stained through his t-shirt.

I felt almost as shocked as Jared. It wasn't enough to put him down though. He bent to pick the bat up.

Scared or not, I knew it was my one and only chance. I leapt forward, pivoting around him, and grabbed his head in my hands as I shoved the washcloth over his mouth.

Please work. Please pass out, I chanted in my head. My mind played back images of Jared snapping Henriette's neck.

Jared grabbed my arm. It was the same grip he had on me in the totem park earlier. This time he meant to break it. I felt it in his bone-crushing grip. I pressed the washcloth against Jared's face with everything I had.

14

GETAWAY

JUST AS MY BONES FELT ready to snap, Jared's grip relaxed and he fell face first onto the carpet.

A sob I'd been holding back gurgled up my throat. I stood up and jumped back as though Jared might revive himself instantly and come after me, but he lay motionless on the ground.

I caught Valerie's movement as she stepped slowly out of the bathroom. She had both hands wrapped around her gun. She kept it aimed at Jared.

"Do you still have your dagger?" Valerie asked, never taking her eyes off of him.

"Yes," I answered slowly, not sure what she was getting at.

"Finish him off."

My jaw dropped. "He's our team leader."

"He tried to kill us."

And he killed Henriette, Andre, and Etienne without pause. But I wasn't about to stick a blade in him. "It's Melcher's call," I said.

"Screw Melcher! If you won't do it, I will." Valerie leveled her gun at Jared's head. Her anger took me aback.

"Leave it for Melcher," I said. "We've been through enough this evening, and we have to get out of here. I'm surprised we haven't heard sirens yet."

That got Valerie's attention. She hesitated a moment, then

pocketed her gun. I thought the situation was diffused, but then Valerie began kicking Jared and screaming, "You son of a bitch!"

"Val!" I yelled.

She stopped and looked at me.

"We need to get the girl in the car."

"You're shitting me."

"What if he wakes up before her?"

Valerie grabbed the bat beside Jared, took it inside the bathroom, and tossed it beside Giselle's unconscious body. The aluminum clanged against the tile floor. "There," she said. "If she wakes up first then she can finish him off for us."

"We're not leaving without her."

"Well, we need to go," she said.

"Then grab her ankles." Cussing seemed to get Valerie's attention. She scowled at me, but at least she obeyed and grabbed Giselle's legs while I went for her arms.

We didn't talk after that. We carried the body successfully down the hall and stairs, setting her down for a moment on the second floor, then brought her down the last set of stairs leading into the garage.

We stopped and set the girl down while I opened the door to the garage. At least she was skinny.

There were four vehicles inside the garage. I looked at the SUV wistfully.

"Which one?" Valerie asked.

"The Mini."

"You're kidding me."

"Nope," I replied, feeling the first hint of a grin since the whole ordeal began.

I unlocked the Mini and pulled the passenger's seat up as

151

far as it would go. While I did so, I heard a loud *slap*. I twisted my head around in time to see Valerie pulling her hand away from the girl's face. "Valerie, what the hell?"

Valerie shrugged. "Worth a try. It would be a lot easier if she could get inside herself."

I sighed. "Let's just get her in the car and get out of here."

I took Giselle's shoulders again and backed my way into the Mini, taking her with me. Valerie held her legs while I did all the lifting and pulling.

"Hey, you're the one who wanted to bring her," she said when I let out a groan.

The Mini was too short to lay the girl across the backseat. I did what I could, bending her legs to make her fit. Once her feet were clear of the door, I scooted back the way I'd come in, bumping my head on the roof before making it out. I stepped out of the car and moved the passenger seat back into the sitting position. As I did so, I got a glimpse inside the front of the vehicle. "Crap!"

"What now?" Valerie asked.

I pulled my head out of the car and looked back at her. "It's a stick shift."

Valerie held out her hand. "Give me the keys."

I handed them over and climbed into the passenger's seat as she made her way to the driver's side. I clicked the garage door opener attached to the visor inside the car. The door groaned as it lifted.

Valerie started the car. She grabbed the stick and rammed it into first gear. We jerked out of the garage. She pulled the stick back and the car jerked again. I didn't care so long as she didn't kill the engine. We careened down the hill, passing our rental car parked at the vacant house.

"We have to get off this island," Valerie said.

"Agreed."

"Do you think Jared left the plane tickets in his room?"

"It's possible."

"Okay." Valerie sounded more assured. She stayed the course, backtracking to the hotel. It didn't take long seeing as we were trapped on a small island.

Valerie parked in the far corner of the lot, leaving the keys in the ignition.

I looked back at the girl. She was still unconscious. "What about her?"

"She didn't see our faces. She'll wake up wondering what the hell happened, drive home, and have to deal with finding out her vampire family is dead." Valerie didn't sound particularly sympathetic. "She should be grateful she's alive, but somehow I doubt she'll appreciate that fact."

In my opinion, family was family whether they were vampires or humans. This loss wouldn't come easy. It might be worse. This girl had spent generations with her family. Then to lose every single one of them suddenly…. Then again, I had my own problems to deal with and Valerie was right—she was lucky to be alive.

Valerie got out of the car first. Before I slipped out, I pressed the self-lock button on the Mini's key fob, securing Giselle inside the car.

We walked up to the hotel in silence. A middle-aged man wearing a pair of black framed glasses stood at the front counter, tapping at the computer in the deserted lobby. "Leave this to me," Valerie said. "I'll get Jared's spare key and meet you back at our room."

I nodded once. We split apart.

I quickened my pace in the hall, wanting only to get to the room and feel safe, but once I reached it, I wanted to grab my things as fast as I could and get the hell out of there. Jared knew where our room was. This was the least safe place in all of Sitka.

Most of my things were still in my duffel bag. I tossed in the items that weren't. That completed, I went into the bathroom.

Valerie had her junk all over the countertop: hair dryer, big round brush, hairspray, lipstick, mascara, toothpaste, and toothbrush.

I looked up, staring into the mirror. My face seemed paler than usual. Although I didn't have any open wounds to clean this time, I turned on the faucet and splashed cold water over my face. Rubbing my skin dry with the hand towel reminded me of how I'd chloroformed Jared.

And Valerie had shot him.

If he ever caught up to us, we were dead. Not undead. Dead. Goodbye cruel life!

Maybe I should have let Valerie kill him. It's not the kind of decision I had wanted to make with only seconds to spare. We needed to get back to Anchorage, and we needed to tell Melcher what happened.

I froze and stared into the mirror, locking eyes with myself. I had big pupils. People were always telling me they made my eyes look black the way they practically covered my irises. I looked into those black spots and tried to control the tremble that had started in my legs.

Jared was a rogue agent now. A rogue *vampire* agent! He knew our operations. He knew our names. No matter where we went, he knew where to find us. Melcher would expect us to finish him off. He was a threat to us all.

Is that how Agent Crist died? Had she discovered his secret?

Perhaps she'd been on her way to tell Melcher. And Mike? That still didn't add up. Jared didn't seem to have a clue about Mike.

I slipped my dagger out of its sheath, holding it in front of the mirror much the same way Valerie had held her dagger and gun in front of the window.

"It has to be done," I said to my reflection. I returned my dagger to its sheath and waited for Valerie in the bedroom.

She returned, grinning as she held up a piece of paper. "Found our flight confirmation inside the bastard's baggage."

I frowned. "Valerie…"

Valerie's smile dropped. "What?" she asked impatiently.

"We have to go back."

Her entire face contorted in disdain. "The hell we do!"

"You know we can't let Jared wake up."

"Wait a minute. Now you're telling me you want to kill him? I told you that back at the house. You had your chance, Aurora. It's too late now." Valerie made a sound of disgust and stormed over to her suitcase. She reached into her coat pocket and pulled out the revolver. I heard the bullets clink together inside her suitcase as she emptied the chamber.

I took a step toward her, stopping at the edge of her bed to give her space. "If we don't take care of him, we're leaving ourselves in danger, not to mention Noel, Dante, and every operative in our unit. I think he killed Agent Crist." I was sure of it. And how convenient to remove her cross after killing her and plant it at the Morrel's house. Hell, he didn't even have to plant it. He simply waved it in front of our faces and told us what he wanted us to believe. The only thing I wasn't sure of was Mike. How would Jared have tracked him down and why? And if he had killed Mike, why not pocket a memento of his, like his class ring, and use it as part of his charade? That simply didn't add up. It's like two unrelated killings had occurred, but then why had both bodies been found dumped at the same location and time? Argh! I felt like my mind was going to explode.

"Probably," Valerie said in answer to my theory about Crist. She tossed her gun inside her suitcase, stormed past me, and disappeared into the bathroom. Her toiletries clacked together as she gathered them up. She returned a moment later, carrying a striped bag which she tossed in her suitcase. The zipper made a ripping sound as Valerie closed it. She set it on its wheels and met my eyes. "There's nothing we can do. The police are probably there by now. Melcher can have someone take care of him while he's inside a cell."

"We should call Melcher."

Valerie snorted. "Right. I'm sure he's sitting behind his desk in the middle of the night waiting for our call." She held up the piece of paper she'd snagged from Jared's room. "What we need to do is get out of here. Lucky for us, our return flight leaves at 6AM. So let's say we get our asses to the airport and off this damn island."

I opened my mouth to speak, but Valerie cut me off. "It's our only option." She moved briskly to the phone on the nightstand. "Yes, this is Ginger in room 102," she said into the phone. "We're going to need a taxi to the airport. Thanks." She set the phone in the receiver. "Let's wait out front. I want to put this place behind me as soon as possible."

I didn't argue. Valerie was right. What could we do at this point?

I hoisted my duffel bag over my right shoulder and followed Valerie into the hallway to the lobby.

Our breath came out in foggy puffs as we waited for the cab outside. This early in the morning, the sky was as black as the

Prince William Sound after the Exxon Valdez oil spill. Valerie's hand shook slightly as she lit a cigarette. For the second time in my life, I felt like asking for a drag.

I think we both breathed a sigh of relief when the taxi pulled up.

"To the airport?" our driver asked once we'd tossed our luggage in the trunk and taken our seats in the back of the car.

"Yes," we said simultaneously.

"How long is our layover in Juneau?" I asked once the wheels on the cab began moving.

Valerie studied the flight conformation. The paper hadn't left her hand since she walked into the room with it. "Our flight lands in Juneau at 6:43 a.m., departing Juneau at 12:27, and arriving in Anchorage at 2:05 p.m."

I leaned into Valerie, doing some quick calculations as I stared at the flight confirmation. "Six hours." That was a long time to stick around the capital twiddling our thumbs. I thought briefly of Mendenhall Glacier. I definitely was NOT in the sightseeing mood. I felt like I was running for my life, which was ridiculous. Jared was the one in the wrong. Jared should be the one afraid. Melcher hunted vampires. Well, not personally, but he had a team of hunters at his beck and call.

I still wanted to know how Melcher recruited *The Recruiter*. And no more of his cryptic, bullshit answers. Our team leader had nearly killed us.

15

TAKEOFF

After we checked in, we settled into two scuffed up chairs in the farthest corner of the terminal. We had a little over two hours to wait until boarding. As soon as we sat, Valerie whipped out her phone.

"What are you doing?" I asked, alarmed. "You can't go telling Gavin what's happening."

Valerie looked up from her phone and gave me a menacing glare. "He thinks I'm in California visiting my mom and annoying sisters."

I pulled my own phone out and sent Dante a quick text message.

Aurora: Jared's a vampire. Valerie and I are on the run. Call me when you get this.

As if that last sentence was needed. I wished I could see the look on Dante's face when he read the text. How many hours until he saw it? The time read three twenty-five. It would be a while yet. He might think I was playing around again.

I looked over at Valerie, still busily texting. "What do you think Jared will tell the police when he wakes up?"

Valerie stopped typing. Her bottom lip turned down. "I don't know. He'll come up with something."

I didn't doubt it. "Do you think the officers are safe?"

"They've probably locked him in a cell for questioning. I

158

mean, they found him with a gun inside a house full of dead bodies."

"Is there anything linking us?" I asked. "What if they trace Jared back to the Westmark? We're under his reservation."

"Under false names."

"But if they questioned the clerk on duty he'd tell them we left for the airport."

"Then let's hope he doesn't wake up anytime soon." Valerie crossed her leg and began jerking her foot around.

"What if they notice the rental car and trace it back to the hotel?"

Valerie's foot stopped. She turned and glared at me. "Will you give it a rest already? You're making me nuts. There's nothing we can do besides sit here and wait for our flight to board." She made a point of holding her phone up to her face.

I fiddled with the bear claw.

Valerie lowered her phone and watched me for a moment. "What is it with that thing? I saw it on Dante before we left."

"He lent it to me."

"Is it like a promise ring or something?"

I squished up my face. "No. We're partners. That's all. At least we were until Melcher forced you on me."

Valerie narrowed her eyes. "Sooner or later Dante's going to tire of your prudish games and move on, you know, and I'd bet my bootstraps you aren't going to like it when he does."

"I hope Dante does find a nice girl," I retorted.

Valerie placed an arm on the armrest between us, leaning in closer than I liked, her fire engine red lips inches from mine. Only Valerie would find the time to reapply her lipstick while running for her life. "Dante doesn't want a nice girl, and you don't want a nice boy. Why do you think you were attracted to Fane?"

My first thought was that it wasn't any of her damn business. My second was that no words came readily to mind.

"When did you notice Fane?" Valerie asked. "Before or after the accident?"

"He's a little hard to miss," I said sarcastically.

"No. When did you *notice* Fane?"

I stared at the empty rows of chairs in front of us.

I noticed Fane the first time I laid eyes on him, sophomore year. He'd looked exactly the same back then, which made sense now that I knew he couldn't age. Even his hair had been the same—that unnatural shade of black, cropped on both sides, and mop of blond flipped back on top. I noticed Fane the first day he walked into English late. I'd gotten goosebumps as he breezed by my desk toward the back row in his long leather coat. My arm hair had prickled as though I'd just been passed by a ghost.

I'd noticed him as someone to avoid.

It wasn't until after the accident that I wanted him to notice me. That's what changed. I wanted Fane to see me. I didn't miss the way he looked at the rest of the student body as though they were faceless, nameless drones going about their day. Back then he only had eyes for Valerie, and it had given me the shivers to see how much attention a boy could give a girl.

Then, by some twist of fate, Mr. Mooney paired us up in gym class. It had only been for one class period, but it had been enough. Fane saw me as no one else had since the accident. And then I'd run into him in front of the video store and he'd walked me home. I didn't know him at all, but he put me instantly at ease. After that I'd wanted to jump his bones, but I didn't. I jumped Scott Stevens instead. *Yuck*. Good one, Aurora.

Fane wasn't available when I made my stupid list of New Year's Resolutions.

I did get to kiss him though. A lot. That is until Valerie put a stop to things. To be fair, I'd put a halt on kissing once I discovered he was a vampire. Those lips had sucked blood from human veins. It didn't bother me as much now.

"You are thinking way too hard," Valerie said. "Fine, you don't want to talk about Fane. It's probably best, all things considered. At least you're not as big of a pansy as I originally thought. But back to my original observation. Dante doesn't do nice and neither do you. It's the vampire blood. Deny it all you want, but you're sick. We're all sick. Noel, too. The agents made us this way."

"What way? What are you talking about?"

"I'm talking about rabies and TB. It's not a lot, but it's enough to increase our sexual appetites."

Sounded like a convenient excuse to me. Sure, Valerie wasn't a sex addict by choice; blame the viruses flowing through our bloodstreams.

"Where are you getting your information?" I asked. It wasn't like there was a manual on vampire traits and characteristics.

"Boot camp. Hasn't Melcher talked to you about it?"

I shook my head.

Valerie smirked. "I guess he's not convinced you have what it takes."

"Fine by me. I don't want to go to vampire boot camp."

"Anyway," she said, ignoring me. "Part of training included a course on understanding the enemy. Has Dante not told you anything?"

"A little. It's a lot of information." I'd like to see Valerie try mentoring a new hunter. There was a lot of ground to cover.

"I thought he would have shared the sexual stuff with you right out of the gate."

I'm glad he hadn't. We'd talked about sensitivities to garlic and sunlight, not sex. I wanted to know more without having to ask. Luckily, on this subject, Valerie was happy to elaborate. "Tuberculosis causes periods of fatigue. It also increases sexual appetite. Rabies is worse. The disease messes with the part of the brain that helps people sleep at night. It kicks their sex drive into fifth gear."

Valerie lifted a finger. "We have the same blood." She lifted a second. "We have the same viruses." A third. "We have the same symptoms." She sat back in her seat, shooting me a triumphant look.

I didn't know what there was to be happy about. In a sense, we were vampires. The only difference was that we were aging vampires.

It was nice talking to someone else who noticed the symptoms—even if that someone was Valerie.

"What about blood?" I asked suddenly. "Do you ever get cravings?"

Valerie smiled. Her eyes took on an unnatural shine under the florescent lights. "I don't see why vampires should get to do all the sucking."

"You sucked someone's blood?" I asked, alarmed. Cravings were one thing. The thought of biting into someone's skin was too horrific to contemplate.

"No, stupid. I can taste my own blood on vampires' tongues after they've bitten me."

"Ew."

"Grow up, Aurora. It's time to take off the granny panties and wear the thong." Valerie turned her attention back to her phone. I didn't know why I felt disappointed. Maybe because out here Valerie was all I had.

"Are you from California originally?"

Valerie lowered her phone slowly. Her expression started taking on the familiar hostile look. "Why do you ask?"

"That's what you told Gavin—that you were in California visiting your mom and sisters. I wondered if your family really lived there."

"You want my advice, Aurora? Don't meddle in other people's lives, especially trained assassins." She stuck her face inches from mine. "I know I'm technically an informant, but I've had the training and I've done the killing. So back off."

Whoa, okay then. I leaned away from her.

She stood up, slipping her purse over her shoulder. She left a larger handbag on the seat. "Watch my bag while I'm in the powder room."

Unlike Jared, I wasn't worried that Valerie would split. She wanted off this island as much as I did.

After Valerie returned freshly perfumed, she pulled out her *Blood in the Snow* novel.

"How can you read that?" I asked.

Valerie looked from her book to me. "The world is an ugly place, Aurora. You gotta face the facts." She opened the book to the last spot she'd dog-eared and lifted the paperback halfway to her face.

"Doesn't mean I want to read about it," I mumbled.

I spent the rest of the wait shuffling through songs, searching for ones that might calm me. I wasn't having much luck listening to a single song all the way through.

More passengers entered the terminal. When a small crowd had gathered near the gate, Valerie lowered her book, dog-eared the corner, and slid the paperback inside her bag. She got up and I followed suit.

As soon as the airline's agent walked behind the gate's counter, Valerie edged her way to the front of the crowd. I stuck to her side. Once boarding began, we were ready with our passes to get on first.

We were in row fifteen on this flight. Valerie charged in first, so I didn't bother protesting when she took the window seat again. I just wanted to be wheels up already.

I slid into the middle seat beside Valerie. Somehow, I felt like if I sat in Jared's seat he'd appear to claim it. Valerie checked her phone again, but from her frown I guessed Gavin hadn't been responding. Her foot tapped the floor until the captain came on the intercom and said, "Flight attendants please seat yourselves for takeoff." Then it stopped.

The plane taxied to the runway. I couldn't see much out the window. It was still dark this early in the morning.

My entire body thrummed as our plane sped up, faster and faster, then lifted off. I breathed a sigh of relief the moment the wheels left the tarmac.

Valerie unclicked her seatbelt as soon as we were at cruising altitude. "Let me out."

My jaw tightened. She didn't need to pee. I knew that much. "Do you seriously want to tamper with the smoke detector and risk having the captain turn this flight around or hold us in Juneau?"

"Fair enough." She sat back in her seat and hummed to herself a minute before opening her book again.

We were only in the air for thirty minutes before landing in Juneau. The cities weren't that far apart, but the airplanes ran at slow speeds between the two towns. I wasn't nearly as far away from Sitka as I'd like to be. Six hours was way too long of a layover. Plenty of time for Jared to wake up. Luckily the next flight out of Sitka wasn't until 6:20 p.m. Even if Jared somehow got out of jail that morning, he wouldn't be able to catch up to us.

Valerie unbuckled before the plane came to a complete stop at the gate. I didn't know what the hurry was. Once we reached the terminal, she began walking in long determined strides. I hurried to keep pace. "Going somewhere?"

"To the check-in counter."

"But we're already checked in through to Anchorage."

"I'm not going to Anchorage."

"What are you talking about?" The feeling of panic swept back in.

Valerie stopped in the middle of the hall. There weren't a whole lot of people around, and the ones who were easily moved around us. Valerie's expression took on a look of almost childlike excitement. Now she was really scaring me.

"Now's our chance, Aurora."

I had a good idea where she was going with this, but I asked all the same. "Our chance to what?"

"Fly the coop. Escape."

I didn't consider it for a second. Oddly, I felt appalled by the idea. Fleeing meant running...forever. Without the monthly antidote I'd lose my humanity. Become one of the diseased for all of eternity, or until Melcher or his predecessor found me. And the same went for Valerie.

"You know we can't do that," I said.

"Speak for yourself."

"Without the antidote you'll turn into a vampire."

Valerie's lips pursed. "I'm already dead as far as my friends and family are aware, so why not? Why the hell not?"

I couldn't think of a response as I stared at her. It wouldn't have mattered anyway. Valerie's mind was made up. She grinned when I didn't answer. "You know I'm right." She began walking again.

I fell into step beside her. My thoughts were running a million miles a second. It's not that I was considering anything, it's just that I couldn't believe she was really making a run for it.

"Melcher will find you."

"No, he won't."

"Of course he will. He has unlimited resources."

Valerie smirked. "I have resources, too. One of the perks of being an informant. I have contacts. Lots of them."

"Is there a big network of vampires or something?"

"That's for me to know and you not to." Her smile widened.

"You're serious about this?"

Valerie began walking. I'd never seen her look so happy. "I think I'd make a great vampire—gorgeous for all eternity."

Sure thing, Evil Red.

I didn't know if I liked the idea of Valerie becoming a vampire. Working with her had been hard enough. Facing off?

I pictured her holding her dagger and gun in front of the window. Her love of brutal crime stories. The way she stabbed the vampires who killed the pizza boy in Anchorage. Her general attitude. No, I didn't like it one bit.

"Don't do this, Val."

She gave me a pitying look. "I've played by their rules long enough. It's time to take back my life."

"What am I supposed to tell Melcher?"

"Hell if I care."

"You're putting me in a really difficult position."

"Then come with me. I can hook you up. Wherever you want to go there's always someone who knows somebody." She snickered. "Don't tell me Alaska's your dream destination."

"It's my home." More importantly, it's where my mom was. If I left, I could never see her again. I didn't think my mom could handle losing both me and my dad. She'd already come close to losing me once. That's the whole reason I was in this mess. She'd made a deal with the devil, and like it or not, I was in on that deal.

Suddenly Valerie frowned. "Don't tell me this is about Fane because you can kiss that fantasy goodbye for good."

I gnashed my teeth together. "This isn't about Fane. My mom's in Anchorage."

She raised a brow. "The woman in the bathrobe?" she asked coldly.

I don't know why I expected to receive an ounce of compassion or understanding. I always knew this wouldn't be a bonding mission, but after everything we'd been through, you'd think Valerie would be slightly less hostile toward me. And what did she care about Fane? Not only was she taking off, she had Gavin now.

I followed her up to the check-in counter where she immediately launched into a story about having just received an emergency call from her mother in the states. Her sister had been in an accident and Valerie needed to get home at once. I wondered if she even had a sister. She struck me as more of an only child.

The clerk was very polite and didn't have much trouble finding a flight departing for Seattle in three hours. Lucky.

While the clerk leaned her head into her computer, Valerie turned to me. "Last chance."

16

PAYBACK

I MET VALERIE'S EYE. SURPRISINGLY, I had no interest in taking off. I wanted to be free, sure, but not like this. "I can't," I said.

"Figures." After that, Valerie turned her complete attention to the clerk while they made arrangements to have her luggage pulled from the baggage bound for Anchorage.

Yep, couldn't flee the state without her handy-dandy dagger and gun.

I stuck by Valerie, even after she'd received her new boarding pass. I wasn't sure what else to do. Were we enemies now? I mean, officially? What would Melcher want me to do in a situation like this?

For now, I supposed the only thing to kill was time. "Want to get a coffee?" I asked.

"Why not?" she said.

We ordered the largest coffee they had from a stand and settled into the nearest seats with our tall paper cups. I took the lid off mine so it would cool faster.

I checked my phone, feeling my forehead crease when I saw there were no new texts or messages. "I'm surprised Dante hasn't called me."

Valerie shrugged. "Maybe their vampire is Crist's real killer."

"Jared killed her. I'm sure of it."

Valerie shrugged again. "Doesn't matter to me."

"Maybe I should try Noel."

Valerie let out a heavy sigh. "Can you just leave it alone? Let them do their job. Or whatever it is they're doing." She grinned wickedly. "Maybe those two hooked up. Noel usually prefers vampires, but as you pointed out, Dante is only one injection away from becoming a full-fledged member of the undead. Noel might make an exception for him, and Dante might make an exception for her. You did get him all worked up last night, and guess who happened to be nearby and handy?" Valerie sneered. "Little 'ol Noel Harper."

I glared at Valerie.

"Don't tell me it hasn't gone through your mind."

No, actually, it hadn't. Noel and Dante were the last two people I could visualize hooking up. Still couldn't.

Maybe Valerie's departure was for the best. No more snide comments or bitchy retorts. I wouldn't mind living a Valerie-free life. There was only one problem. "What will you tell your contacts about our operation?"

"Nothing."

"You expect me to believe that?"

"I'm already on the run. Do you think I have any desire to make myself even more of a target than I already am once I step foot on that plane? All I want is to live my own life and answer to no one but myself."

"What will you tell Gavin?" I demanded.

"I'll say that I'm a vampire. That's all he needs to know."

I snorted. "You're just going to spring it on him. Hey, not only am I your suck buddy, I'm a vampire. What will be your explanation for keeping it from him before?"

Valerie's bold red lips came closer to mine when she leaned forward. "Because I didn't know I was a vampire until someone tried to hunt me down. That's why I'm on the run." She leaned back, satisfied.

"And what is your backstory on how you became a vampire?"

"I died a year ago," she answered coldly. Her jaw tensed. "I was murdered."

"What?" I nearly spilled my coffee. I had a feeling she wasn't making this part up. "Who tried to kill you?"

"If I knew that, he'd be dead."

"What happened?" This was crazy. I couldn't believe she'd finally shared.

Valerie's fists tightened. "Psycho came at me from behind when I was having a smoke outside a club one night. Didn't ask for a thing. Didn't try to rape me, either. He stuck his knife in here," Valerie said, touching a spot behind her shoulder. "And here." She touched behind the other shoulder. "And back here." She reached her arm around her lower back. "What really pisses me off is I had a gun in my purse, and I couldn't even get to it."

My eyes widened. "What were you doing with a gun?"

"I'm from L.A. You don't stand alone outside at night without some kind of weapon or at least pepper spray. I'm not stupid." Valerie's fingers curled back into fists. "I never saw him coming. Never even heard him until he had me by the neck. I couldn't even scream. After he stabbed me three times, he tightened his fingers around my throat and choked every last breath out of me. The next thing I knew, I was in this suck ass state."

"How did you get here?"

"I was flown up, obviously." She shot me her trademark glare.

"But how did the government find you?"

170

"Like I know."

I thought of Jared, master of recruiting. Sounded more like he did the killing than the recruiting to me. Right place at the right time, my lily ass.

He could tell Melcher he found Valerie after she'd been strangled and mugged. He could tell Melcher anything he wanted.

A sick feeling twisted in my gut. The image of him grabbing Valerie from behind in the hotel room raced across my mind. Sharing any hunches with Valerie didn't seem wise. She'd want to turn back around and kill Jared if she had any suspicions. But first, she'd want to murder me for stopping her from killing him in the first place.

This whole Jared thing was getting creepier by the hour.

He'd claimed to be at my accident scene as well. Had he done something to my brakes? No, my car had been fine. It was the oncoming vehicle that had slid into my lane.

I pictured Jared polishing the ice on the corner where I'd bitten the dust.

Ridiculous notion.

Maybe he messed with the oncoming vehicle's brakes?

Again, ludicrous. Even a vampire couldn't plan the exact moment two cars would pass inside an icy curve.

Still, something wasn't right. Melcher owed me answers and this time he better be more forthcoming.

"Anyway, the experience taught me that humans are psychos, not vampires," Valerie said. "Melcher tried brainwashing me into thinking otherwise. I played along. Did the summer boot camp. Combat training. Learned everything I could about fighting and vampires. I became an informant. Met my first vampire. Met more vampires. And bided my time for a day like today."

"What about going to college? I thought you wanted to sign up for classes at UAA."

"You think the University of Alaska Anchorage is an incentive to stick around? Fuck that! Fuck you! And fuck this state!"

"Well, whatever," I said.

"Yeah, whatever."

We sipped our coffee in silence.

"Want to see me off?" she asked at a quarter after nine.

"Why not?"

We walked slowly to her gate. It felt like a dream. It's not like I'd gotten any sleep that night, and I was starting to feel it now that things had calmed down. I kept expecting government agents to rush in and grab us, but the airport was eerily quiet. Even our conversation came to an end.

Valerie and I stood watching the gate together. We watched passengers milling around; watched the agent take her place behind the counter; watched the plane land, taxi in, and unload; watched two stewardesses roll their luggage to the gate and disappear behind the door leading from the jetway to the plane.

Valerie turned to me. "Melcher knows about Fane."

A shockwave went through my brain. "What?" Oh, I'd heard her all right, but I couldn't process the information. The last twenty-four hours had been filled with too many surprises. This one nearly knocked me off my feet.

"Francesco Donado," Valerie said wistfully.

My chin dropped. I gaped at her, but Valerie gazed into the distance like her memories were hovering at the far end of the terminal.

"He was my first assignment. God was he goth." She chuckled softly to herself. "I wouldn't have given the time of day to a guy like that in California." Valerie puffed up suddenly and looked at me. "I could have any guy back home." She snapped her fingers. "Like that."

I rolled my eyes.

"When my blood transfusion didn't have the desired effect, Melcher ordered me to become a vampire whore."

My jaw dropped. "But…" I couldn't finish. I didn't know what to say. Guess I shouldn't complain about being a hunter. Obviously, there were worse things. Maybe Noel wasn't as into Henry and Gavin as I thought. Maybe she'd been ordered to do whatever it took to get close to the enemy. The whole thing made me sicker than sick.

"What did Melcher want from Fane?"

Valerie flicked a strand of hair out of her face. "Names."

"Did you get any?"

"Some."

My heart knocked against my chest wall. "Is he in danger?"

Valerie snorted. "Fane's too valuable to kill. He's been around a long time, and he's traveled extensively. He knows a lot of vampires. I'm not the first informant Melcher tried to set on him." She gave her hair another toss, smiling wickedly. "The girl before couldn't get him to bite. They transferred her to Fairbanks."

"Janine?" My jaw dropped.

"Who? Anyway, I completed boot camp, enrolled at Denali High, and *snap*, hooked the elusive Fane Donado. He wasn't as hot as my exes back home, but the things he could do with his tongue…" Her grin widened.

She was trying to upset me with the tongue thing. From the way my jaw ached, I supposed it was working.

The flight agent announced they would be boarding soon. Valerie hoisted her purse over her shoulder and moved toward the line forming outside the jetway.

A sudden thought occurred to me. "So that's why you needed me to break up with Fane? You had orders to be with him."

Valerie smirked. "That was payback. No one breaks up with me. Not even a vampire."

The flight agent opened the door to the jetway. Passengers encroached around our space. At this point, I couldn't see the point in responding to Valerie's jibe. She was who she was—a backstabbing vixen to the end.

"Well, good luck to you." I didn't know what else to say.

"Yeah," Valerie said. "Watch your back."

I couldn't be sure if she meant in general or because of her. It didn't matter. The moment she headed down the jetway, she aligned herself with vampires.

I didn't stick around to watch Valerie's plane take off from the window. I didn't envy her. She wasn't headed for freedom but a life on the lam. A life of eternity. I couldn't understand the appeal of it. Live forever? What was the purpose? What was so special about life that made someone want to hold on to it indefinitely?

I wasn't going for dark or moody at the moment. It's just that life had ceased to bring me joy. Why prolong that?

I heaved a sigh and headed out of the terminal. I could use a breath of fresh air, even if it was drizzling. The mist turned to rain when I stepped outside, followed by falling slush. The overcast sky tinged the outdoors in a damp gray.

I walked across the parking lot, which was small like the airport.

It was thirteen miles to town. Too far to walk. I didn't want to get too far from the airport, anyway. My flight would board in a little over an hour. I stopped when I reached the sidewalk. I tried calling Dante, but it went to his voicemail. Where the hell was he?

I tried Noel next. Not like Valerie could stop me now. But Noel's phone went to voicemail, too.

My heart sped up. What if something had happened to them? Even if their vampire wasn't the right suspect, he was still a vampire, ergo dangerous.

I called my mom next and let her know when I was landing.

"Good. You're done then," she said.

Done? As though I'd ever be done.

It felt weird flying back home alone. I had an entire row to myself. This time I took the aisle seat. Didn't want to feel trapped or have someone from a full row nab the empty seat after takeoff. I don't think so!

I tried to look at UAA's class schedule again, but it was useless. I couldn't concentrate.

I lay across the seats thinking, "I won't be able to sleep but at least I can rest." Somehow, I managed to drift off. I was having one of those dreams where you feel yourself freefalling. I woke up with a jerk. The plane was descending.

I sat up and rubbed my eyes, then leaned over the seats and looked out the window. I saw mountains covered from top to bottom in snow. Back in familiar territory.

My mom wasn't waiting in the terminal or baggage claim. No surprise. Hopefully I wouldn't have to call her for a pick-up.

I yanked my duffle bag off the baggage carousel when it came around. The arctic wind blasted me the moment I stepped through the sliding doors to the sidewalk lining the arrivals lane. Mom's car was nowhere to be seen, but a black sedan waited out front.

The tinted window on the back door moved down and Melcher leaned forward. "Get in, Aurora."

I shot him a tight frown in response, hoisted my duffel bag further up my shoulder, and walked around to the passenger's side door.

Gee, thanks, Mom. Could have warned me.

"Are you taking me on base?" I asked after clicking my seatbelt shut.

"I'm taking you home, but first we're going to drive around a bit and talk." Melcher smiled. Since he always smiled, I had no way of telling if I should take it as a sign of reassurance or one of displeasure—as in I was in big trouble.

I hated how the stress crept into my consciousness. Melcher's the one who sent me off with a psychotic vampire and defective informant.

The driver put on his blinker and rolled slowly forward. From behind, all I could make out was the collar on his blazer and dark cropped hair.

I watched a man greet a woman as she emerged from baggage claim. She dropped her suitcase and threw her arms around him. Behind the reunited couple, a man helped take a teenage girl's bags off her hands, giving her a warm welcoming smile. Why couldn't I be any of these other people?

The driver eased out of the arrivals pick-up lane. He turned left at the first major intersection—the opposite direction of home. At least it wasn't the route to the base, either. I had no desire to discuss things in Melcher's office, even if it did seem slightly sadistic to meet with me in a moving vehicle given the nature of my accident.

Melcher folded his hands in his lap. I saw his jaw move as he readied himself to speak.

"Jared's a vampire," I said.

Melcher showed no emotion except to lower his head as if in silent prayer. "That is correct, Aurora. Jared is one of the damned, but he is atoning for his sins."

Melcher knew. Why wasn't I surprised? "By killing humans and vampires at will?" I cried out.

"Humans?" Melcher lifted his head. He studied me with green eyes.

I squeezed my three middle fingers so hard the tips turned red. "I think he attacked Valerie in California and who knows how many other recruits."

"Did you and Miss Ward discuss this?" Melcher asked.

"No, but someone attacked her, and then suddenly she's in Alaska undergoing training."

"And you assume Jared did this?"

"Did Jared recruit Valerie?" I asked back.

Melcher turned away. He cleared his throat softly. "That is a heavy accusation, Aurora."

"Yeah, well, I just witnessed him on a murderous rampage."

The driver took a sharp turn. I grabbed the door handle to keep from leaning toward Melcher. I looked out the window after the car straightened out. I knew this road. Mom, Dad, and I once biked it to get to the Coastal Trail. Eventually, we'd hit Point Woronzof Road. The last time I'd been out this way was with Fane.

This is where it had all ended.

It's where I'd gotten a glimpse of Fane the Vampire. Fane, the predator who chased girls through the woods. Fane, who would have bitten me if he hadn't been shocked to see bite marks across my skin after he ripped my scarf off.

But then he'd been so sweet afterward. He'd answered my questions and given me space. He said he'd never killed anyone, and I believed him. Even though he couldn't bite me, he still wanted to be with me.

I'd asked for time to think. He asked how much, and I countered with, "What do you mean how much time? You have all the time in the world."

"That doesn't make the seconds away from you go by any faster."

What happened to that guy? The nice one? Vampires seemed to have a bit of Dr. Jekyll and Mr. Hyde in them. Except in Jared's case. He was all Hyde.

"Jared was doing his job," Melcher answered evenly. "Something he told me you and Miss Ward failed to do."

That jerk!

"We were a little too busy defending ourselves to carry out Jared's command to execute an innocent girl."

Melcher started talking the moment I finished. "I assure you that Giselle Morrel is no innocent girl. Her killing spree has spanned the better part of two centuries, and now she remains on the loose."

Lovely. At least she hadn't seen our faces.

I straightened in my chair. "Maybe if you'd briefed us, we would have known what to expect. Better yet, maybe we wouldn't have freaked out if you'd told us Jared was a vampire and you were okay with that."

Melcher frowned. "Jared's status is classified. It appears he could have gone about things a little better, but if you had stuck to his plan, Giselle would have been put to rest and Miss Ward wouldn't have panicked and taken off."

Again, I supposed it should come as no surprise that Melcher didn't need to wait for me to arrive to have the full bloody scoop on what had gone down. Still, he'd better give me a chance to tell my version. Not that it looked like he cared much.

"So you've spoken to Jared?" I asked.

Melcher nodded once. "As soon as he woke up."

"I suppose you had him released."

"He's on his way back tonight."

I wrapped my arms around my chest tightly and stared out my window. The snow-covered trees and mountains across the inlet looked like a scene from a postcard.

Wish I wasn't here.

"How did you pull that one off?" We'd left Jared in a house full of bodies practically holding a smoking gun.

Melcher glanced at me briefly. "I told the police what they needed to hear. Jared is an undercover agent who spent the last year tracking down a family with terrorist ties. He showed up to investigate and they opened fire. He had no choice. The girl got away."

How convenient—for Jared. "I'm afraid of him," I admitted.

Melcher did the head bob again. "You should be. He's one of the infected but a necessary evil all the same. Jared started out as my top informant. He knows vampires from centuries back—all around the world. Even with the resources I have at my fingertips, I could never come close to identifying and tracking the vampires Jared has led me to. After he proved his loyalty to this unit, I promoted him to top recruiter."

My head snapped in Melcher's direction. "And it's never struck you as odd that *accidents* just happen to occur the moment he's around?"

"Accidents happen all the time," Melcher said calmly. "The world works in mysterious ways."

In other words, Melcher had granted Jared carte blanche. I glared.

"I'll look into it," he said. "I'll even put Jared on suspension

179

while I do. I hold him responsible for last night's failures. As team leader, it was his duty to get the job done and return with every member of his team."

"What about Valerie?" I asked.

"I know that she took flight sixty-two to Sea-Tac International, which landed…" Melcher checked his wristwatch. "Twenty minutes ago. This isn't the first time a member of this unit panicked. She'll come back on her own or I'll send an escort. Miss Ward knows the rules."

That's just the thing. I was pretty sure Valerie was playing by her own rules now.

I leaned forward in my seat, feeling anxious for the driver to turn the car around and take me home. A shower would be nice. So would sleep. If I actually could sleep knowing Jared was on his way back.

"Have you called Dante and Noel back to town?" I asked.

"Dante and Miss Harper have come across some interesting information. I'm keeping them on stakeout for the time being."

I felt my shoulders sag. I wanted people I could talk to. I wanted my friends back.

"What about Mike?" I asked.

Melcher gave me the same blank look Jared had. This was really starting to unnerve me. "Jared claims he found Crist's cross at the Morrel house, but he didn't find any link to Mike."

"The case is closed, Aurora," Melcher said in one of his most clipped tones. "It was a double homicide and justice has been served."

"But how are they linked? The last time I saw Mike he was at Marcus's party."

Melcher sighed. "I am not at liberty to discuss the details,

Aurora, but it is likely Agent Crist was patrolling around Marcus's townhouse the night of the party."

I relaxed my arms and fidgeted with my fingers in my lap. "Did she do that often? Go out on patrol? I didn't think she was a field agent."

"I am not at liberty to discuss Agent Crist's involvement in our unit, Aurora," he repeated. "Our work has its dangers. It's one of the greatest duties on the planet. At the end of the day, Agent Crist was privileged to sacrifice her life in the line of duty."

I tapped my leg in agitation. And Mike? What about him? I doubted he'd consider it a privilege to die for no good reason before he got a chance to live his life.

According to Melcher, justice had been served. I still couldn't swallow it. Jared had said nothing about Crist or Mike when confronting Henriette and Andre. Wouldn't he have mentioned it? Maybe whatever past hang-ups they had were more important in the eleventh hour than two more dead bodies.

I stopped tapping my leg. "Jared knew the Morrel's," I said. "They called him Xavier. He used to be married to Henriette."

"How do you know this?"

"I overheard them talking."

Melcher muttered something under his breath. His next words were as calm as ever. "Since you are already aware of Jared's connection to the Morrel family, there is no harm in filling you in on a few details. I feel at this point it would be worse not to."

Okay, so fill me in. I urged Melcher with my eyes.

He took a deep breath that came out like a sigh.

"Back in the eighteen hundreds, Jared was a vampire in Paris. His name back then was Xavier. Henriette posed as his wife, Etienne and Giselle as their children, and Andre as Xavier's brother. They were body snatchers."

"Body snatchers?"

Melcher nodded. "Grave robbers. They dug up fresh corpses and sold them to medical schools for dissection."

I wrinkled my nose.

"A body snatcher could make over a thousand francs in a single night. A small fortune back then. But the Morrel's didn't stop at corpses. In their greed, they began murdering people then selling their bodies for even more profit."

I shivered involuntarily.

"This practice was known as burking, named after the Irishman and murderer William Burke. Victims were smothered and suffocated, resulting in a speedy death with no signs of violence. This also produced the freshest possible corpse. In an era without refrigeration, you can begin to understand how a steady supply of fresh corpses was in high demand among the medical community."

Yep, sounded like Jared all right. There it was again, that sick feeling in the pit of my stomach.

Melcher had a similar look of distaste on his face. "Xavier was caught and taken to La Force prison to await trial."

"What happened?" I asked, leaning forward.

"There was a cholera outbreak. Most of the prisoners died. Xavier did not."

"And then?"

"He was released."

I stared at Melcher, but he didn't continue.

He could be really maddening at times—like *all* the time! He leaned forward and caught the eye of the driver in the rearview mirror. Melcher made a circular motion with his finger. The driver turned into the parking lot at Point Woronzof and looped around. "I'll take you home now," he said.

"Do I need to worry about Jared?"

"Once Jared has been debriefed I am sending him to the lower forty-eight. You have nothing to worry about, Aurora. I can terminate Jared at any time, and he knows it."

What? Like some kind of kill switch in his brain? It wouldn't surprise me. I bet Jared loved that. Maybe Melcher was the one who should watch his back.

"If you're up for it, you can go to school tomorrow." He flashed me a smile.

I wanted to graduate and all, but I would be lying if I said I wasn't dreading my return to West with Noel gone and Mike's letterman jacket still in my locker.

Maybe I could skip going to my locker the rest of the week. I only had two days to get through. I could make it.

"Aside from letting Giselle go, I want you to know you did well, Aurora. You didn't panic. You came home, and that says a lot about your commitment to the program. That is why I am happy to tell you that you've been approved for summer training once the school year ends. You'll even get to go out of state."

Did he really expect me to jump for joy over spending my summer stuck at boot camp? "Is this mandatory?"

"It's not only mandatory, but it's also a step up to official agent status. It also means you'll be eligible to mentor new recruits after you have a few more missions under your belt."

Just how many young AB-negative people did they antici-pate biting the dust each year? Is that why Jared was being sent away? To speed up the recruiting process?

I narrowed my eyes, studying Melcher's unblemished face.

Did he believe in the cause enough to actually hurt young people in order to get them in the program?

Melcher kept smiling. "Don't worry. You'll do great."

"Where are you sending me?"

"I can't tell you that until it's time to go."

"Of course not," I said with a grumble.

"And we'll have you back in plenty of time to start your college classes." Melcher leaned toward me. "You did still want to go to college, didn't you, Aurora?"

"Yes."

He sat back. "Good."

We drove back in relative silence. I turned my head away from Melcher and stared out my window. My breath spread across the glass in a fog that lingered then disappeared.

"What if Valerie doesn't come back?" I asked while we waited for traffic to pass before turning onto my road. I glanced at Melcher. Not that I needed to. I could see the smile on his face in my mind before my eyes ever reached him.

"If she doesn't come back, we'll bring her back."

I just hoped that wasn't why Jared was headed to the lower forty-eight. I wouldn't wish him on anybody. Not even Valerie.

As soon as Melcher dropped me off, I sent her a quick text. I didn't know why, and I didn't know if she'd even get it, but it was something I had to do.

Aurora: Melcher knows which flight you're on.

17

IT'S COMPLICATED

I WOKE UP LATE THURSDAY. WELL, to hell with school. One more day wasn't going to make a difference. As soon as I saw the time on my digital clock, I stuffed my head under my pillow. Third period could go on without me.

I bit the bullet Friday and went to school. I hadn't made it past third period when one of Mike's friends got in my face and yelled, "What happened to Mike? He said he was meeting you at a party and then he ended up dead!"

I cowered at the accusation in his voice. Me, Aurora Sky, vampire hunter let a high school boy intimidate her in the hallway.

"I'm so sorry," I stammered. "I don't know what happened."

"Well, he's dead because of you." Such hatred in those eyes. Boy did he know how to make an exit. He said his lines and left, leaving them to linger in my brain like a scar I was stuck living with for the rest of my life.

People in the hallway stared. Let them. This wasn't my high school. I had no friends here. I had no life. Just passing through.

I couldn't wait to get my damn diploma and get out.

At the end of the day, I waited until the school emptied out to open my locker. I swear that the small metal enclosure had become permeated with Mike's scent. I yanked his letterman jacket off the hook in the far back and wadded it into my hands.

Halfway down the hall, I saw a big plastic wastebasket. I clutched the jacket to my chest and then dropped it the moment I stood over the trash bin. I looked over my shoulder. Why did it feel as though I was disposing of a body?

Outside, my mom waited at the curbside for a change. I got into the car and yanked the door closed behind me. "How was school?" she asked.

"Sucky," I said, staring out the front windshield.

"At least it's the weekend."

Yeah, so? I kept staring out the window. Mom did her loop around Benson Boulevard. "Taco Bell again?" I asked.

"I have a lot to deal with right now," she said defensively. Her voice went back to normal when she rolled down her window and ordered a taco salad, Mexican pizza, and nachos. "What would you like?" she asked in her even voice.

"I'm not hungry."

"You need to eat something."

"Maybe I should drink blood instead." Mom wasn't the only one whose mood was slipping. I felt myself going to a dark place. I'd been there before, and it never did me any good.

Mom added a bean burrito and a pink lemonade freeze to the order. Right, 'cause I really wanted to drink something with the word "freeze" in it.

Once we were home, I changed into my running gear. Instead of going through the woods, I ran down the street to the bike trail across the road. I had my earbuds in but no music playing. I jogged up to the corner where I'd had my accident and then paced along the curve, staring at it from every angle.

I could still see it in my head: the frosted trees along the road, the oncoming vehicle, my dashboard, the windshield…

186

then nothing.

I pictured Jared driving along a couple of seconds later, happy to see another person about to lose her humanity.

"Another One Bites the Dust" by Queen started spinning through my mind.

I ripped my earbuds out, but it kept going. It was all in my head.

Mom had *The Vampire Diaries* on when I returned home. The pink lemonade sat on the kitchen counter where she'd left it, the slush slowly turning to liquid, condensation dripping down the side to form a wet ring. I took a shower, blew my hair dry, and stuck my earbuds in, and listened to music while carefully applying makeup. Nothing too heavy-duty. Just a bit of eyeliner, shadow, mascara, and lipstick. I left Dante's bear claw in the top drawer of my nightstand.

I dialed Marcus and stared at my phone for several minutes before hitting send.

"Black beauty," he answered.

I took a steadying breath. "Hi, Marcus. You wouldn't happen to be throwing a party tonight?"

Marcus chuckled then stopped. "It's Friday."

I'm pretty sure that meant, *what do you think?* "Great, so you don't mind if I show up?"

"Are you coming alone?"

Oh God, I didn't want to have to talk about Mike. Marcus probably already had his hopes up. If I told him Mike had died after stopping by, he might take it as a personal affront again and try to hunt down the offender. My lips twitched. It would serve Jared right if Marcus went after him. Jared had tried to pin it on the party host, after all. If anyone could take on Jared, I'd put money on Marcus. He'd killed Renard for abducting a guest. Jared had actually *killed* a guest—Andre.

"Yes." But I didn't plan on being alone for long.

Mom wasn't too happy when I told her I'd arranged for an uber to pick me up so that I could go "check on something for work."

Or when I told her not to wait up.

I called Fane on the ride over. I didn't even hesitate. Valerie was right. It was time to wear the proverbial thong. I'm sure this isn't what she had in mind, but she'd skipped town and taken her threats right along with her. Not that it mattered anymore. Not if Melcher already knew about Fane and wanted him alive for information. Like Jared. I doubted Fane would work for Team Vampire Hunter if Melcher approached him. I'd just have to hope Melcher never gave him an ultimatum.

"Aurora Sky," Fane answered in his mocking tone.

"Hello, Fane," I replied back. "I'm just on my way to Marcus's. It would be great to see you again. I so enjoyed our last meet-up."

"Are you drunk?" Fane asked suddenly, his voice changing.

"No, but I will be," I said, and hung up. I turned my phone off before dropping it inside my purse.

If Melcher could fraternize with vampires and bend the rules, so could I.

I threw my arms around Marcus as soon as I entered the palace. He let out a deep laugh and patted my shoulder. "Rough week, my pet?"

I nodded. "You can't begin to imagine."

"Come," he said, taking my arm. He escorted me into the kitchen, which had quite the gathering.

I hesitated but Marcus kept pulling. None of the faces looked familiar. There were a couple of teenagers and some older twenty-somethings. Everyone looked clean-cut and casual chic.

"Allow me to present Aurora Sky," Marcus announced.

I hoped my lips were smiling. They had a tendency to grimace all on their own when I felt uncomfortable. Luckily, everyone in the group introduced themselves, though I forgot each name the moment a new one entered my ears.

"Aurora is a student at West," Marcus continued. "She wants to relax after a long week."

"Relax? It's Friday night!" someone said.

I found myself laughing with everyone else. Probably just nerves.

"Will you drink a whiskey with us, Aurora?" a guy to the right of me asked.

"That sounds perfect. Thank you."

The boy turned to Marcus. "Gorgeous and polite. Where did you find her, Marcus?"

My face heated at being called gorgeous.

Marcus chuckled. "She found me."

"Lucky man."

"Tell that to Francesco," Marcus said. He left my side and joined a young man in the corner who began giggling the moment Marcus started speaking in his ear.

The boy poured two shots of whiskey and handed one to me. "Then I suppose we'll only be drinking whiskey together," he said, lifting his glass.

I hit my glass against his, careful not to spill.

Don't do it, Aurora. Not again. It never leads to anything good.

I threw back the glass and coughed.

The boy's eyes widened slightly at how fast I downed it. He chuckled then drank his in one fluid motion before refilling both our glasses. "What do you think?" he asked.

"It's disgusting."

He laughed and handed me the full shot.

"I like the way it burns, though," I said. Much better than pouring freezing slush down my throat.

I let the whiskey slip down my throat slowly this time.

Conversations resumed around us. It made me feel better now that I wasn't the focal point.

"What was your name again?" I asked the boy.

He grinned. "Thomas. You can call me Tom."

"It's nice to meet you, Tom."

Tom lifted the whiskey bottle and raised a brow. I nodded. "Thanks." I felt more relaxed with each sip. I did a lot better one on one than in bigger groups, and Tom seemed nice.

"How long have you and Fane been together?" he asked after we'd done another shot.

I felt warm inside. It felt good. I leaned against the counter. There were only two other people who'd lingered behind and that felt good, too. More room to breathe.

"Not long," I said, running my hand along the countertop.

Tom watched my fingers as I stroked the smooth black granite. "It's not like Francesco to leave his woman unattended."

"Yeah? Well, our relationship is complicated."

Tom looked me up and down, a glint in his eyes. "Giving Francesco a run for his money, are you?"

For some reason that made me laugh. Once I started it was hard to stop.

Oh yes. I was giving him a run for his money all right. The vampire and the vampire hunter. I began laughing harder.

Tom laughed too, thank God, so I didn't look like a madwoman laughing on my own. "Can I get you a glass of water?" he asked when we'd regained our composure.

"No thanks," I said, leaning more weight into the counter. "I feel good. Do you go to school, Tom?"

"Nah," he said with a wide grin. "I don't get nostalgic like some of these other vamps. High school sucked. Why would I go back for more?"

"That deserves a toast," I said, grabbing the whiskey bottle. I filled Tom's glass too quickly and ended up spilling on the counter.

"Don't worry about it," he said.

I stopped halfway on my glass to avoid a second spill. I lifted my shot. "To life after high school."

"The only kind of life," Tom said.

I managed not to spill as we clinked glasses.

"We should all go out some time," Tom said after he finished his shot. "Movie night or something. Double date."

Double date? I nearly snorted whiskey out of my nose. This felt surreal.

"Got any friends interested in meeting a polite young man?"

"My friends are in the dark about all this," I said. Better than admitting to being a loner. "Except Noel Harper. Have you met her?"

"Yes, I have. She's sweet on Gavin." Tom laughed. "Maybe I should enroll in high school."

"Forget that," I said. "Stick to your guns."

Tom poured us each another shot. I left mine on the counter. I felt warm and good-humored at the moment, and I wanted to keep it that way.

"What about you, Aurora? What do you have planned for life after high school?"

"College." Tom laughed with me.

"College and drinking?" he asked, raising a brow.

I wavered slightly. Definitely feeling the whiskey. I hoped I hadn't gone too far. "College and dancing. I love dancing. How come there's no dancing at any of these parties?"

Tom's eyes lit up. "You're absolutely right. There should be dancing! Come on." He grabbed my hand and led me to the living room. I stopped when Tom stopped on the edge of the sunken living room. "Marcus, Aurora and I want to dance."

Marcus turned away from the young man he'd been conversing with. I thought he'd show annoyance, but his lips lifted into a full grin. He clapped his hands twice. "Dancing! Excellent idea!" Marcus grabbed a remote off a speaker in the corner of the room. A moment later, "Ring My Bell" by Anita Ward began playing.

"Where's the disco ball?" someone yelled.

"Bedroom," Marcus answered.

We all laughed. Tom took my hand, and together we stepped down to the living room. The furniture and statues made it challenging, but we managed to groove in place, lifting our arms in unison to ring our "bells." Tom moved side to side with a goofy smile. It made me laugh.

I felt my limbs begin to loosen up.

A guy next to us snapped along with the beat. Just about everyone had started dancing. The whole room and everyone in it was rocking. I cranked my arm in the air.

Smiling, laughing, dancing—this is what I needed, not drinking.

I shimmied in front of Tom. He laughed and shook his arms in return.

"I think I was born in the wrong era," I said. I mean, how could anyone not enjoy themselves with disco blaring from the speakers?

The song ended too soon. "YMCA" by the Village People shot out of the speakers. The room erupted in laughter.

"Oh my God," I said.

Tom shook his head, his smile reaching all the way to his eyes. "Vampires."

"My party, my music," Marcus yelled over the singing.

I shrugged and began doing the YMCA. The Bee Gees "Stayin' Alive" cranked through the living room of the palace when Fane walked in and took in the scene. Marcus had gone into full John Travolta *Saturday Night Fever* moves. Fane looked more like John Travolta from *Grease* in his black jeans, black tee, and black leather jacket—and a sly smile on his lips. Somehow, I doubted he'd start shaking his ass and grabbing his crotch.

Fane did remove his jacket in one smooth motion and tossed it aside. It landed on the back of a chair. Way smoother than Travolta.

Fane walked up to Tom and me. Before I could say anything, he jutted his chin toward Marcus. "Now there's a sight I haven't seen in a long time."

"Not long enough," Tom said.

The guys laughed, but the way Fane looked Tom up and down was far from friendly. He glanced at me then back at Tom.

Tom stopped dancing. "Don't worry, Francesco. I didn't lay a finger—or tooth—on her." Tom shot him a cocky grin.

Fane looked at Tom with his own bemused smile. "Lucky for you." Fane turned to me. "Now that I'm here, what do you say we go somewhere a little less seventies?" He glanced at the spiral staircase leading to the rooms above.

"I'm all yours," I said in a flirtatious voice.

"Tom, thank you for the drink and dance."

"My pleasure," he said. "Let me know if you ever want to

hang out. Francesco has my number."

"Sure, why don't I give you Tom's number," Fane said under his breath as we walked away. "Shmuck."

I glanced over my shoulder. "I thought he was nice."

"Thomas? Thinks he's James Cagney."

I frowned. "Who?"

"James Cagney," Fane repeated impatiently. "American film legend." He made a sound of disgust in the back of his throat. "God, I'm getting old."

I chuckled softly. "No, actually, you aren't."

"Thinks he's James Dean," Fane tried again.

"*Ah*, Rebel Without a Cause."

"Exactly."

"What movies was the other James guy in?"

Fane's lips twisted in thought. I loved those lips. "The Public Enemy. Angels with Dirty Faces. Love Me or Leave Me. Yankee Doodle Dandy."

"Nope," I said, shaking my head. "Didn't see any of those in film class."

"Film class?"

"Yeah, I'm taking it with Noel."

Fane's lips curved. "I should tell Joss. It might motivate him to give high school a try." He stretched his hand out for me to go up the staircase first.

I stopped abruptly, causing Fane to bump into me. I turned around, momentarily breathless when I found myself against his chest. "I need another drink." All that dancing had started sobering me up. I needed at least three more shots. I needed to be able to blame the alcohol if something happened between us. Something that involved tongues not teeth.

18

STEP THREE

"**I** SEE YOU'RE BACK IN SELF-DESTRUCT mode," Fane said, staring at my throat when I threw back my first shot of whiskey.

"I'm just having fun. Don't I deserve to have fun?" I smacked the glass onto the granite countertop.

Gloria Gaynor began singing "I Will Survive" from the living room. Lately, I felt like every song on the planet had been written specifically to mock my life. Aurora Sky: The Musical. One big bloody harmonic extravaganza.

Fane's gaze moved to my eyes. He stared. Okay, that wasn't unnerving. "Kill any vampires while you were away?" he finally asked.

"Actually, I saved one." Never mind that I'd probably live to regret it. If Giselle Morrel sniffed out any clue as to my involvement in her family's death I could have another Renard on my hands. Angry vampire hunting me down in Anchorage. My favorite kind. At least she didn't look that intimidating. I'd like to think I could take on a skinny blonde who collected stuffed animals and fairy figurines. Then again there'd been swords on her wall. Hmm.

"So now you've been transferred to vampire search and rescue?" Fane asked in a mocking tone.

I narrowed my eyes.

"Didn't think so," Fane said.

I poured myself another whiskey. "Want one?"

"Whiskey isn't my liquid of choice."

"Right," I said, rolling my eyes. "You prefer blood."

"Wine, actually." He backed against the counter and folded his arms low over his chest. I could feel Fane watching my eyes as I stared at the outline of his abs. He might have questionable hair, but Fane's abs were rock solid and utterly dreamy in the dark. Not that I'd gotten a good feel recently.

"I owned a vineyard in France for many years," he continued. "Another life."

My hand stilled as I reached for the whiskey bottle. I recalled what Valerie had said about Fane having contacts all around the world. Had he known the Morrels back then? I had to force myself not to dig for more. *Not an informant. Not my problem.* Instead, I asked, "If you enjoyed it so much, why did you leave?"

Fane stared at me a moment before answering. "It is one thing to spend a lifetime in the same place, another to spend an eternity."

"So you won't stay in Alaska?" My chest suddenly ached.

"Forever?" Fane chuckled. "I never stay in the same place for more than fifty years. Sometimes less than five."

"And your plan is to what, keep going from city to city, country to country?"

Fane's eyes met mine. "It's worked out so far."

I reached for the whiskey bottle, but Fane grabbed it first. He moved away from the counter faster than I could've anticipated. "Hey."

He opened a cupboard and shoved the bottle inside. Then he pulled out a large glass and filled it with water from the tap. "Drink this," he said, handing it to me.

Something about the way he said it made me drink. Halfway through the water, I set the glass down. "I feel sick." My

196

organs had started coiling in on themselves, or maybe the dancing, drinking, and water had all mixed together and reacted violently. I placed a hand on my abdomen.

"You should drink the rest of the water," Fane said calmly.

I made a face. "If I drink any more water I'm going to hurl."

"Good. You'll feel better."

I narrowed my eyes. "Do you enjoy watching me suffer?"

"Not at all." He sounded sincere. If I hadn't felt so sick all of a sudden, I would have wanted to kiss him. How humiliating. This wasn't part of the plan. The plan was to loosen up and feel sexy.

It hadn't worked with Scott Stevens, and it was failing dismally with Fane. I should have known better.

I eyed the glass of water. Even the thought of another sip caused my stomach to protest. I brought this on myself.

I grabbed the glass suddenly and chugged down the remaining water. My stomach rolled as though riding the waves of a storm.

I set the empty glass down shakily. "I'll be right back." I started toward the living room.

"There's one to the left of the front door," Fane said.

"Thank you," I said.

I hurried to the front entrance and shut myself inside the bathroom. I lifted the toilet seat, chanting in my head, *never again, never again, never again*. My stomach held on stubbornly. At this point, I felt so miserable I just wanted to get it over with. Saliva gathered in my throat. I spit into the toilet. It foamed on the surface of the water.

"How romantic," I said, and nearly burst into laughter.

There is no worse feeling than throwing up, except maybe the agony your stomach puts you through before you do it.

At some point you're begging for it to be over, no matter

what you have to go through to get to the other side.

Finally, my stomach let go. Luckily I found a bottle of mouth-wash in the cabinet below the sink. I rinsed my mouth, splashed water on my face, and dabbed my cheeks and forehead dry.

The face in the mirror only looked half-human, but I felt as though I'd returned to the land of the living.

Fane had his jacket on when I returned to the kitchen. If it had been any other guy I might have been humiliated, but this was Fane. We'd been together. We'd made out. Not for very long, but long enough to create something of a familiar bond between us—no matter how much he pulled back.

"Want to get out of here?" he asked.

"Yeah."

We didn't bother saying goodbye. I'm sure Marcus and the crew would survive without us. Ha, ha.

"How did you get here?" Fane asked when we stepped outside.

"Uber."

"Where's Noel?"

"I'm not at liberty to say." Right, so I totally lifted that line from Melcher.

"Noel trusts me, unlike you," Fane said, his words hard.

Ah, yes. Noel had spilled our little secret in a moment of panic, not that I wasn't grateful. If Noel hadn't shown up with Fane I would have bled to death after being gutted by Renard's evil crony.

But I had to admit, it was interesting how Noel's role of informant went both ways. Had she told Henry or Gavin? If Gavin didn't know already, I'm sure Valerie would fill him in. I didn't like the thought of that. Pretty soon every bloodsucker in the state would be onto us, and I wouldn't be able to cross the street without looking over my shoulder. Fine, so long as they all knew I hadn't signed up for this!

I followed Fane to his car, The Tank. After grabbing the handle on the passenger's side, I stopped and looked over the hood at Fane. "Noel panicked."

Fane shot me a lazy smile. "Noel knew exactly what she was doing."

I frowned and lowered myself inside the car. A feeling of nostalgia settled into the pit of my stomach as I buckled myself into the worn seat. "I see The Tank's still running."

Fane patted the dashboard and grinned. "She's managed to keep up with me so far."

It tugged at my heartstrings to see Fane flash one of his real smiles. His full upper lip looked so sexy when he did. When he smiled like that he came to life. He didn't sparkle (are you kidding me?), but he had this glow about him.

I stared at his slim, white fingers as he turned the keys in the ignition. Even now, the sound of a car starting caused a jolt of panic, but it no longer made me reach for the vehicle's handlebar.

Fane stared out the windshield as he asked, "Where to?"

"Surprise me."

He grinned and put the car in drive. Fane headed toward home but passed my exit. He kept going south on the highway. His house then? That's what it looked like from the exit he took, but he passed his neighborhood. Denali High loomed in the distance. That feeling of nostalgia crept back inside me.

We approached the empty parking lot, lit from above by all the high-powered lights. The lot had been plowed, the snow pushed to the sides in hill-shaped mounds, forming walls on all four sides of the parking lot. It reminded me of a hockey rink.

Fane pulled in and put the car in park. We idled in the parking lot, facing the school.

"Do you miss it?" Fane asked softly.

"Why would I?"

"Someday you might." He held the steering wheel, even though we were parked. He kept staring straight ahead. Did he want a picture or something? It was a high school, not a castle.

Finally, he let go of the wheel and leaned back. "Going to school, hanging out with people, it helps me hold onto my humanity. I've seen a lot of my kind lose that. I had my life stolen from me, but I won't give up my humanity."

I tried to think of a response worthy of what he'd just said, but none of my thoughts seemed up to the task, so I remained quiet until the silence got the better of me. "Why did you bring me here?"

Fane turned to me and smiled. "Auto rehabilitation. We covered step one and step two, but we never made it to step three."

Speaking of genuine smiles, it had been so long since I'd truly smiled it made my jaw ache. I covered my mouth with my hand. "Oh my gosh."

"You didn't think I'd forget, did you?" Fane asked. "You've had plenty of time to practice step one."

Step one: Get inside the car.

Fane smiled when he saw my eyes on his lips. I was already thinking of step two: kissing. *"The surest way to get over a car phobia is by creating positive associations,"* Fane had told me.

My heart began thumping against my chest. It took all of my willpower not to wet my lips.

We'd had some epic make out sessions in this car.

I'd wanted more than kisses. Fane wasn't the only one who

felt like he'd lost his chance.

"What's step three?" I asked, hoping my breath was steady.

Fane shot me a sly grin as though he'd known what I was thinking all along.

"Step three: drive the car."

19

I SAT UP STRAIGHT IN MY seat. "Are you crazy?" The thought of driving still terrified me—as in cold sweats and mass panic.

Fane turned to me, resting an arm on the steering wheel. "Just around the parking lot. No one's here, Aurora. And you can go as slow as you want. Five miles per hour if that's what you're comfortable with."

I stared at the steering wheel. He made it sound so easy. Sweat gathered under my arms and I shivered. "I'm not ready."

"The longer you wait, the harder it gets. Take the next step. Joss never got over his death and look how he turned out."

My head snapped up. "Are you comparing me to Joss?" Fane's roommate only happened to be the most sullen vampire I'd ever met. He chuckled in reply.

I surveyed the parking lot through the windshield. Patches of flattened snow gripped the pavement, but I couldn't make out any ice. "Fine," I said, unbuckling my belt. "I can drive from one end of the parking lot to the other if it will make you happy."

"It's not for me," Fane answered with that same infuriating smile.

I scooted to the middle seat and shot Fane a pointed look. He grinned and opened the driver's door. As soon as he stepped out, I settled into his place. He walked around the front of the car.

After I clicked my seatbelt in, I heard Fane chuckle again. Ignoring him, I pressed my foot down on the brake. I felt proud of the way I put the car in drive without hesitation. But as soon as I had it in drive, I froze. I pressed my foot firmly on the brake, and I jammed down so hard my leg began to tire. As I reached to put the car back into park, Fane touched my shoulder gently. "Aurora, let go."

I took in a deep breath and nodded.

I returned my right hand to the steering wheel and squeezed. Slowly, I lifted my foot off the brake. It stayed in place, and I laughed with relief.

Fane chuckled. "She's a tank, remember? You gotta give her gas."

"Uh-huh." I felt much better. I lowered my right foot slowly to the gas pedal, hovering right above. My heel touched the floor. I rested it there. Much more comfortable. Then slowly, I lowered the ball of my foot to the pedal. I barely touched it the first time. The car didn't move. I laughed again. Nerves.

Fane said nothing as I hesitated each time I came close to pressing down. That's the great thing about vampires. They have all the time in the world.

I took in another breath and straightened in my seat. Eyes on the parking lot. "All clear. All mine. No one but me. No big deal. Not at all. I can do this. I can totally do this."

Fane played the gentleman and didn't comment as I spoke aloud.

I stared at the snowbank at the far end of the parking lot. Even if I somehow panicked and pressed down too hard, there would be a nice white mound at the end to cushion the blow. What was there to be afraid of? "Nothing but fear itself," I whispered.

I pressed the gas pedal gently. The car moved forward. I took my foot off the pedal, and it rolled to a stop. A nervous laugh ripped through my lips. Fane remained silent.

I pressed down again and again, and the car moved forward. I pressed down harder. It wasn't fast. My eyes were on the pavement, not the speedometer, but we couldn't have been going over ten miles an hour.

A sense of exhilaration built inside my chest. I braked gently in front of the snow bank and put the car in park.

Fane and I sat staring at the wall of snow. I didn't care about the big grin on my face.

"See?" Fane said. "Like riding a bike."

"Yeah," I said, a bit breathless. "Well, if I ever need to get to one end of a parking lot to the other I'll be fine."

Fane laughed. "Now that you've made it from one end to the other, how about turning her around and making a full circle?"

I shook my head.

"No?" I heard Fane ask beside me.

"That's enough auto rehabilitation for today."

"Very well," Fane said. "I'll drive you home."

"No."

I was staring straight ahead into the snowbank so I didn't see Fane's expression, but I could see that he'd turned his head to look at me.

"You want to give it another go?"

If only he knew. "I don't want you to drive me home."

The only sound in the car came through the air vents. I kept my eyes forward, feeling suddenly shy. What happened to badass Aurora? The one who straddled Fane on the public bus? The one who pushed him back on the bench of this car and gyrated against his body while slipping him the tongue?

And what about Fane? Where was the tough talker now? He had to go and ruin things by being nice.

The silence was unbearable. The sound of my seatbelt when I unclicked it amplified in the quiet of the car. I paused a moment then scooted toward Fane. No turning back. Someone had to take the reins.

"Aurora." His voice stopped me.

"Yes?" I asked innocently. I turned and faced him.

"Not a good idea."

I frowned. "Why not?"

"You're a vampire hunter."

"I'm not hunting you."

"Do you have your dagger on you?"

Did he really expect me to hang out in a house full of vampires without one? "Of course I have my dagger on me."

Fane stared out the windshield at Denali High with all its interconnecting hallways. "If you can't trust me, this can't work."

"I don't trust anyone right now." I mean, take Melcher. I didn't trust him one iota. And he wasn't even a vampire.

"All the more reason why this is a bad idea."

"Then why did you bring me here?" I asked, waving a hand in the direction of my old high school. "Why are you picking up where we left off?"

"I'm trying to help you move on."

I sucked in a breath. Fane might as well have punched me in the chest.

"What we had was good," Fane continued. "Let's not ruin that."

Tears slipped down my cheeks. It happened so fast I never felt the moisture gathering in my eyes.

Why did my heart have to get all gushy over a vampire? If

it broke apart it was my own damn fault. Vampire hunter, Aurora. Vampire *hunter*, not *lover*. God, I felt like such a fool.

I put my face in my hands.

"Aurora?"

"Just take me home." There was no masking the tears in my voice now.

I heard Fane move toward me then stop, hesitate, and pull back. The car door opened and closed. I took that opportunity to hurry and move over. I didn't want to be anywhere near Fane when he opened the driver's door.

He got inside the car. "If anything happened between us, you know you'd regret it in the morning."

I sucked air in through my nose and blinked rapidly. "You're the one who would regret it, not me, Fane. I'm not the one hung up on vampires. You're the one who has a problem with me!" I felt angrier as the words came out. "The moment you found out what really happened after my accident you treated me like I had the plague."

His lips twitched slightly.

"You think that's funny?" I demanded.

He straightened. Eyes narrowed. "There's nothing amusing about the plague."

Right, probably not the best analogy. It was possible Fane had actually caught the plague and now had to live with it the rest of his life. I wondered what kind of predominant symptoms vampires with the plague displayed. Maybe not the best time to ponder.

"I've never regretted our time together," I said.

"Haven't you?" Fane's words sounded like ice.

"When I broke up with you I was confused and scared for your safety."

"My safety?" Fane said with disbelief.

"There's an entire unit of the government that exists to hunt down and kill people like you."

Fane turned to me. "Then I guess it's a good thing I have someone on the inside to look out for me."

I swallowed. "There's only so much I can do."

"At least you don't want to stake me." He faced forward again.

Before I could answer, he put the car in reverse and made a sharp backward U-turn. We faced the entrance. How many times had I driven out of this lot, happy to have completed another day in so many leading up to graduation?

The emptiness of the school grounds seeped deep inside me. I would still graduate, only not with my original class. The students at Denali High had felt as familiar to me as family not so long ago. Now I was the new loner girl who had gotten a boy killed at my new high school. The tears pooled in my eyes again. I blinked rapidly. Better to wait and torture myself with these thoughts later inside my room with a box of tissues by my side. I wasn't going to humiliate myself in front of Fane twice in one night.

We drove in silence the rest of the way. As Fane drove up my hill, he half-heartedly asked, "How are things at home?" He was only being polite. That's all. I could hear it in his voice.

"Fine," I said.

"Good."

I figured I'd leap out of the car the moment Fane came to a stop in my driveway, but I didn't. I sat staring at the dark house the way I'd stared at my old high school. "I asked my mom if I could move into my own apartment."

"I can't imagine she liked that."

"It doesn't matter. In another couple of months, I can start making my own decisions." I reached for the door handle.

Fane stopped me by putting his hand on my thigh. "Aurora." My heart responded with erratic beats. "It's not that I don't want to. Far from it. But deep down I know you're not ready to cross that line."

I pulled my leg away. "Good night, Fane." I hurried out of the car. I didn't want to hear another word from his mouth. I focused on reaching the front door.

Once inside, I went straight to my room, curled into bed fully clothed, and cried myself to sleep.

20

TASTINGS

Dante FINALLY CALLED LATE SUNDAY night. So late I'd already brushed my teeth and gotten into bed to rest up before a full week back at Hell High.

"Finally," I said in place of "hello."

"I'm back, baby!" Dante said.

I propped my pillow against the headboard and leaned against it. "Melcher said there was some activity in Fairbanks?"

"We went panning and came up with gold," Dante said with barely contained excitement.

"Did it have anything to do with the death of Crist or Mike?"

"Melcher said you all solved that," he said. His voice dropped an octave. "I loved your last text, by the way. Almost as much as the other ones. Humor is highly undervalued in our line of work."

So he thought I was joking, did he? "I wasn't kidding."

"Really?" Dante didn't sound alarmed in the least.

"Yeah, really. Jared tried to kill Valerie and me, and now she's taken off."

The line was silent a moment before Dante said, "I bet she tries for France. She's got that French chic thing going on."

Not to mention the attitude. "Hopefully when the agents catch up to her they'll be as lenient as they were with you."

Dante had once split for Amsterdam. Lucky for him, the

agents gave him a second chance to prove himself, otherwise, he might be stuck working in some underground lab. I couldn't picture Valerie confined like that any more than Dante.

"So cool, Jared's a bloodsucker. Must be Melcher's secret weapon. Did he show you his fangs?"

I'd almost forgotten how nearly impossible it was to have a serious conversation with Dante.

"What made him go after you and Red? Did he skip a meal? Get hungry?"

"I don't know." I sighed. "Things just sorta spiraled out of control."

"That's fieldwork for you." Dante chuckled. "Well, I'm glad you made it back in one piece."

I rested my cheek against my shoulder and suppressed a yawn. "Me too. I'm glad you made it back, too. So, you struck gold?" I didn't want to talk about Jared anymore. Not right before bed and not over the phone. This was a conversation Dante and I needed to have face-to-face.

The excitement returned to his voice.

"If only you'd been there, Sky! We started out taking tabs on this dude, Buck, who was at that party you went to. Melcher's like 'This is a stakeout, no engaging with the enemy.'" Dante stopped to chuckle. "Anyway, we *accidentally* bumped into Buck. He and Noel had their "Oh wow, what a coincidence running into you here" moment, and next thing you know we're drinking brewskis together, chilling."

So while Valerie and I were being terrorized in Sitka, Noel and Dante were sitting back drinking beers in Fairbanks? Damn, why did I always have to draw the short end of the popsicle stick?

"That's only the beginning," Dante said, voice dropping. "So

Buck's this good looking dude with an even better looking girl-friend—human. They start telling us how Nicole, the girlfriend, makes the big bucks working these ritzy vamp parties. Tastings, they call them."

I scooted up in my bed. "Tastings?"

"Tastings," he repeated. "Upscale shindigs for fancy pants vampires who like their blood laced with fine wine."

I shivered and pulled the covers up to my neck. "That sounds messed up."

Dante laughed. "And I didn't even have on my lucky bear claw. You still have it, right?"

"Right here in my nightstand."

"You should keep it."

"What?" I sat up straighter. It wasn't exactly a sapphire necklace, but it still felt a little too much like a boyfriend gift.

"I want you to have the claw. I don't need luck charms. I attract luck all on my own."

"It's a nice gesture, Dante, but you earned it, not me." I cleared my throat. "So, you were telling me about tastings."

"Right, tastings. There's this master organizer who sets these things up all around the state. It's more of a fall and winter thing. Buck said we lucked out because it was the last one of the season."

"Lucky you," I said, rolling my eyes even though Dante couldn't see.

"What did I tell you?"

"Let me guess? You attended the party."

"We did." His voice was filled with smug satisfaction.

"Just like that? You show up in town and they roll out the red carpet for a couple of curious humans who just happen to be passing through?"

"I didn't go as a human," Dante said.

"What does that mean?"

"I went as a vampire."

"Say what?"

"It was Harper's idea from the very beginning when we first approached Buck. I posed as her vampire boyfriend."

A big burst of air rose in my chest. It came out of my mouth as one big gasp of a laugh. Better to laugh myself to sleep tonight than cry. "You're kidding?"

"Nope. Harper isn't squeamish. I'll tell you that much."

Harper? Dante's use of Noel's family name meant she'd earned his respect.

"And they bought it?" I asked.

"Well, I mean, I had to do some biting."

"Dante!" I gasped.

"Hey, I was undercover. My hands were tied."

I rolled my eyes. "And I'm sure you didn't enjoy it in the least."

"Don't be jealous, Sky. You know I only have eyes and teeth for you."

A chill went through me. "That's not funny."

"Come on, what did I tell you about humor being a key ingredient to this job?"

Right, humor and blood. Funny how Dante had brushed off my question of blood cravings and here he was biting people.

"Anyway, we attended the party, and I got on the list."

"The list?"

"I'll be receiving invites starting this fall to tastings around the state." Dante whooped. "Can you believe that, Sky? You should have seen Melcher's eyes light up. I should have asked for a promotion."

"Congratulations," I said sarcastically. "I'm glad you'll have something to keep you busy. I plan on starting college this fall."

"This won't get in the way of school," Dante replied.

"Of course not."

"Melcher wants us working together again. They already think I'm a vampire. We just need to get the organizers to hire you as one of their wine girls."

"And how exactly does that work?"

"The way Nicole explained it to us is that each girl is assigned a vintage. You drink several bottles, enough to knock you out, but not make you sick, lie on top of a bed in your designated room, relax, and let the vamps filter through one at a time sucking the wine from your blood. Bam! You poison them, I pop them."

I gathered my blanket in my free hand while Dante spoke, squeezing the edge inside my tightening fist. "Why me?" Noel's the one who made the discovery with Dante. She didn't have the poisoned blood, though. Still, there had to be other vampire hunters Melcher could put on assignment. I wasn't even twenty-one yet. I shouldn't be drinking. Scratch that, I was done with drinking.

"Because Melcher wants the A-team on this one," Dante said proudly.

"I don't want to drink myself into a coma," I said. "More importantly, I don't want a bunch of vampires drinking from me. How many are we talking about anyway?"

"I don't know. Maybe fifty total?"

"Fifty!"

"Don't worry. There are strict rules about not overly puncturing the bodies. The vamps have to drink from the same watering hole, so to speak."

I let go of my blanket. An instant visual of a group of sexy male vampires licking and sucking my naked body flashed through my head. For some disturbing reason one of them looked like a teenaged Robert Pattinson. I shuddered, and it wasn't purely out of disgust. "And how much did you partake in these *tastings*?" I scrunched up my nose on the last word. That was something I couldn't and didn't want to visualize.

"I wasn't on the list at that point. I got to attend the party but wasn't allowed to sample any of the offerings. I mean, there is a limit. Can't have too many vamps sucking all the juice out of the women. Then there's the price to taste…fifteen hundred dollars."

"Fifteen hundred dollars!" If Dante wasn't exaggerating about the fifty tasters, that thing brought in seventy-five grand in one night.

"I told you we struck gold," he said smugly.

"You said you had to do some biting."

"Oh, that," Dante said and laughed. "Buck bit his girl-friend in front of us, so I bit Noel. I just sorta got caught up in the moment and went with it." He started laughing again. "We told him I was a newbie vampire. We all had a good laugh when Noel had to point out a vein. Buck insisted I give Nicole a bite. That was a couple nights before she got juiced up for the party. I wonder what wine-laced blood tastes like."

"Dante!"

"Buck says they should do a beer spinoff. October Blood Fest. What do you think?"

I groaned and rubbed my forehead with the palm of my hand. "I think I should go to bed and try and process all this in the morning."

"Good idea," Dante said. "Let it soak inside your brain a bit."

"Yeah, sure."

"Sooo," he said, changing his tone. "Are we going to talk

about the sexting?" I groaned again. Dante chuckled. "Where are you right now anyway? Did I catch you in bed?"

"I'm not having this conversation with you."

"Don't get me wrong, I enjoyed your dirty little messages, but you know what's even better than texts? Phone sex. And know what's better than phone sex?"

"I'm hanging up!" I hit "end" on the call but not before hearing the rumble of Dante's laughter.

Right. Time for bed. I turned my phone off in case Dante had the bad idea to call me back. I pulled my pillow down and moved around, trying to get comfortable under the covers. Problem was, the moment I closed my eyes I saw myself lying naked, wearing only a black lace thong, atop a king-sized bed with crimson sheets. Candles blazed from dozens of pillars surrounding the room, casting dark, sensual shadows against the walls.

My hair spilled over the covers as though it, too, was a shadow in the room. The cool, dry air touched every part of my body. I felt as though I'd slipped into a blissed-out state of relaxation.

A vampire stepped inside the bedchamber, moving slowly around the bed. He bared a striking resemblance to Tom, and he was on the bed with me before I knew it, crawling toward the center where I lay sprawled across the sheets.

"Have you come to suck my blood?" I asked breathlessly.

"Blood is overrated." The Tom lookalike smiled seductively. He made his way to my legs. I felt his breath and then his tongue as he ran the tip from my thigh to my knee then back up.

The sheets rubbed against me when I squirmed.

Tom lifted his head and grinned before dipping back down. All I could see was the thick waves of brown hair at the top of his crown. His fingers brushed the thong's narrow strip of lace aside and then his tongue was on me, flicking and tasting.

I nearly levitated from the bed, moaning as I did.

Tom looked up with a wicked grin before returning to his prize. I balled the covers inside my fists, thrashing from side to side. Tom gripped my thighs firmly and pushed his tongue inside me. I gasped and clutched at the sheets.

I turned my head and saw Henry watching us from the side of the bed.

"Henry," I rasped in surprise.

He leaned forward. "I have a confession to make, Aurora. I've been waiting for this moment since the night we met."

I swallowed. "You have?"

Henry nodded slow and sensually. He lifted his knee onto the bed, followed by the other. The mattress dipped down. "I've been waiting a long time to bite you."

"But you can't." I gasped when I felt Tom's tongue extend deeper. My eyes closed briefly. When I reopened them, Henry was on all fours at my side.

"Can't I?" he asked. He lowered his lips the hard peak of my breast and bit down gently.

Waves of heat shot through me. I cried out. My body stretched over the covers as though reaching for more.

Henry wet my other nipple with his tongue then blew gently on the tip. It tightened in response. Not to be outdone by Henry, Tom's tongue flicked inside me faster and faster. A blissful cry rose from my lips.

I lifted my head. The sight of Henry at my breast and Tom between my legs nearly drove me over the edge.

Then I noticed Fane. He stood leaning against the back wall, arms crossed over his chest, watching me. The moment our eyes met he smirked and shook his head. "You're not ready to cross that line."

"Don't listen to him." Dante stepped in front of Fane and walked to the foot of the bed.

Henry and Tom lifted their heads toward Dante simultaneously. "Hunter," they hissed in low, hostile voices.

Dante's grin widened. "Scram."

They moved aside, disappearing into the shadows of the room. Dante lifted a brow, flashing me one of his cocky grins.

My heart rate quickened when he climbed onto the bed and walked toward me on his knees. I could no longer see Fane. Dante suddenly filled the entire room. He straddled my legs, not stopping until he'd positioned himself at my hips.

"I know exactly what you want." Dante looked down at the bulge in his pants and grinned.

I propped myself up on my elbows. "Get over yourself."

His grin widened. "I'd rather get over you." He leaned beside my ear. "Over and inside of you."

A raspy breath left my lips at the same time my eyes rolled back in my head. Dante went for his zipper and this time I didn't clench.

I jumped in the shower first thing before breakfast the next morning. It looked like a rash had spread over my cheeks. I put on my clothes as soon as I'd dried off and stared at my reflection in the mirror while I yanked a comb through my wet hair.

You've got a sick mind I told my reflection. Sick, sick, sick.

Once downstairs, I shoved a piece of bread into the toaster and poured myself a glass of orange juice. I pushed aside a stack of magazines on the table and took my first bite of toast.

On my fourth bite, I heard Mom shuffle down the stairs.

"Good morning," she said, sleep clinging to her words.

"Good morning." I bit into my toast.

She shuffled to the kitchen in her robe and slippers. After she prepared her glass of ice and soda, she returned to the table. Mom moved a stack of unopened mail aside so that she could take the spot in front of me.

I crunched down on each bite of toast. Mom sipped her soda, blinking the sleep from her eyes. She looked at me, looked away, then quickly looked back. "Are you feeling okay, sweetie? Your face looks a bit feverish."

"I'm fine," I answered, feeling my cheeks get hotter.

"Are you sure you aren't coming down with something?"

"Yeah." Nothing to worry about, Mom, just a case of crazed vampire lust. According to Valerie it couldn't be helped. Then again, maybe I was just a normal eighteen-year-old with raging hormones. At least I practiced safe sex. It didn't get any safer than fantasy sex.

I grabbed my red scarf and wrapped it loosely around my neck before we headed out. Now that Mike's jacket was no longer in my locker, the sick feeling in the pit of my stomach wasn't as pronounced when I spun the combo on my lock. I still felt it when I went to history class.

During lunch hour I checked the library hoping I'd find Noel behind a row of bookshelves, but no such luck. I really *really* didn't want to check the cafeteria. If I saw Henry, I might combust on the spot. How could I have a normal conversation with him without blushing my cheeks off?

Guess I'd have to wait until film class to see Noel. I took my sack lunch into an empty classroom and pulled out a peanut butter sandwich. Bread and peanut butter was starting to get old.

I'd spread a thin layer of blueberry jam on it to try for a different taste. I usually went for strawberry or raspberry. As I ate, I started on my class readings. I hadn't missed too much the week before.

As usual, I went to film class early. I hoped that today Noel would, too. She didn't. In fact, she didn't show up at all. Weird. Dante was back in town, which meant Noel had to be back. She probably felt tired, but I wouldn't think she'd want to miss any more school.

As soon as school ended, I tried calling her, but it went to voicemail. I sent a text while I waited by the pick-up lane in front of the office.

Aurora: Hey. Missed you at school. Everything OK?

When I looked up, I saw my mom parked along the curb. I stuck my phone in my pocket and made for the car.

"Hi, honey, did you have a good day?" she asked before I'd buckled in.

"Yeah." It took me a moment to notice that she'd put on a pair of jeans and a nice sweater. "You look nice. Is Dad coming over?"

Mom sniffed. "I haven't heard a word from him."

What is it then? A date? My mom didn't appreciate jokes like that so I kept it to myself. I didn't have to wait long. Mom had never been the secretive sort, except when it came to Agent Melcher. "Your grandmother called."

"Oh?"

"She arrives in Anchorage this Thursday."

I turned in my seat. "Isn't that a bit early?" Like two months early. After Gramps retired, he and Gran became snowbirds. Unfortunately, Grandpa didn't stick around very long to enjoy his retirement, but winters in Florida certainly agreed with Grandma. She'd made a vow never to set foot in Alaska before the month of May.

Mom nodded solemnly. "You know how she likes to meddle. She thinks I'm in need of her advice."

"Can't she give it over the phone?" I loved Gran and all but in small doses. When she smelled trouble I swear she made it worse.

"She's given me an earful over the phone for hours every day," Mom said tightly. "Now she's on a mission to straighten out this mess with your dad."

I nearly laughed. The only thing Gran would do is send Dad running for the hills. I was so lost in thought I didn't notice Mom pass up the fast food chains until we were halfway home. I almost said something then decided against it.

The moment I walked into the house I felt a sense of space and order. The countertops were cleared, the carpets vacuumed, everything was put in place and clean. Mom had gone to town.

A feeling of panic shot through me. "Gran's not staying here, is she?"

I swear my mom's look of horror mirrored my own. "No. No. Thank God."

"Okay." My shoulders relaxed. Guess it was a good thing I hadn't talked my mom into letting me live in Grandma's apartment. I'd be moving right back out. My mom had her issues, but she left me alone for the most part, unlike Gran who got her kicks giving orders. As if I didn't get enough of those in my life.

21

BOYFRIEND MATERIAL

NOEL DIDN'T RETURN TO SCHOOL Tuesday or Wednesday. Nor did she return my calls or texts. By Thursday I'd stopped expecting her and that's when she walked into film class and slid into the seat beside me without a word.

"Hi," I said.

Noel turned her head slowly. "Hey."

That's it? Hey? "You never returned my calls," I said.

Noel studied the surface of her desk. "I'm sorry. I had family stuff to deal with."

I didn't know much about Noel's family since she always shied away from the subject. I only knew she didn't live with her family. "I hope it wasn't anything too serious," I said. It wasn't exactly my most hospitable voice, but I felt hurt that she didn't trust me enough to talk about it.

She merely shrugged and stared sullenly down at her desktop.

My parents are getting a divorce! I wanted to yell. My drill sergeant of a grandma gets in this afternoon, and I get to spend the rest of senior year being bossed around whenever she's around.

Noel wasn't the only one with family problems. If she didn't want to talk about it, neither did I. So maybe I was being overly sensitive. But I thought we were friends. More than friends—blood sisters.

Noel took out a spiral notebook and began tracing the letters of her name over and over.

"Dante said things went great in Fairbanks," I said.

She stopped tracing. "Yeah, we got some good leads," she said without looking at me. "He asked a lot of questions about you."

I momentarily forgot Noel's sulky behavior. I wanted to ask what kinds of questions, but I resisted the urge. Two could play the silence game. I pulled out my own notebook and straightened it on top of my desk.

Mrs. Campbell walked in and glanced at the big round clock on the wall.

"How did it go in Sitka?" Noel finally asked.

I snorted. "Jared tried to kill us and Valerie took off." I enjoyed seeing the shocked look on Noel's face right as the bell rang.

Mrs. Campbell walked to the front of her desk. "Last week we watched *Apocalypse Now*. Today we will be watching *Hearts of Darkness: A Filmmaker's Apocalypse*, Eleanor Coppola's documentary about the making of the film."

Noel and I faced forward the rest of the period. As soon as the bell rang at the end of class, Noel turned to me. "I'm sorry I didn't return your call sooner. Things have been…well, crazy, but it sounds like you've been through all kinds of crazy, too. Can we talk after school?"

So now she wanted to talk? "Can't, my grandmother's coming to town."

"Tonight?"

"She's staying with us all evening. What about tomorrow night?"

Noel looked at me funny. "Are you going to Marcus's?"

"The palace? I'm done with that scene."

Noel nodded once. "Well, call me when you're available, I guess."

I accompanied Mom to the airport to pick Grandma up. We waited in the terminal until Gran walked out holding an oversized aqua purse. She wore khaki capris and a silk scarf tied fashionably around her neck.

She stopped in the middle of the terminal when she saw us and threw out her arms. "My darlings!"

Oh, and dramatic, too. Sometimes I wondered if Mom and I were really related to her.

"Hi, Mom," my mom said, walking up to Gran and giving her a hug. "Did you have a good flight?"

"Every year I forget how long it is," she answered. She turned to me. "And let's take a look at my granddaughter. Oh my, you're so pale." She turned to my mom. "The two of you should come out and see me more often." Gran took both our arms and steered us toward the escalators leading down to baggage claim.

She pointed out her luggage as it passed on the carousel. I pulled each of her three heavy suitcases off. I took two, mom took the extra one, and we rolled them through the terminal. Grandma froze in place as soon as we stepped through the sliding doors into the parking garage. "Oh dear," she said.

"What is it?" I asked.

"I'd forgotten how cold it was this time of year." She shivered for emphasis.

I laughed.

"I told you to wait until summer," Mom said.

"My dear," Grandma said, turning to my mom aghast. "You wouldn't have lasted the spring without me."

Welcome home, Gran.

She wanted to drop her things off and freshen up at her apartment first. I still found it comical that I'd tried to snag the place for myself. Grandma had her own vehicle she kept garaged during the winter. She said she'd drive herself over for dinner.

"Are you sure?" Mom asked.

Grandma gave her a look of exasperation. "I will see you at five."

Mom sighed when we got back inside the car.

"I'll help you make dinner," I said.

"Thanks." Mom didn't usually want my help. I think today she wanted company more than the actual help.

The moment we returned home I got to work on the mashed potatoes. Mom was on her own with the turkey. We'd stopped at the bakery for a loaf of fresh bread and lemon meringue pie— Grandma's favorites.

"I don't know how she eats like this and stays skinny," Mom said, setting the temperature on the oven.

I stood at the sink, scrubbing the potatoes. "I'm guessing it has something to do with her inability to sit still. She's probably the only seventy-two-year-old whose metabolism hasn't slowed down."

Mom laughed and then nodded at the potatoes. "You know she doesn't like skins."

"That's where all the nutrients are." Plus it meant I didn't have to peel them. "You can blame it on me if she complains."

Mom sighed and got the turkey out of the fridge. Once the potatoes were clean, I got started on a chopped salad with lettuce, celery, apples, and walnuts.

She surveyed the kitchen. "We're going to have a lot of food for just the three of us. Maybe you should invite Dante."

I didn't grimace the way I would have before. A smile crept slowly over my lips. "I'm sure Gran would *love* that." She was something of a flirt—a charming one, at least, not the embarrassing kind.

Mom and I looked at each other and started laughing. "I think I'll save Dante for another night. Who knows what Gran's got up her sleeve?"

Mom nodded thoughtfully. "Good point."

It was a good thing I didn't invite Dante. Grandma arrived full of energy and ready to draw up battle plans as I suspected. I tried to stay out of the conversation as much as possible. It was up to Mom to stick up for herself. Gran had surprised us both by urging my mom to sign the divorce papers and move on with her life. Her advice could have swung in either direction, and for some reason I thought it would swing in favor of a fight to win Dad back. Grandma did love herself a battle. But that's not what she said after passing the salad bowl to me.

"He's obviously moved on. It's high time you did the same."

Mom's jaw dropped. "You think I should give up on twenty-one years of marriage? How can you say that?"

"Honey," Gran said, lowering her fork. "Things between you and Bill haven't been good for a while. The first thing you ought to do is put this house up for sale. It's much too big for just the two of you, anyway. Soon there will only be you."

Mom pushed her food around her plate with her fork. It was a real shame she couldn't enjoy the fruits of her labor.

"Aurora, why aren't you eating any turkey?" Grandma asked suddenly.

"She doesn't eat meat," Mom answered for me. I appreciated the firm tone of her voice, especially since my mom had never been a big fan of my eating choices.

"Since when?" Gran demanded. She turned back to me,

sucking in a dramatic breath. "My dear, I didn't want to say anything before, but you do look rather sickly since the last time I saw you."

"Well, it is the middle of winter," I said. I'd always been better than my mom at answering Grandma's jibes. My diet was the same as it had been last summer. Grandma hadn't noticed anything to complain about then, well not with my looks anyway.

Thankfully, Grandma let me off the hook. "Yes, winter is dreadful. Don't remind me." She turned back to my mom. "It's simply no good staying in this house. Until you move out, you can't move on."

Mom sat listening with a frown on her face for most of it.

Before Grandma left for the evening she invited us out for dinner the next evening. More of a summons, if you asked me.

Noel wasn't at school Friday. What the hell was going on with her? If she had something she wanted to tell me, it was up to her to make a move. I'd already left several messages and texts while she was out of town and more when she hadn't showed up to school at the beginning of the week. It was hard not to take personally.

Rather than make Mom drive to midtown twice, I walked to Gran's townhouse after school.

"Aurora!" Gran cried as soon as I made it to her front door after being buzzed inside the building. I stepped into her arms and hugged her then stepped back.

"Hi, Gran."

"Come in! Come in! How was school?"

I shrugged. "They haven't kicked me out."

She hooted with laughter. Our best bonding moments involved humor. I followed her into the open kitchen.

"I made us some snacks."

I liked the way Grandma said "made" to describe the store-bought cookies she had arranged on a ceramic platter. Mom hadn't inherited her love of cooking from Gran, that's for sure.

"Thanks," I said, taking one to be nice.

"Can I get you something to drink?" she asked. "A Red Bull or Mountain Dew?"

"Uh, water's good."

Gran got a glass out of the cupboard and handed it to me. "I'm going to have a Red Bull," she said.

I held my glass under the faucet and filled it with tap water.

"I'm glad you came over early so just the two of us girls could talk," Gran said. She opened her Red Bull and drank from the can. "Shall we get cozy in the living room?"

I nodded and followed her to the white sofa overlooking Westchester Lagoon. That's where they'd found the pizza delivery boy. If only Gran knew what my life had been like since she last left.

"Your mother tells me you're still not driving," Grandma said.

I felt my defenses rising. Here we go. "I'm not ready," I said.

"You're not ten anymore, Aurora. You shouldn't need your mother to drive you around."

I forced myself not to glare or sound petulant. Gran was just being Gran—stepping on toes and butting in where she didn't belong. "She won't have to for long. I'm going to live on campus as soon as I graduate."

Gran jumped on that immediately. "What happened to Notre Dame? I cannot for the life of me understand what made you give that up. You can't mean to stay in Anchorage and babysit your mother. I can tell you right now it won't do either of you any good."

Grandma sounded pretty fired up, more than usual. My jaw ached from clenching my teeth together. It's not like I wanted to stick around, not that she had any clue of that.

"My mind's made up." I didn't know what else to say.

"I just don't understand it," Gran said, shaking her head.

I watched her take a sip of her energy drink. "I'm not staying for Mom," I said before thinking out my next words. "I'm staying for my boyfriend."

Gran's eyes lit up when she faced me. She'd worried on more than one occasion about what she viewed as my lack of interest in the opposite sex. Apparently, a boyfriend held more value than a top-rated college.

"Tell me about this boy," she said, her voice rising with excitement. "What's his name?"

"Dante," I said without thinking twice. Maybe his name came so easily because this was the second time I'd used him as a fake boyfriend. That ought to concern me.

"And his last name?"

"I don't know. I don't think he has one."

"Everyone has a last name," Gran said, some of the chiding returning to her voice. "But never mind that. Is he handsome?"

"Extremely."

She let out what sounded like a squeal. If she didn't have a beverage in her hand, I swear she would have rubbed her palms together. "I insist he come out with us tonight."

"I can see if he's available."

"Why don't you call him right now?"

"Okay," I said. "What time and where?" It was better to sound perfectly confident in front of Gran.

"Five thirty at the Crow's Nest."

Speaking of crows, Gran had the whole early bird eating thing going on. Plus, she hadn't adjusted to the time difference yet. Five thirty in Anchorage was nine thirty in Florida. No wonder she was chowing down on cookies and chugging an energy drink.

I pulled my phone out of my coat pocket, smiling inwardly as Gran watched. I bet she thought I was bluffing. I dialed Dante. He answered immediately. "Oh good, we didn't get a chance to finish our conversation the other night. I think your phone died."

"Right," I said, laughing softly.

"I believe we were talking about sex in all its forms: written, verbal...physical."

I cleared my throat. "Dante, my grandmother is in town, and she'd like to take you, me, and my mom out to dinner. Five thirty at the Crow's Nest. Can you meet us?"

"That's early."

"Gran's on Florida time." I looked at my grandma. She gave me a big smile.

Dante chuckled. "Well, you know me. I can always eat."

I found myself smiling into the phone. "I know."

"Tell your grandmother I would be delighted."

I lowered the phone. "Dante says he'd be delighted."

If anything, Gran only looked more pleased. I lifted the phone back to my ear. "Right answer."

Dante laughed. "Then I'll see you soon...in the flesh."

I shivered slightly. "Yep. See you soon."

Grandma set the can aside while I said bye. Now she really did rub her hands together. "Oh, won't this be fun!"

"I hope you like him."

"I know I will. He obviously has good taste to go out with you."

I felt my cheeks warm. "Gran..."

"What? It's true." She got up and headed back to the kitchen. "Do you want another cookie before I put them away?"

"I still have mine, thanks." It sat uneaten on a coaster on the end table by the couch. "Need help?"

"No, dear, I'll have this cleared in a jiffy."

While Gran put the cookies back inside their boxes, I sent Dante a text.

Dante: One more thing. My grandma thinks you're my boyfriend.

Dante texted back a moment later.

Dante: No problem, kitten, but this time it's going to cost you.

Aurora: ?

Dante: You know what.

I sucked in a breath as I stared at the screen on my phone. I waited to see if he'd say anything else, but he didn't. I quickly put my phone away when my grandmother rejoined me in the living room. I could feel my cheeks heating again, as though I'd been caught looking at a dirty magazine in my grandmother's living room.

"I cannot wait to meet this Dante fellow," Gran said. "He sounds like quite the gentleman."

I nearly snorted but recovered quick enough to nod. "He makes me laugh."

Gran took a seat in the recliner and leaned back. "Humor goes a long way, my dear."

22

ALWAYS LEAVE THEM WANTING MORE

GRAN WASN'T THE ONLY ONE pleased about my new-found boyfriend. As soon as she'd been buzzed in, Mom went right along with it when Grandma asked why she'd never mentioned Dante before.

"They just started going out," Mom answered, giving me a quick questioning look.

Gran did the squeal thing again. "Oh, isn't it wonderful I came home early? Now tell me everything there is to know about Dante."

"He's a freshman at UAA," I said.

"Already in college," Grandmother noted, raising a brow. "Well done, my dear."

"You'll love him," my mom said. "He's entertaining, well-mannered, and extremely good looking."

"Mom!"

She smiled. "What? It's true."

And so the conversation went the entire drive downtown. Dante won extra points for, as my mom put it, having a hearty appetite the one time she asked him to stay for dinner. Of course, what we both left out is the reason behind that first visit. Dante had arrived on our doorstep to introduce himself as my vampire hunting mentor then haul me off to Fairbanks for my first mission in the field with no warning.

"Is that him?" my grandmother asked suddenly when my

mom drove down a side street beside the Captain Cook Hotel looking for a parking spot.

And there stood Dante, waiting in front of the hotel's double doors, dashing grin upon his face. He looked like a young, fit Chris Pratt, only better.

Dante wasn't just winning points with my mom and Grandma. From the moment I landed eyes on him I liked what I saw, but there was more to it than that. Dante made me smile. He made me laugh. Wasn't that better than a guy who made me cry?

And he was reliable. No question. He came out tonight because I asked him, and here he stood, waiting at the entrance with a big welcoming smile.

I felt a pitter-patter inside my chest. Oh yeah, there was a definite attraction going on between us. Our first face-to-face since the whole sexting thing in Sitka had my nerves deep-fried and sizzling.

As we got out of the car, Dante approached, his cheeks dimpling as he smiled even bigger. "Mrs. Sky, it's been too long." He walked right up to my mom and hugged her.

"Hello, Dante. It's good to see you again." Mom was all grins. I swear this was her dream come true for me. She took a step back and looked at Gran. "Dante, this is my mother, Abigail Williams."

"Mrs. Williams, I am delighted to meet you."

"Oh, the pleasure is all mine," Gran said. Dante reached out his hand, but Grandma took him in her arms. "Let's have none of that. You're family now."

Luckily no one saw my face. I felt ready to burst into laughter and give us away. I doubt Gran would be thrilled to watch me erupt into hysterics. I bit my tongue. Hard.

"And there's my girl," Dante said energetically, honing in on me. His lips quirked upwards. He'd seen the laughter on my face.

"Hey," I said casually, trying not to look too amused by the situation. I had to admit it was much more entertaining than awkward. That is until Dante stepped up to me, dipped me back, and kissed me full on the lips.

My eyes widened. Dante made sure to get what he could out of the kiss before lifting me back up. He smirked the moment he took in the dazed look on my face. Before I could think of anything to say, he offered his arm to my grandmother and launched into a conversational tone. "Aurora tells me you came in from Florida, Mrs. Williams. How long are you visiting?"

"Call me Abby, dear. I have a place in midtown where I stay six months out of the year."

"Ah, so you're a snowbird. Can't say I wouldn't mind taking off south myself when the big freeze comes in."

Gran squeezed Dante's arm. "You and Aurora must visit me next winter."

"We'd love to."

Mom and I fell into step behind Dante and Grandma. Mom raised a brow at me and I shook my head. She answered with a smile.

Our small group tromped through the lobby up to the elevator. Inside the elevator Dante pressed the button for the restaurant on the top floor, then took a place beside me.

When we reached the top floor, he held the elevator door open. My grandmother stepped out first. Before following Mom out, I leaned back and whispered to Dante, "Thank you for doing this."

"Anytime. Shall we?" Dante reached for my hand.

When our fingers laced together, it felt like the most natural thing in the world. We walked down the corridor toward the restaurant's lobby. Mom glanced back at us and smiled.

I should have known Grandma wouldn't let Dante off the hook completely. "What's this I hear about you keeping my granddaughter behind to attend an in-state college?" she asked after we'd been seated.

Dante didn't miss a beat. He smiled slyly. "Couldn't let her run off east and fall in love with another man."

Gran looked Dante over closely. "Aurora must think highly of you to stick around Anchorage."

He chuckled. "You know what they say. Who needs a dream college when you've got your dream man?"

I smacked Dante playfully on the shoulder. "And so humble."

Gran looked between the two of us and smiled. "I can't say I was too happy when Aurora told me she no longer planned on attending Notre Dame, but at least now I can begin to understand why."

Dante may have gotten the Abigail Williams stamp of approval, but that didn't absolve him from the background check. Gran asked about his family, education, and upbringing in Fairbanks.

Dante and I didn't get much chance to talk, and maybe that was a good thing. I did try to ask him about Noel at the end of dinner as Mom and Gran gathered their hats, gloves, and jackets.

"Did something happen in Fairbanks that upset Noel?" I asked.

"Harper? No, why?"

"She's been acting withdrawn at school."

Dante looked up in thought. "Nope, can't think of anything. She seemed fine to me. Way peppier than I've ever seen her."

"Hmm."

"Why don't you just ask her what's up?"

"Because that's not how women do it," I said, exasperated.

Dante squinted at me. "Why not? Seems a heck of a lot easier."

"Come on," I said, grabbing his arm. My mom and grandmother are waiting."

Dante put a hand on top of mine. "Why don't I drive you home?"

Alone with Dante. I'd done it plenty of times before and felt perfectly safe but that was before the sexting and his starring role in my erotic fantasy, and the pretend but oh-so-real-feeling relationship and date out with my family.

I felt the tremble even in my fingertips. I hoped Dante didn't.

I cleared my throat. "My grandmother just got into town and is expecting Mom and me to come over for a while. Not to mention she's going to want to have me around so she can gush over you."

Dante straightened up and smiled. "Well, in that case." He chuckled. "You know, Aurora," he said slowly, "if your grandma's going to believe the whole us being an item story, it would be much easier if it were true."

I gave him a hard stare.

"Am I not good boyfriend material?" he asked when I didn't answer.

"You're great boyfriend material," I said quickly. "But we work together."

Dante grinned. "That's what I call a bonus. Come on, Sky. Let me take you out on a date. A real date."

"A date," I repeated slowly. The guy I'd been fantasizing about was asking me on a date.

"Sky," Dante said, low and seductive.

"What?"

"You're blushing. That means you want to say yes."

I looked him in the eye. "Fine. One date. It can't be more dangerous than a vamp mission, right?"

"In my case, biting is optional."

I groaned. "I'm so going to regret this, aren't I?"

Dante lowered his voice. "I guarantee you'll love every minute."

A shudder ran through my body. I pulled my hand away from his and hurried to catch up to my mom and grandma in front of the elevators.

Dante was all smiles when he joined us. "Mrs. Sky, Abby, dinner was delicious. Thank you for inviting me."

"Of course, Dante," Gran said. "I hope to see a lot more of you in the coming months."

"Well, you won't see much of me," I responded. "I still need to survive the last couple months of high school."

"That's right," Dante said. "We want Aurora to graduate and join me at the U of double A. I look forward to many late-night cram sessions."

Gran tittered. I didn't doubt she caught Dante's double meaning. I felt that familiar wave of heat rush over my body.

Dante walked with us to the car, opening the door for Gran. "It was so lovely to meet you, Abby."

"Where are you parked, Dante?" Mom asked.

He grinned at her over the hood. "I'm on the other side."

"We can take you around."

"That's okay, Mrs. Sky. I don't mind walking."

"Well, it was so good to see you again," she said.

Mom got inside the car, leaving me beside the passenger door next to Dante. He raised a brow. "Kiss goodbye?"

I looked sideways at the car then back at Dante, my heart doing a flip-flop. "Only because my grandmother is watching."

"Right," Dante said, a big smile on his face as he stepped up to me.

His expression turned serious as he stared at my lips. I thought he would have rushed in for the kiss before I changed my mind. Instead, he set my nerves buzzing as he stared down at me, inches from my face. I took in shallow breaths. He leaned in slowly with the sort of dark expression that made me shiver all over.

Our lips met.

He'd taken me off guard with the first kiss. This time it was like he wanted me to anticipate what was coming and dangle it in front of my face like a carrot in front of a moose.

Two could play that game.

I moved my lips over Dante's, tilting my head as needed to change the angle, adding pressure. I was much more confident about my kissing skills thanks to Fane. My heart accelerated when I heard his intake of breath. I pulled back and shot Dante a grin. "Good night, babe."

"Oh, you're bad." Dante said. "You know this isn't over."

I chose to smile rather than answer. I got inside the car, shutting the door gently. As my mom pulled away, I glanced over my shoulder and saw Dante still on the curb watching us go.

"Well, my dear," Gran said from the front seat. "I can see why you've elected to stay in town. You'll need to keep an eye on that one."

I glanced over my shoulder, but Mom had already put downtown behind us.

23

SURVIVAL INSTINCTS

I SHOULD HAVE KNOWN GRAN WOULD be back at it when she came over for dinner Saturday night. At least we were eating Thursday night's leftovers and only had to reheat stuff. Gran had arrived early and watched Mom and me as she sipped an iced tea.

"You really need to get behind the wheel again, my dear," she said. Yep, she was back on me about that. "Look at me. I'm driving around at seventy-two."

When my back was to Gran, I rolled my eyes.

"Aurora will drive when she's ready," Mom said.

"That fellow of yours might get tired of picking you up and dropping you off all the time," Gran said, switching tactics. "A man likes a woman who's independent."

"There's always the bus," I said cheerfully.

"The bus?" Gran sounded horrified. Her expression made me chuckle. "Oh, dear. Oh my. Have you seen the depot downtown? I would be scared for my life."

"I don't ever go downtown, Gran."

"Well, that's a relief."

Mom surprised me by saying, "After graduation we'll look at

She nodded.

"Oh, Mom." I felt tears in my eyes. I dropped the salad spoons in the bowl and threw my arms around her.

She chuckled and rubbed my back. "It's what makes the most sense."

I wiped the moisture under my eyes with my fingers after I pulled back. I could feel the grin all the way up to my nose.

Grandma clapped once. "Now that that's settled, we can decide what to do about the house."

I saw Mom's smile drop from the corner of my eye.

"I told you; I'm not selling the house."

"You should move in with me. We can take long walks on the coastal trail. It's just what you need."

Mom's back was to us as she stirred the gravy at the stove, but if I could see her face, I'm sure it would mirror the horror she felt at Gran's suggestion.

I only half-listened to Gran through dinner as she planned out the next six months of Mom's life—something about cooking classes, water aerobics, and French lessons.

After helping clear the dishes, I tried calling Noel. She didn't pick up. Dante's advice of asking her what the hell was up sounded pretty good the more I thought about it. We hadn't had a chance to fully discuss either of our missions. I felt like if I didn't get it off my chest soon it was going to drive me half mad. Shouldn't Noel be a bit more curious about Valerie skipping town? Not to mention happy about it?

I returned to the kitchen from the living room. "I need to head out."

"At this hour?" Gran asked incredulously.

Mom merely nodded. "I'll drive you."

"You know, if Aurora drove…"

"Mom!"

Gran turned back to her tea and pie. "Better bundle up, dear. It's like one big walk-in freezer out there."

My pleather jacket was better suited to spring and fall, but it's what I grabbed. At the last second, I ran upstairs for my red scarf.

"I'm surprised Gran didn't want to come with us," I said as soon as we'd pulled out of the garage.

Mom snorted. "And miss the chance to snoop around the house?" I glanced at my mom, and we laughed in unison. It didn't last long. "How long will you be out?"

"I don't know."

"Are you on assignment?"

"No."

"Are you going somewhere dangerous?"

I thought a moment before answering with the truth. "Yes and no."

Mom nodded slightly. She kept her eyes on the road. "Do you have protection?"

"Got my dagger, but I don't plan on using it."

"Where am I taking you?"

"Bootleggers Cove."

I had her drop me off at Elderberry Park. No way was I having her drive anywhere near the palace, not after what had happened to Agent Crist when she patrolled the area. Not to mention poor Mike.

"You have your phone?" Mom asked after pulling into the park's small vacant lot. Her body became rigid as she stared through the windshield at the deserted playground. At night the statues looked rather creepy, like creatures crouched in the shadows.

She had to have seen my phone in my hand, but I held it up for reassurance. "Yep. Right here." I stuffed the phone inside my coat pocket, leaned across the car, and kissed her on the cheek. "I'm just going to talk to a friend."

She nodded tightly. "Be safe."

I unbuckled. "You, too. Gran's in full battle mode."

Mom's shoulders relaxed and she laughed. "Don't remind me."

"Will *you* be okay?" I asked.

"I'll manage."

At least Mom didn't look so tense when she drove off. I started down the hill toward the inlet and N Street, zigzagging my way across patches of dry pavement. Both sides of N Street were lined with condos. I stuffed my hands inside my coat pockets, sharing space on one side with my phone.

The humidity from my breath looked ready to freeze in the air. I pulled my scarf up to my nose, capturing the moisture in the fabric where it cooled instantly. We had to be in the negatives tonight.

I walked a couple blocks then turned right.

I hoped Noel had come out tonight, but what if she hadn't? I guess I'd call an uber after killing enough time for Gran to leave our house. She couldn't stay much longer. It was already late for her.

As I approached Marcus's townhouse, it began to strike me that coming over tonight wasn't the best idea. What friends did I really have here? I could hardly pretend to be with Fane, not after the way he'd cast me off.

I walked up to the hand-carved wooden door with the stained-glass panels on either side and stared at the door knocker. I heard footsteps behind me and glanced over my shoulder. A young man walked up. Maybe one of the guys who'd been in the kitchen? I couldn't tell in the dark. "Don't be shy," he said, nodding at the front door.

I pulled on the door handle and walked in ahead of him onto the slabs of sand-colored stone in the entryway. The first time I'd been to the palace Henry told me Marcus imported the stones from Jerusalem. Now here I was walking on them in Anchorage, Alaska. Surreal.

I took my jacket and scarf off and hung them from one of the curly iron hooks along the wall of the entryway.

Latin music played on low from the direction of the living room. No disco tonight.

I pulled my tunic sweater down over my skinny jeans and headed for the kitchen. I tried play it cool when I walked in and found Gavin pouring a drink inside a martini shaker. I fought the urge to ask if he'd heard anything from Valerie.

"Aurora," he said evenly.

I stared at the martini shaker, waiting for him to shake it from side to side, but he didn't. "I don't suppose you've seen Noel around tonight?"

"Are you looking for Noel or Fane?"

My heart flopped. I put a hand on my chest. It didn't feel especially good. "Fane's here?"

"I suggest you check the October room," Gavin said.

"Why's that?" I asked coldly.

"Go see for yourself," he answered, matching my tone.

I hated the hard look on his face. Even more than that, I hated that I felt compelled to do the very thing he obviously wanted me to. I certainly didn't want to stick around the kitchen with him. As soon as I turned my back, Gavin began shaking the mixer.

My feet carried me to the living room. The surroundings had

begun to take on a dreamlike quality, all hazy around the edges.

Marcus stood leaning against the iron banister of the spiral staircase in one of his silk shirts, half-buttoned, chatting with a fellow to his left. He nodded at me in greeting, and I nodded in return. I passed him and stared at the first step of the staircase. Marcus broke off his conversation. He turned to me. "Are you sure you want to go up there?"

"Yes," I replied firmly.

He gave me a knowing smile. I'm not sure what he knew. It wasn't good, whatever it was, but there was no turning back.

With each step I took, I had that feeling in my gut that I really didn't want to see what I was about to, but I couldn't turn away. I reached the landing and passed the giant shower with its mosaic tile artwork.

The door to the October room loomed in the distance, the silver bat hanging heavy from the knob. I approached with even steps. I did not pause to listen when I reached it. My hand moved for the knob as though gliding on the strings of a puppeteer. It turned easily in my hand. I pushed the door open and stepped inside.

They sat on top of the bed in the flickering candlelight. Fane and Noel.

Noel's top had been dragged down her shoulder. A drop of blood beaded at the fresh puncture wound on her pale smooth skin. Not on the neck, but lower, right by her shoulder blade.

Fane's eyes were half-closed. It took him a moment to notice my intrusion. When he did, it looked like he was slowly beginning to wake from a dream. His expression cleared into one of recognition. Our eyes locked.

I couldn't speak. Neither, apparently, could Fane.

Then Noel saw me. "Aurora!" she cried. Horror filled her

face. How comical. Noel Harper horrified that I'd walked in on their disgusting display of betrayal. I swear I hated her even more than Fane at that moment. "It's not what you think!"

I didn't give her time to explain.

I gave Fane one last look, one I hoped would haunt him for the rest of his everlasting life, then turned in place and walked out, shutting the door behind me.

The last thing I wanted was Fane or Noel coming after me. If I had to look at either of their faces or hear their voices, I'd fling myself off the balcony into Marcus's living room. And I just might have to if I wanted to make it downstairs in time.

I looked side to side frantically. All the doors had silver bats hanging from the knobs. I just needed a moment to avoid Fane and Noel and compose myself. I didn't want anyone to see my face until I'd had time to mask my emotions.

I hurried down the hall. Those stupid bats mocked me from each closed door. I quickly rounded a corner. At least I'd reached an area that couldn't be seen from the door of the October room. Even a bathroom would do at this point. I'd lock myself in and wait until I felt certain it was safe to come out. I didn't care if I had to wait all night.

A door at the end of the hall caught my attention. It was closed but there wasn't a bat hanging from the knob. I walked up to it and reached for the knob then stopped. My hand wasn't as adamant about going into this room. Then I heard a door open. This would have to do.

I yanked the door open and shut myself quickly inside.

I leaned against the door. My breath came out in ragged gasps. I fought to control my breath and listened. I thought I heard footsteps in the distance but then they died off.

Fane and Noel. I wanted to cry. I wanted to scream. I wanted to punch myself in the face and knock the image of the two of them together right out of my head. My lip curled back. Traitors, both!

How could Noel? She knew what it was like. She was worse than Valerie. At least Valerie did her backstabbing out in the open, not behind closed doors like Noel.

I clutched my stomach. Fane and Noel. The two of them together made me physically ill.

I stormed up to the window and glared at my reflection. The girl in the glass looked haunted. I wanted to smash through her face. I turned away from her and walked the few steps to the king-sized bed, dropping to my knees at the side as though in prayer. I shoved my face into the satin cover spilling over the edge. I pressed my mouth against the fabric to muffle my sobbing screams. I let it all out. I had nothing better to do, and I couldn't leave with the party in full swing. How could I show my face downstairs?

I stood up slowly and went back to the window. Too far above ground to make my escape. I guess I was just stuck waiting until morning. Hours of mind torture. What a Saturday night!

I felt an insane urge to call Dante. I was sure he'd happily charge through the front door and get me the hell out of here, but noooo, I had to go and leave my phone in my coat pocket.

I paced the room, muttering angry curses.

"Not ready to cross that line." I grumbled under my breath. "Not like Noel!" I snarled at the door, punching my fist in the direction of the October room. I quickly covered my mouth and listened. When no one appeared at the door, I resumed pacing, muttering, and mocking everything he'd said to me the last time we were together.

"*What we had was good. Let's not ruin that.* Oh, you ruined it, buddy boy. You chewed up every good feeling I ever had for you and spit it back out!" I swung my arm in the air as though cracking an invisible whip. "*Good thing I have someone on the inside to look out for me.* Yeah, Noel! I see she's looking out for alllll your needs."

Maybe there was a perfectly good explanation for this. Maybe Noel was just doing her job. Even if Melcher had instructed Noel to take Valerie's place with Fane, I couldn't let it go. There wasn't any room for rationalization inside my head when it came to him.

"All right, Aurora. Time to get a grip. Head held high. Let's get the hell out of here."

I stopped beside a statue, noticing for the first time the bust of a muscled chest ending at the groin. I looked around the room. A watercolor of two men seated naked beside one another hung at eye level beside the window.

On the opposite side of the room, oil paintings depicted full male nude frontals. The adjoining wall featured more whimsical and modern portraits, including an Asian silk screen with two men: one in black leather pants and another in red, thigh-high heeled boots.

"Oh wow," I said in a whisper. "I really need to get out of here."

I turned quickly away from a nude drawing of Peter Pan wearing spiked wrist cuffs and bumped into Marcus's dresser. My knee hit one of the artsy iron handles. I cursed.

"Ow, ow, ow, ow, ow." Pain shot up my leg. I'd hit the worst spot on my knee.

I gripped the dresser, breathing in and out, waiting for the wretched pain to pass. As it subsided, I straightened up, both palms firmly planted on the dresser's surface. I looked down and saw a box with swirls and squares intricately carved into the dark wood.

Jared claimed to have found Crist's cross inside a wood box in a bedroom.

The same feeling of dread I'd had as I approached the October room came over me. I lifted the lid and pushed it back gently. Inside I found leather and silver bracelets, pendants, a gold chain, large gothic rings, and even diamond cufflinks. And then there, nestled inside the box, I caught the glint of an orange oval gemstone. It practically flashed me in the eye.

My heart dropped to the floor. I felt sick all over again.

My fingers reached inside in slow motion. I lifted the ring in front of my face. The name "Mike" was carved into the silver on one side—an eagle, our school mascot, on the other.

My hand shook. My breath caught in my throat. At that moment the knob of the door began to turn. I fisted the ring, but I didn't have time to shut the lid on the jewelry box.

Marcus stepped inside. His expression darkened when he saw me. "Who do we have here?" My heart raced to unnatural speeds inside my chest. "This room is off limits."

I swallowed and tried to control my voice. "I'm sorry. I needed privacy. I was upset."

"And what or who has caused such upset, my pet?" His voice amplified inside my ears as he approached. There was no hair on Marcus's chest, only rock-solid muscles where his shirt gaped open.

"Fane," I whispered. I hoped he mistook the panic in my voice for heartache, but that wasn't what made my heart pump its way up my throat as I stood trapped inside Marcus's bedroom. Marcus, Mike's killer. Mike's real killer. And that possibly meant Crist's killer, too.

"Francesco and Noel," Marcus said knowingly.

"Do not worry your pretty little head over Francesco. There are other bats in the sky."

"I'll keep that in mind," I said, meeting Marcus's eyes. "I'm

247

sorry I intruded on your personal space." *Move feet, move*. I took my first step toward him, then the next, and began to pass. My heart called out to the open door. I could make it. I'd never felt so close to escape.

"Aurora, what is in your hand?"

That should have been my cue to run, but I froze in place. My fist tightened. I turned around, not wanting to keep my back to Marcus. "Nothing."

Marcus chuckled. "Why is a human's first reaction to lie?"

I shrugged. "Survival instinct?"

Marcus smiled. "A good instinct to have." He nodded at my fist. "Let's have a look."

I fought the urge to glance at the open door. No sudden movements or visible signs of panic seemed like the best advice in this situation. I lifted my fist slowly, trying to buy myself time. My fingers curled back. Mike's ring sat in my palm.

"Ah," Marcus said.

"Why did you kill him?" I asked calmer than I thought was possible.

"I didn't kill the boy, Aurora. You did."

I screwed up my face. "How do you figure that?"

"You brought him here."

"He followed me," I said defensively, despite my predicament. Just because Marcus had me cornered didn't mean I was going to let him pin a murder on me. Why couldn't vampires own up to their actions? "The moment I saw him, I escorted him out. I walked him to his car. How did you get to him?"

Marcus stretched, at ease as always. His neck popped when he leaned to the side. "The boy came back for his jacket."

"I told him I'd bring it to school."

"He came back," Marcus said firmly. "And because he knew you and had come here, I thought he knew of our existence. So I invited him on a personal guided tour. I found us a cozy little room and went in for a bite. Do you know what happened, Aurora?"

I felt my throat closing. I shook my head ever so slightly. I didn't want to hear. I closed my eyes for one brief moment.

"He started screaming."

I opened my eyes and looked into Marcus's cold gaze.

"I had no choice," he said, devoid of emotion. "*You* left me no choice."

I shook my head. Tonight wasn't my night to feel guilty. It wasn't my fault. I didn't want Mike to like me. I didn't want him at the palace. I didn't want him to die. The culpability stabbed at my insides.

"And you leave me with no choice now," Marcus said. He sighed and grabbed my arm. He was so quick he had his hand clamped over my mouth before I could scream. Mike's ring fell from my fingers, clattering against the floor.

24

WE DIE YOUNG

Marcus hauled me with him to the door before slamming it shut. I struggled to break free of his hold. His grip tightened and I stomped on his foot. He squeezed my arms so tightly, tears leaked from my eyes. He had the same brutal strength as Jared.

I kept waiting for him to bite me so I could put an end to this nightmare evening, but he didn't. Naturally I'd get the gay killer vampire.

He pulled me down as he squatted in front of his dresser. My knees hit the floorboards. He pulled open the bottom dresser drawer. It was filled with leather bondage material.

My eyes widened as he pulled out a roll of duct tape, ripped a piece off with his teeth, and slipped it over my mouth, sealing my lips together.

When I squirmed, Marcus simply said, "It's not time yet."

He looked so determined, it nearly took my breath away. Not that I had any breath with my mouth taped shut.

Marcus wrapped my wrists in duct tape, pushed me on the bed, and taped my ankles together. It reminded me of Thomas—human Thomas—the boy I'd taped to a chair in Fairbanks before Dante interrogated and killed him. Karma was one twisted bitch.

I tried to pull my wrists free while Marcus closed the door

and rummaged through his closet. He returned with a stepladder and steel bar attached to chains and a snap hook.

Oh hell no.

Marcus grinned slightly as he unfolded the stepladder near the foot of the bed. He moved up the steps, reached up and attached the snap hook to a metal hook in the ceiling. My eyes expanded in my head. I would have preferred a disco ball, that's for sure.

Once the bar was hanging in place, he stepped down. While Marcus crouched over his drawer of playthings, I rolled across the bed. I meant to stop at the edge, lift up, and hop toward the door, but in my panic, I rolled right off the edge and hit the floor with a wham. Maybe someone downstairs would hear. Ha, fat chance.

The leg I landed on throbbed. Marcus didn't bother turning from his drawer until he'd found what he wanted. He pushed the drawer closed and stood up. He turned, holding leather wrist cuffs and a pair of scissors.

It was useless, I knew, but I tried to scoot away from him.

Marcus crouched beside me and began snipping away the tape around my wrists. I tried to beat him with both hands bound together. I didn't care if he cut me. Maybe he'd see the blood and give it a lick.

Somehow, he managed to cut through the tape without cutting me. Once my hands were free, I attempted to punch him, but he caught my right fist and shoved it inside the first handcuff. Marcus tightened the strap around my wrist. All the while I struggled. Clearly, he'd had practice.

He grabbed my second wrist and shoved it in.

Marcus cut the tape around my ankles then lifted me to my feet and toward the ladder. I thrashed against him.

I hated the way he didn't so much as grunt, as though

dragging an unwilling victim across the room wasn't anything out of the ordinary.

He hauled me up the steps and yanked my right arm up so hard I was afraid he'd pull it out of the socket. A chain rattled overhead as he hooked my cuffed wrist to the suspension bar. I beat his chest with my left fist, but Marcus captured it easily and hooked it to the other side of the bar. Thus secured, he stepped down, taking the ladder with him.

I hung suspended by the wrists from Marcus's ceiling, a foot off the floor.

He refolded the stepladder gently and propped it against the wall.

Marcus stood in front of me, surveying his work with a smile of satisfaction. I tried to kick at him, glaring all the while. Marcus took a step back. "Now, feel free to struggle all you want. It won't do any good. I should know." Marcus let out a deep throaty laugh. "I wish I could offer you a playmate, but this will have to do until my guests depart." He looked me up and down. "I never did give you the full tour, Aurora. Once we're alone I'll show you my music room."

I stopped struggling and stared wide-eyed at him. Marcus shook his head grimly. "Such a pity."

He backed out of the room. I tried to scream his name before he walked out the door, but it was no use. The door clicked shut behind him.

I twisted from side to side. That wasn't any use, either, but I wasn't exactly in the mood to just hang around. The chains groaned over my head. I tried swinging forward, reaching my foot out to grab the edge of the bed. The only thing I managed to do was wiggle like a worm on a hook. My nostrils flared as I inhaled and exhaled rapidly.

I needed my dagger. I kicked my feet, but the motion added extra strain on my outstretched arms. I tried bending my legs backwards. Even if I could touch the sheath around my waist with my toe, it wouldn't do any good. There's no way I could get under my sweater, get the blade out with my toes, and then magically lift it with my feet to my wrist and cut through the leather cuff. I wanted to laugh at the absurdity of it, but again, my mouth was taped shut!

Where the hell was Fane? How could he miss my red scarf hanging from the hook downstairs? The steel suspension bar above me creaked. Maybe I didn't want Fane to find me this way. Talk about humiliation.

I stopped fidgeting. I needed to save my energy for Marcus. Just one bite, that's all it took. I closed my eyes and concentrated on calm breathing through my nose. Clearly, I had the disadvantage. My arm muscles screamed with each passing second. Hopefully I wouldn't need my arms, but who knew how long Marcus would keep the party going downstairs? I might be hanging here all night.

Oh God, is this what the rack felt like back in the day?

I tried to think about other things to get my mind off my aching arms.

I would not die tonight. I refused. Hell would freeze over before I allowed my last moments on earth to involve walking in on Noel and Fane's suckfest.

That's right, Aurora. Concentrate on the anger, not the pain. After a while, I didn't have the strength to think.

By the time Marcus returned, I was happy to see him.

Tears ran down my cheeks. After opening the door, he took

one look at my face and frowned. "My poor, sad pet. I tried to get them all to leave sooner, but they wanted to stay."

He grabbed the stepladder from against the wall. As soon as he'd unfolded it, I set my feet down and started crying anew at the relief in my arms. I held still while Marcus unhooked me, even though I hated having his body pressed against mine. Through my nose I inhaled the smell of sweat and alcohol.

Marcus helped me to the edge of the bed. It didn't take much coaxing to get me to sit. While I did, Marcus removed the cuffs and gently massaged each wrist. He stopped, looked me in the eye, then ripped the tape off my mouth in one swift motion.

Without warning I began crying. Even worse, Marcus started rubbing my back. "There, there."

I needed this moment to compose myself. My arms felt limp and tingly. At least Marcus wasn't in any hurry to kill me.

Once I had my sobbing under control, I glanced at the open door.

"Where's your partner?"

"This week it's an art show in New York."

"Does he know that you murder people when he's out of town?"

"I keep Richard in the dark for his own protection. Now I'm very sorry," Marcus said, "but it's time we adjourned to the music room."

I cried out when he took me by the arm. I didn't think he meant to be rough, not yet anyway, but it didn't hurt any less. Once the blinding pain passed, I asked, "Why did you kill Crist?"

"Who?" He paused with me in the doorway.

"Tall woman, dark brown shoulder-length hair. Late twenties or early thirties. Frown on her face."

Marcus chuckled softly. "I think I left you hanging too long."

Understatement of the year. The only reason I let him lead

me down the hall is because I didn't want pressure or pulling of any kind on either of my arms.

"Up or down?" I asked at the landing.

Marcus studied my face. "You're taking this rather well, pet. You always were unusual."

"Yeah, well, why fight the inevitable?" I answered.

"Wise beyond her time. Such a pity," Marcus said again. "Ladies first."

I took the steps one at a time. The last thing I needed was to trip and break my neck. I watched my feet the whole way down. Even though my arms were now free they felt about as useful as spaghetti noodles. I made it down the last step and looked into the living room.

The lamps glowed eerily from low bulbs. I'd never seen that area deserted. Fane really had left me here.

I quickly blinked back tears.

"To the right," Marcus said.

I had never noticed anything to the right of the staircase. A narrow hall skirted the far wall. I followed Marcus down the corridor into a small room. As I suspected, there were no instruments in the music room but there were a couple giant speakers surrounding a massive stereo system.

The walls had gray sponge-like padding on them. Once I'd stepped inside, Marcus closed the door behind us. The familiar grip of terror seized my heart. This room reminded me way too much of my initiation room.

"What song would you like to die to, Aurora? Staying Alive? Somehow, I don't think that's appropriate tonight." I glared at him. Vampires really sucked at humor. "No last requests?" Marcus asked.

"Just one," I said looking him square in the eye. "Bite me."

Marcus grinned slowly. "I like you, Aurora. I always have. It's such a pity to have to kill you, but you've given me no choice. I tell you what," he said, leaning in closer. "Before I do, I'll grant your last request."

I leaned toward him like a lover leaning in for a kiss. I needed him to suck my blood. My life depended on it.

From the corner of my eyes I saw him go for my neck. Marcus's teeth pierced through my skin instantly. It felt like a clean break compared to the ones before. Should have known Marcus would be smooth to the end.

His lips formed a suction on my skin. He sucked. The sensation caused me to momentarily forget my predicament and shudder. Marcus kept his hands on me while he sucked.

The warmth of his lips left my neck. He took a step back and stared me in the eye.

A second later he spit my blood out on the ground, his upper lip curling back.

I stared from the splatter of blood on the floor to Marcus in shock. He looked equally spooked. "You taste like death."

"Marcus, I…" Oh God, he hadn't swallowed my blood. I took a step back.

"Why didn't you say anything?" he asked.

I shook my head. "I don't understand."

"You're new, aren't you? When did you die?" Marcus asked.

I shook my head again. What the hell did my blood taste like? Like Renard's? Like the guy in the vamp house? Not quite human. Vampire.

It's not as though I'd had an opportunity to ask before. Usually, vampires swallowed after tasting my blood, which led to convulsion and death.

Did all AB blood taste this way, or did it have to be activated by a virus? And how the hell did Marcus know what vamp blood tasted like? My guess? He'd sampled vampires and humans alike!

He walked to my side and stroked my hair. "I should have known, my pet. I mistook your apprehension for something else. You must not worry about the boy. It was his fate to die. It is the fate of all humans, whether by our hands or the hands of time. The end result is the same."

I suppose I should have felt relieved, but I was still trapped inside a padded room with an admitted killer, and he still had his hand in my hair.

All I had to do was go along with his theory. Play the newbie vamp card and be on my way. I tried to think of what to say. *Yep, sucks to be human. Glad I'm not.*

Marcus's fingers slid over my hair again and again as though petting me. His hand suddenly stopped. I held my breath.

Marcus gathered a chunk of my hair in his fist and pulled. I screamed.

"What have you done to me?" His body began to shake, but he didn't let go of my hair and he didn't fall to the ground.

I tried to push away from him, but my arms felt like jelly. Instead, I dropped to the ground. My scalp screamed as a chunk of hair ripped out. I rolled quickly away the moment I hit the floor and took a quick survey of the room.

Marcus grasped pieces of long black hair in his hand, staring in disbelief. His shoulders and head twitched. "I know what you are," he said, looking at me. His voice had changed. He spoke to me like he would a stranger—an extremely unwelcome one.

Marcus lifted the strands of my hair in front of his face then let go and watched them fall to the ground. He walked slowly to the stereo system. With his back turned toward me, I reached around my waist. I willed the feeling back into my fingertips as I groped for my dagger.

Marcus lifted a remote in a shaky hand. An electric guitar screeched through the speakers followed by heavy drums and a deep, raspy snarling voice from Alice in Chains' "We Die Young." Our disco days were definitely over.

I used my elbows to lift to my knees and then feet, clutching the hilt of my dagger in a death grip.

Marcus turned. The convulsing put him at a disadvantage but made him look manic the way he shook all over. I didn't think he even noticed my weapon; his eyes were narrowed in on my face. It was beyond creepy the way he moved toward me at the same time Layne Staley sang that scary was on his way—like the whole thing had been choreographed. Is this how Mike died? No, I didn't want to think about that right now. -

One side of my brain screamed at me to run for the door, but I couldn't leave Marcus alive. What little blood he'd swallowed might wear off at any moment. Marcus knew a lot of vampires. I couldn't allow him to alert any of them if I went running. Also, he'd killed Mike. And Crist. Maybe.

This whole double homicide had been playing Tetris inside my brain from the start. I kept trying to make all the pieces fit only to be bombarded by new information and uncertainties. It still didn't stack up. The one thing I could be certain of was Marcus's hand in killing Mike, and that's what I needed to focus on right now. My head pounded with the music.

I backed away from Marcus. He came at me slowly and we circled the center of the room. Bloody déjà vu.

The song ended abruptly. A second of silence ensued before

the next Alice in Chains song started. Marcus and I locked eyes, saying nothing.

I squeezed the handle of my dagger. I should attack. Every time I readied myself to spring forward, my fear reined me back in. It was like trying to psyche myself to bungee jump off a cliff. The moment I got too near the edge I panicked. If I didn't take the leap, Marcus would push me himself.

My heart lodged itself in my throat as I charged and rammed into Marcus with my shoulder. I hoped to knock him to the ground then plunge the blade into his heart as soon as I had him on his back, but even convulsing, Marcus was all rock-solid muscle mass. He stumbled back a foot but didn't fall.

His lips curled back. Without taking a step toward me, his hands shot forward and grabbed me by the neck. He began squeezing, crushing my windpipe.

The music drowned out my choking sounds.

Marcus squeezed harder. Another song ended and started.

I lifted my dagger and jabbed at Marcus. It struck flesh.

He let go of my neck and roared in fury.

I gasped and sucked in deep breaths. I looked at Marcus with his hand pressed firmly on his thigh. His head bent to survey the damage.

Now, Aurora. It's time to jump.

I pulled my dagger back, took two swift steps up to Marcus, grabbed his shoulder with my left hand, and plunged the blade into his heart with the right.

His head snapped up, the whites of his eyes expanding to unnatural proportions. He tried grasping for my hair, but I shoved him backward.

I walked to Marcus's side, watching to make sure I'd hit my

mark. His lips opened and closed. The twitching stopped. His eyes stared at the ceiling, unblinking.

I waited. His body didn't move. His expression didn't change. "Angry Chair" filled the room. The volume had been cranked so high I felt the notes vibrate inside my body. I grabbed the remote where Marcus had left it on a speaker and hit stop.

The silence provided a momentary respite. I glanced down at Marcus one last time then fled from the padded room of horror.

I hurried past the living room to the front entrance and found my jacket and scarf, the only ones hanging from a hook.

I yanked my phone out of my coat pocket and dialed Melcher's number. Hysteria overcame me the moment he answered. "I killed Marcus! He killed Mike and then he tried to kill me. So I killed him. He's dead! Marcus is dead!"

"Aurora," Melcher answered calmly. "Where are you?"

"I'm at Marcus's townhouse!" Where the hell did he think I was?

"Stay put and stay calm. I'll send someone over."

I paced the entryway, clutching my phone in case Melcher called back. I walked in and out of the kitchen, briefly considering a swig of whiskey. I picked up my dagger where I'd set it down on an end table before calling Melcher. In the kitchen, I ran it under the faucet, shook the water off the blade, and then wiped it with a kitchen towel. I pulled my sweater up in back and slid the dagger into its sheath.

Back in the entryway, I pulled my scarf and jacket off the hook and put them on, slipping my phone back inside my pocket. I stood on the edge of the living room.

I heard tires whine to a stop outside and waited, my breath suddenly erratic. I turned my body around to face the door. The knob clicked as the person outside grasped the handle.

I watched the door open, and Jared walk in. He was dressed casually in jeans, a black tee, and a blue bandana tied around his forehead as though he'd been hanging out right before receiving Melcher's call.

I recognized that bandana. I'd focused on it in the seconds before my crash. The other driver's face had been hazy, an afterthought as I took in the vehicle coming at me head on.

The bandana brought everything into focus.

Jared's eyes locked on mine without a trace of sympathy.

25

LOST SOULS

My BREATH CAUGHT IN MY throat as Jared started toward me. I couldn't move, no more than I could when his vehicle had come crashing into me that fateful afternoon when I lost three organs and my entire life to the agents.

I wasn't meant to die. Jared had done it. That psychopath had all but killed me.

This night kept getting better and better.

I didn't have time to react. Jared grabbed me by the arm as he'd done at the totem park, but the chance of him letting go this time was slim. He crushed my bones between his fingers, but I barely felt it, not after hanging from the rafters thanks to Marcus. Oh, how I wished they were both dead. I wished I could rewind time and pop Jared myself.

I couldn't tell if he'd worn the bandana to try and jog my memory or if it was simply part of his casual attire. In Sitka he asked if I recognized him as though he wanted me to or maybe he'd been feeling me out. Keeping quiet felt best at the moment.

Jared squeezed my arm.

My lips curled back. I crushed my teeth together, wanting so badly to bite him. "Do it," I said. "Break it."

Jared squeezed harder.

"Let her go," I heard Melcher's voice behind him.

Jared kept me in his grip. I felt his hesitation, knew my chances were fifty-fifty. He might obey, or he might break my arm to spite Melcher. He turned his head slightly to look at Melcher. His eyes returned to mine, and somehow, I knew the final decision was mine once more.

I smiled at him, my front and bottom teeth crushed together. I imagined it looked rather ugly and that made me smile bigger.

Jared studied me a moment then slowly released his grip on my arm. Inwardly I winced, but at least he hadn't broken any bones. "Don't ever disobey me again," he said.

I looked at Melcher all spiffy in his suit. Did he have it on when I called, or did he change at warp speed like Batman when he responded to a distress call? What was he doing here anyway? I wouldn't think he'd want to sully his hands with a mess like this. That's what assassins and cleaners were for.

"Where's Marcus?" Melcher asked.

"I'll show you." I led Melcher and Jared to the music room.

Melcher walked straight up to Marcus's body and looked down. He stood silently for several minutes.

I looked at Jared who had leaned against the padded wall to survey the room. He didn't speak.

"Marcus had Mike's ring in a jewelry box inside his bedroom," I said. I waited for Melcher to ask what I was doing in Marcus's bedroom. When he didn't, I continued. "He found me with it and confessed to killing Mike, but he wouldn't own up to Agent Crist."

"Andre Morrel killed Crist," Melcher said. "He had her cross."

I narrowed my eyes. If I had to come up with a theory, I'd say Jared killed Crist and used her death as an excuse to execute Andre and his entire family. If they'd left him in a prison to hang, as Melcher explained it, then Jared had plenty of motives to get revenge. He didn't strike me as a forgiving kind of vampire.

"But why was Crist's body found with Mike's?" I asked. It all led back to the dump, and once more the pieces scrambled and refused to fit inside my brain.

"It appears we had ourselves two separate killers," Melcher said. "For all we know Andre asked Marcus for help disposing of Crist's body."

Jared snorted. "Wouldn't that be Marcus's luck—a ready volunteer to take care of his own problem."

"And Andre wouldn't know where to dump a body being from out of town," Melcher said.

Now that made sense, except for one thing. "I still don't see what motivation Andre had for killing Crist…or how he even bumped into her." I glanced quickly at Jared.

Melcher stared at me a long time. "Aurora, you remember the *occupation* I told you the Morrel family used to engage in?"

"Yeah."

"Those instincts don't go away. Andre Morrel has always been a hunter. He doesn't get his blood from the blood bank."

"So he just happened to bump into Agent Crist, who just happened to be patrolling this neighborhood?"

Melcher didn't blink. "The murder is solved, Aurora. End of story."

Yes, sir! If you say so. Did Melcher really believe that load of crap, or was he covering for Jared? I doubt Crist ever set foot in this area that night. Jared stalked people for a living. He probably followed her off base, broke her neck, and then stumbled upon an interesting surprise when he tried to ditch her body at the landfill.

Melcher crouched beside Marcus and closed his eyes gently.

I watched as Melcher hovered beside Marcus's body. He began to speak in a low voice. I couldn't tell what he was saying at first then realized it was a prayer. "By the power of God, cast into hell Satan, and all the evil spirits, who prowl about the world seeking the ruin of souls."

I cranked my head back and looked at Jared. He barely glanced at me before stifling a yawn. I looked back at Melcher as he said, "Amen." He stood, looking solemn. "We can't pass this off as suicide."

Jared grunted and pushed away from the wall. "This is what happens when you let rookies go solo."

"What's the problem?" I demanded. "Marcus killed Mike. I killed Marcus. Isn't that how it works?"

Jared leaned into my face. I forced myself to take even breaths. "The problem, you little fool, is that Marcus was a prominent figure within the vampire community. Rumors have already been circulating about what we do. He's been stabbed in the heart. Why not put up a neon sign while you're at it? Vampire Hunter was here."

"So make him disappear," I said. "Bury him at the dump."

Jared snorted. He looked at Melcher. "Can you imagine the vamp hunt to track down Marcus's whereabouts?"

Melcher nodded, his expression far away, focused somewhere beyond that room. "You should have called it in first, Aurora."

I balled my fingers into fists. I felt like shaking one in Melcher's face. "And how was I supposed to do that after Marcus chained me to his ceiling?"

Jared snorted and smiled at Marcus's body. "Marcus chained you to the ceiling?" He looked overhead as he asked, searching for hooks, no doubt.

"Not here," I said, grinding my teeth together. "Upstairs in his bedroom."

Neither man asked if anything else had happened or if I was okay. Barbarians, both. "What is Jared doing here, anyway?" I asked Melcher. "I thought you were sending him out of state."

"Jared isn't going anywhere," Melcher said. "I want him where I can keep a close eye on him."

Jared snorted again. "Whatever you say, boss."

Melcher looked at me, his expression grave. "Aurora, how many people saw you here tonight?"

My lower lip dropped. I didn't answer immediately. I couldn't. In the battle against Marcus, I'd blocked out the other consequences of this evening. "Everyone," I said. "Everyone who was here earlier."

Henry's words echoed in my ears. *You seem to have a knack for drawing unwelcome attention.*

Gavin had seen me head toward the upstairs and never return. Then suddenly Marcus ends up dead. No, I'm sure he wouldn't find that odd in the least. I hadn't gotten a look in the living room as I passed. For all I knew Henry and Tom had seen me, too.

"Aurora," Melcher said carefully. "I think it would be best if we sent you out of town for a while."

"Out of Anchorage or Alaska?"

"Out of state."

"Really?" My voice lifted. I hadn't thought anything could brighten my mood tonight, but there was nothing I wanted more at that moment than to get the hell out of Alaska. Away from Jared and Melcher. Away from Noel and Fane.

"What about school?" I asked.

"I'll get you everything you need to obtain your G.E.D.

through correspondence," Melcher said. "I know it's not what you wanted, but having you stick around at this point isn't a good idea."

"It's fine," I said. "Can you reassign me to another state permanently?" Indiana? I could still attend Notre Dame. Perhaps there was such a thing as second chances. Melcher certainly owed me. If Jared had gotten to me, it was only because Melcher gave him the resources to do so. I wasn't about to ask Melcher what he knew about Jared's recruiting practices. I trusted Melcher about as much as I trusted his new sidekick.

"No, we need you up here."

I felt my heart drop even though I knew the verdict before Melcher delivered it. "We'll send you away to finish your education, followed by boot camp as planned. You'll be back by the end of summer and can attend UAA if you still choose to."

"Where are you sending me?"

"Don't worry about that," Melcher said.

"I mean, should I pack flip flops? A bikini?"

Melcher walked out of the room instead of answering. As I passed Jared, he leaned into me and said, "Nice try, Raven."

I kept my expression neutral.

It didn't matter where Melcher sent me. I was going to give boot camp everything I had, and when I got back, Jared better watch himself.

He had run me down and taken my life so that I would be forced into killing vampires. Well, that's exactly what I planned to do. Kill Jared. It might be too late for me, but that didn't mean I couldn't save countless other targets on Jared's list of potential AB negative recruits.

Melcher stepped into the living room, lifting his phone to his ear. "Send in the cleaners," he said into the speaker. He lowered the phone, glancing at me. "I'll have one of my men drive you home."

"Don't bother," I said. "I'll have my mom pick me up on L Street. She's expecting my call. She isn't aware of this address," I added.

Melcher nodded. "Very well." With that he turned to Jared and started talking as though I were no longer there.

Fine by me.

As I approached the entry, the front door opened and two men in biohazard suits walked in wearing masks. I tried not to stare. I'd never actually stuck around long enough to see the cleaners. Not that I could distinguish anything beyond their facemasks.

They didn't spare me a glance as we passed over the stones of Jerusalem. I looked over my shoulder one last time. No more disco. No more parties. No more champagne and blood.

Melcher had forgotten to say his customary lines. Justice had been served.

Despite this being the shittiest of shit nights in the whole history of my life, I knew I'd done the right thing, and I'd continue to fight the battle even if I had to start a war from within.

I stepped outside and breathed in the night air.

As soon as I'd put several blocks between myself and the townhouse, I sent Valerie a text in case she was checking.

Aurora: We have unfinished business to take care of.

I jammed each ear bud deep inside my eardrums.

There wasn't a cloud overhead. The aurora borealis, for which I was named, weaved like a river in the sky. Usually, it was too cloudy to see them, but tonight shades of dark blue, faint purple, and white swirled across the expanse overhead.

I selected "Running Up That Hill" by Kate Bush and began the long walk home.

The occasional car zoomed by, otherwise the streets were deserted. The digital clock on my phone showed the hour approaching one in the morning.

I didn't want a ride home. I wanted to feel the hard ground beneath my feet, the frigid air going down my throat.

I sucked it in.

It didn't chill me one bit.

AURORA SKY CONTINUES...

Don't miss STAKEOUT, an Aurora Sky: Vampire Hunter novella about Noel and Dante's assignment in Fairbanks. Learn the truth about what happened between Noel and Fane, along with a secret that changes everything.

Noel Harper got a second chance at life when the government recruited her as an undercover vampire informant. Since the day they brought her back from the good-as-dead, she has wanted to prove herself worthy.

When a member of her investigative unit is murdered, Noel is paired up with Dante to spy on a suspect in Fairbanks. The problem? They're not the only ones on stakeout. Taking down murderous vampires is one thing. Dealing with the past is another. But this time, Noel isn't letting fear win. She's calling in help from the other side and discovers a shocking secret along the way.

SAY HELLO!

Sign up for Nikki's spam-free newsletter. Receive cover reveals, excerpts, and new release news before the general public; enter to win prizes; and get the scoop on special offers, contests, and more.

Visit Nikki's website, nikkijefford.com, to put your name on the list, then confirm your email so you won't miss out.

See you on the other side!

SLAYING, MAGIC MAKING, & RULING ACROSS REALMS

Discover your next fantasy fix with these romantic, coming-of-age titles by Nikki Jefford:

ABOUT THE AUTHOR

Nikki Jefford loves fictional bad boys and heroines who kick butt. Books, travel, TV series, hiking, writing, and motorcycle riding are her favorite escapes. She is a third-generation Alaskan nomad who wouldn't trade her French husband in for anyone – not even Spike! The dark side of human nature fascinates her, so long as it's balanced by humor and romance.

f facebook.com/authornikkijefford
instagram.com/nikkijefford/
tiktok.com/@nikkijefford

Made in United States
Orlando, FL
29 March 2024